OUT
of
TIME

OUT
of
TIME

by

Stephen T. Gerdel

Out of Time

by
Stephen T. Gerdel

Published by Watershed Inc.
524 Olympus
Cedar Hill, TX 75104
www.watershedarts.com

Copy Editor
Bethany Swoboda

Content Editor
Sherilyn Gerdel

Cover design by
Katy Tapley

ISBN 978-0-9814541-5-3

Printed by Snowfall Press
Monument, Colorado

This book is dedicated
to my best friend
and beloved wife,

Jan

who with remarkable
patience endured my
long nights,
re-writes,
and
at the end of it all
still loved me.

Special Thanks and Appreciation

Group Source Team
Who brought insight and clarity where it was lacking.

Anne Roth
Arit Essien
Connie White
Gary Van Beek
Gina Borcherding
J. Gregory Gerdel
John Gerdel
Laura Schaefer
Macharr Heisel
Marcia Gardner
Mary Lou Yost
Mary Young
Ray Cousins
Sarah Shaw
Sharon Burns
Shirley Rockel
Tyann Marcink
Terry Rainey

1

I am One. The first.

Emptiness. I am alone. Silence surrounds me. I see shapes. Some are large, frightening, others just shadows. Nothing I like. Nothing I want.

The sound approaches from every direction, rushing over me, pressing down with unbearable weight. I do not know what causes it. The roar is unrelenting, awful when it begins, and maddening when it lasts too long. Sometimes they are near, other times distant, almost gone but never entirely gone. I do not want to hear the noise.

When silence comes it sucks the breath from me. I tremble as I wait for the sound to return with its dreadful shriek.

It doesn't matter how far I walk. It is all the same. I searched for the end, but there was no end. The shapes, shadows, and sounds are always different, unknown, unseen, threatening.

I do not know how I got here. I am aware that things have happened to me, some seem like they were long ago, others recent. I do not understand why. I don't know what I should do. It all seems hidden.

Sometimes one thing happens that is different, and it happens very quickly. The noise is not like the other sounds. It starts from a distance, and goes by in a flash. I hear it approach but, I cannot catch it.

When it returns, it is slower. Sometimes I catch it. Once it woke me. That was the first time I caught it. After it comes, when I catch it, I can sleep. The hurt goes away.

Now, I wait.

*   *   *   *   *

Mark and Jonathan stood beside one of the huge maple trees in the park across from the old apartment. The old park was a silent observer of their past, a sentinel that remained while life unfolded around it. This was an important day, one they had awaited for a very long time.

The late April sun was warm on their faces, but the air was crisp and cool. Maybe it was that they were older, but the cold seemed to find more ways to creep in, silently invade, and chill the two men than in years past. They kept their coats pulled tight around them.

Quietly, they watched the young man leave the apartment. He was bold and confident, even brash. He jogged across the street and paused in front of Gina's Laundromat that was now a bike shop. The men watched as he made his way to the café and sat in his usual place beside the planter, one they both knew well.

The waiter approached and spoke to him. They were too far away to hear what was said. Abruptly, the young man leaped to his feet and sprinted back to the apartment building.

"So, this is where it begins," Mark said softly.

*   *   *   *   *

To most it was just another graduation day, the culmination of years of study and research ending in grand celebration. A landmark where graduates find themselves liberated from their books to face the reality of finding an actual job.

But it wasn't a normal graduation day for Dr. Martin G. Walsh, Dean of Graduate Studies, and former Head of the Mathematics Department at Stephens University. He read the names of the graduates in anticipation for a particular moment, the moment when his son, Jonathan M. Walsh, received the designation of PhD.

The bright mid-day sun was unusually warm for March. As the list of names was read, the P.A. system echoed across the stadium, and squealed when the speaker leaned too close. Each name brought cheers from parents and family and cat-calls from fellow students in the crowd.

Jonathan waited toward the end of the line, with the "Ws." To him, this day of graduation was a crowning moment preceded by years of hard work. His thoughts swirled, mixing memories and dreams.

He remembered the day he stood in the yard outside his father's study at home. As a boy of nine he was determined to draw his dad's attention away from whatever it was that held him so captive. *Maybe if I swing harder, faster, he will see me,* he had thought. He swung hard and fast. Again, Jonny tossed the ball high into the air, watching it closely, hoping to make contact with the bat. Time and again the ball fell into the dust. Dad never noticed. He never came out to play ball.

Years of disappointment evolved into a personal resolve to excel in his studies of mathematics and science. Jonathan's boyhood visions pursued impractical and impossible concepts that he was sure would someday make him great and noticed by his father.

Graduation was the beginning of a journey that he hoped would lead him to greatness, his greatness. Deep in his bones he believed he would discover his destiny on that journey. This was the green flag at the beginning of the race, his license to pursue his vision.

The delay of the moment only heightened the anticipation. He'd grown used to being at the end of the line, the finale. To Jonathan and his father all the other graduates were simply the build-up to the big finish. Everything before "W" was just the warm-up. And then, the moment came.

"It is with great pride that I introduce our next candidate, my son, Jonathan Martin Walsh." Martin applauded his son, now a man, as he approached the podium. The faculty and students stood clapping. Many of the faculty had watched Jonathan grow up, and his scholastic merit granted him high esteem among his fellow students.

One small voice echoed across the crowd.

"Go Jonny!" It was a singular cheer from Jonathan's girl, Maggie Chambers. Many in the crowd turned toward her and laughed warmly as she pumped her fist in the air cheering him on.

Jonathan marched across the platform with long strides to meet his father at the podium. The two men shook hands and embraced. Jonathan took his certificate of graduation, and flipped his tassel to the left of his mortar board.

"Thanks, Dad."

"This a great honor. You make me proud, son. Your mom, too." Martin Walsh and his son shared a sorrow that Alice, Jonathan's mother, had not lived to see this day. She would have cheered loudly right along with Maggie, like two school girls with a flirting crush on the handsome graduate.

Martin cleared his throat. The contrast of sorrow and joy brought tears to his eyes and a lump into his throat, but the moment needed to pass. Five more doctoral graduates were waiting to be announced and recognized. Martin Walsh cleared his throat and approached the podium to call the next name.

*   *   *   *   *

The Walsh home was one of modest elegance, spacious enough for one to be lost in private thoughts and small enough for one to be found when needed. Alice's artful touch and preference for delicate comfort had ruled and was never questioned. It was also reverently maintained.

The guests arriving at the celebration included few from out of town, but for the most part the house was filled with professors, graduate students, and faculty members. Many had known Jonny since he was a toddler, although none of them called him by his childhood name anymore. Today they were gathered to honor Dr. Jonathan Walsh.

Martin Walsh greeted friends, family, and associates as they entered the house. Maggie and Jonathan extended the courtesy by escorting visitors into the dining room with engaging conversation. The room was filled with the aroma of warm food inviting everyone to relax. As the house filled, friends filtered out into the yard and the surrounding gardens.

"So, how's the new Doctor of Fringe Science?" a familiar voice said over Jonathan's shoulder. It was his best friend and study partner, Mark Vaughn, also a newly credentialed PhD.

"Probably not quite as confident as a Doctor of Artificial Intelligence," Jonathan said with a smile as he turned to embrace Mark. "Glad you're here, Mark."

"Wouldn't miss it. Any word on the grant?"

"Not yet. If the committee has the same attitude as my dad, I'm sunk."

"Well, at least your dad was here for the ceremony. You know, my folks won't be back in town for three more weeks," Mark said. "If they remember I graduate this term maybe they'll have a big party for me. I don't know. I guess we'll have to wait and see."

"It'll be one heck of a party, too!" Jonathan added.

"Maybe. I'll believe it when it happens," Mark smiled. "I have to ask myself, why is my field called Artificial Intelligence? Even *I* don't get that. Intelligence is intelligence, right?"

Suddenly, Jonathan was nearly knocked over when a young woman threw her arms around his neck. He grabbed her with his free hand and pulled her to him. "You almost made me spill my drink." Maggie's eyes sparkled as she swayed and laughed at her surprise entrance.

"Intelligence is intelligence," Jonathan echoed. "And hot . . . is hot."

"Okay, that's out of my league," Mark said backing away and holding up his hands. "I can take my exit cue, no problem."

"No, Mark," Maggie said. "Where are you going? You need to stay right here. Besides, I have someone I want you to meet."

"Double exit cue," Mark said smiling as he began walking away. "You know I don't have any luck with women. Especially the ones you keep setting me up with. Think I'd better hit the road."

"You get back here, Mark," Maggie insisted. "You're the absolute worst. Jonny, make him come back!"

Jonathan smiled. "I just love the sound of your voice. I don't know a sweeter sound." The accent, a by-product of her North Carolina upbringing, was the polish on the apple to him. Her beauty was accented by her southern charm and added warmth to her soft, seductive speech.

"No, Jonny! I mean it. Please stop him. Mark!"

"Should I drop you and run after him?" Jonathan replied. "What would people think if I left a beautiful woman and chased a homely varmint like him?"

"Don't you talk like that," she retorted. "I want him to meet a *special* girl. Mark!" she called again.

It was too late. Mark waved from the distance without looking back and walked to his car.

*   *   *   *   *

As the afternoon faded to evening, the well-wishers departed with glad hearts and full stomachs. Jonathan flopped onto the couch in the family room and rested his head in Maggie's lap. She smiled and gently stroked his forehead and temples.

Martin eased his large frame into his chair with a heavy sigh.

"Now *that* was a full day!" he exclaimed with a victorious smile. "I'm proud of you, Jonathan. I know your mom is proud as well."

To his mother he had always been Jonny. After Alice passed away, Maggie continued using *Jonny* affectionately, keeping the tradition alive. Jonathan allowed it.

"Thanks, Dad," Jonathan said. Then he smiled and said, "Sort of felt like she was here."

A gentle peace settled in the room. Everyone missed Alice. Each in a special way, but in every heart and memory a spot was empty. Maggie broke the spell as she sat upright.

"I thought the caterers did a good job," she said. "Everything was delicious."

"Thank you, Maggie," Martin said. "Something else from your mom, Jonny. She always insisted we hire the new guy in town, whether a painter, gardener, or caterer. It was a risk, but she preferred to give a new business owner a chance."

Jonathan feigned a swoon. "Oh man, did you taste those little things on the crackers?"

Maggie giggled. "You dork, there were a dozen hors d'oeuvres on crackers. Which one?"

"You know the ones with the green stuff and sprinkles?" Jonathan paused, looking at Maggie with his best *you-know-what-I'm-talking-about* look.

"Jonny, you are a mathematician—a genius—but when it comes to food you don't quite get it, do you?" she replied mussing his hair.

They all laughed. Every part of the day had been delicious.

"Your mom used to make something similar, as I remember," Martin said. "Don't ask me how though."

"She was a magician in the kitchen," Jonathan added with his eyes still closed.

Maggie playfully slapped him on the head. "Come on, you know I'll never match her skills. You're making me feel bad."

"Whoa! Nothing against you, babe. You've said as much."

Again, silence fell on the trio.

"It's at times like this that I really miss her," Martin said. His eyes rested on the floor in front of his favorite chair, his brow etched with furrows of regret.

"I feel guilty for not paying more attention when she cooked," Maggie added. She glanced at Jonathan as he rolled his eyes. "Really. You creep!"

Maggie swatted Jonathan with a pillow.

"Careful. You're going to break my brand new doctor face," he teased ducking her attack. He scooted across the couch and leaned against the armrest. Maggie moved to his side and snuggled close to him. She played with the buttons on his shirt waiting for her next opportunity to taunt him.

"Oh, have you heard more about your grant?" Martin asked.

"Dad, I don't want to talk about that right now." Jonathan's mood visibly shifted. For weeks any mention of the grant had irritated him.

"Aren't the awards coming out this week?"

"Dad, can we just give it a rest? Please?" Jonathan squirmed on the couch.

"It's a simple question son," Martin replied. "I'm curio—"

"I know, curious to know if they think I'm as crazy and misguided as you do!"

"Jonny, don't—" Maggie said.

"It's the same conversation over and over. You think they won't award me my grant, don't you?"

"No, I simply haven't heard any more about it, and I wanted—"

"Right. What you *really* want to know is if they shot me down!"

"Jonny!"

"No, I—" Martin protested.

Jonathan leaped from the couch and stomped toward the door. "I will *not* be baited right now. Okay, Dad?"

The screen door slammed behind him, echoing through the room. Bitterness reclaimed its territory.

"I'm sorry, Dad," Maggie said softly. "I don't know why he explodes like that." She clasped her hands together in her lap, her eyes downcast.

"No, it's all right, Maggie. He can't help it . . . he's just like me." Martin scowled and looked at his son's lovely fiancée.

Maggie stood and walked toward the porch. She paused at the screen door before going out.

Martin Walsh knew his shortcomings. His memories were marred with the times he had cut off or viciously rebuked Alice. It was the same confrontational attitude he saw in Jonathan. The difference between him and his wife, though, was that he lacked the temperament to deal with his son effectively. Alice had known how. She was a tiny woman but a mountain of grace and patience possessing insightful and piercing wit. In the end, Martin had always apologized. But he knew he would probably do it again.

It was simply part of Martin's make-up, who he was. The attitude that he, and only he, could find the right answer, devise the proper formula, or discover the correct sequence to resolve the problem. It made him a good mathematician, one of the best. However, the trait did not equip him well as a father.

Alice had been his counterweight, and losing her left Martin ill-prepared to communicate with a son possessing the same abrasive personality. Both men were certain they knew the correct answer to the question, whatever the question might be, but each man always found a different answer.

Maggie stepped onto the porch. Jonathan leaned heavily against the rail, gripping it firmly. His knuckles were white under his grasp. He stared angrily at the flowerbed beneath him. She knew he was angry, and that he knew he shouldn't be angry at a simple question. Maggie walked slowly to him.

"Jonny," she began as she touched his shoulder.

"He does that all the time! He doesn't approve, I understand that. But, it's *always* in his tone of voice. That sneering disapproval of my work."

"Honey, he was just asking. It's the next step, the next big event for your project. It was only small talk, no accusation."

"I know," he turned to face her. His cheeks were flush with rage. He sat on the railing. "It's just that when I was a kid, Dad scoffed at the ideas that popped into my head. I was all into third-dimension theories, out-of-body experiences, life after death—it was just a bunch of foolishness spun by weak-minded men according to the great *Dr. Martin Walsh*."

"Jonny, don't."

"Everything that fascinated me was ridiculed. It seems he wanted to condition me to rejection and failure. The more pressure I'm under, the happier *he* is, and I blow up at him faster."

"But Jonny, you've done it. Graduation is a fantastic accomplishment. We just have to wait until the grants are awarded."

Maggie touched his forehead and brushed back his hair. She knew she could quiet the beast inside him. It only took a touch.

The anger lingered in his eyes then softened slightly. "You do it just like Mom. All I have to do is look at you, and I know I'm wrong . . . again." He shook his head and stared at his feet.

"I know it's hard to wait like this. You know the announcement comes out next week," she said. "It's only a matter of time." She put her arms around his waist and rested her head on his chest.

Maggie could hear Jonny's heart pounding an angry rhythm. Then she felt one of his arms gently wrap around her, then the other arm. Maggie listened as his heart slowed. The hammering beat calmed to a regular pulse. She would be happy to stay right there in his embrace.

"I guess I should apologize to the old goat," he said in a soft voice.

"Jonny! You be nice!" she teased. "But I think he would appreciate it."

He sighed without releasing his hold on her. She could feel his smile as the tension melted from his muscles.

"Do you think my dad and I will ever be able to just have a conversation?" It was a serious question, and one that held hope.

"I hope so," she said lifting her face to his. She kissed him. "I know I don't want to go through life as a referee."

2

In contrast to his devotion to math and science, Jonathan loved cars, and oddly enough, so had his mother Alice. After she retired she "went off the deep end" as she told it, and purchased a Mazda Miata. The two-seat, five-speed sports car was her passion. She loved driving with the top down and flying across the winding county roads outside of town. It was the kid in her showing off.

When she died Jonathan inherited the car, her prized possession. The fact that it was Mom's car first would never be forgotten. He cared for it with the appropriate reverence, keeping the perspective that it was, after all, a car.

Jonathan pulled into the graduate student parking lot at the university and parked the Miata in his assigned spot. This could be the day, the day his grant approval would be announced. He took in a deep breath, blew it out, and caught his reflection in the rearview mirror. *How many times did Mom check her make-up in you?*

"Well, Mom," he said out loud. "This is it. This could be *the* day." He paused and cast a doubtful look at his reflection. "Or tomorrow, or the next day, whatever. I'll take sooner over later, thank you." He exhaled a deep sigh and climbed out of the car.

Jonathan restrained himself from skipping across the campus lawn. *Too kid-like*, Jonathan thought. Still, he felt like a child on Christmas morning. Breaking into a jog would get him there more quickly, but it would possibly make him look a little too eager. Simply walking across the grass was prohibited by the bursting of excitement in his chest. So he mixed it up: a little jog, quick steps, and controlled, long, measured strides.

Jonathan remembered the spot on campus where he met Maggie. Every time he walked by that spot he grinned. It was a chance meeting about twenty feet east of the main stairs to the Administration Building, next to a large hosta bed that was shaded by a giant, ancient oak tree. He remembered the time of year because the hostas were in bloom, and of course, classes were about to begin. Now, as he passed, he smiled again.

Maggie had been a freshman from North Carolina away from home for the first time. She hadn't had a clue what to do or where she should go first. Jonathan saw her and was immediately fascinated by her beauty. Her eyes did him in. He had had no choice, he had to help her.

"You look a little lost. Can I help?" he had asked.

"Well, yes, if you don't mind. I can't find the Liberal Arts Building. Do you know where it is?" Her voice had the softest southern lilt he had ever heard, and he was mesmerized.

"I'm sorry, would you say that again, please?" he had asked.

She repeated herself with a calm and clear voice, but it didn't matter. Jonathan was so smitten after the first few words, he still had no idea what she was asking. His second request for her to repeat the question was nearly the fatal blow. Before Maggie could brush him off and walk away, though, Mark Vaughn had come to her rescue. He sauntered between them with a playful tough-guy swagger

"Is this bum giving you trouble?"

"Hi, Mark," she said smiling at his approach. "I was just trying to—"

"You know this guy? You know Mark?"

"Well, yes, we met this morning at the bookstore, and—"

"And as with all beautiful women on this campus she was drawn like a magnet to my sex appeal and charm," Mark teased.

"No, that's really not what I'm think—"

"Hold on there, buster, I believe the young lady has a say in the matter, don't you?" Jonathan turned to Maggie. He looked directly into her eyes and with his best imitation of a southern dialect said, "I am Jonathan Walsh, a junior at this fine establishment of higher learnin'. I apologize for my brutish friend's antics and braggadocio, and willingly offer myself to you as a personal guide to wherever you may want to go. Besides, I just love to hear your enchanting voice."

Maggie shook her head and laughed at Jonathan's attempt, but Mark protested.

"Oh, come on, Jonathan, you can't expect—"

"Why, I am very pleased to meet you, sir. My name is Maggie Chambers," she said in a very slow and thick southern drawl. She blushed right on cue. Then, taking his arm in escort, she willingly yielded to his charm and eloquence, then looking over her shoulder at Mark, she winked. Jonny and Maggie had been together every day since.

During the past semester, he and Maggie had spent hours working and re-working his grant application. He handled the details of his experiment; she remedied his use of spelling and grammar. It was a good way to use their complementary strengths.

The grant postings were in the main hall next to the graduate studies office. A traditional glass case held the list pinned to the cork backing, as it had for decades. E-mail was well understood by the heads of the departments, but tradition was tradition.

As soon as he entered the building, Jonathan saw the small throng straining to find their names on the list. He glanced at the faces of those walking away. More reflected disappointment than celebration. He knew not everyone would win this time around.

Jonathan pressed into the crowd. Of course, his name would be toward the end, at the bottom of the page. Excusing himself, he pushed through the downcast faces until he could read the list.

He nearly gasped when he saw it: Jonathan M. Walsh – Approved. He had his research grant. Now the exciting part of his studies would begin. No more speculation and dreaming.

It was time to bring the theories to life.

*   *   *   *   *

Rachel Armstrong held a master's degree in Library Science. She was hired at the Stephens University library a year earlier, immediately after her graduation. The job offered everything she had ever wanted. She wasn't interested in the corporate world, nor the political aspects of university life. She loved books.

She had had enough politics in her childhood. Both of her parents were politically active, gone a lot, and, in her estimation, were a couple of frauds. Their repeatedly empty promises had jaded her by age ten. When she was twelve she decided her parents and all their friends were the same: all fakes and swindlers. She lost trust and interest. Her passion for the written word drew her studies beyond her original goal of being a librarian.

Books were always the same, constant, never to make unfulfilled promises. Rachel found that books shielded her from people like her parents, and allowing her to thrive in fictional relationships. She did all she could to avoid a real relationship with a man.

During the first week of that term, the same week Maggie met Jonny, Rachel had met Maggie in the library. Maggie had walked to the checkout counter with Jane Austen's *Mansfield Park*. Rachel discerned Maggie's plan to fill a summer weekend that would otherwise be empty of passion and probably void of communication.

"I love this book," Rachel had said to Maggie over the counter. She smiled and introduced herself.

"I think I've read it a dozen times. Maybe someday I'll buy a copy," Maggie replied. She blushed a little. "This book is the story of my life, broken friendships, betrayal, and personal ruin. Maybe it will keep me from getting bored."

"Listen, if you get bored before you get to chapter six, a bunch of us girls are having dinner at my apartment Saturday evening. Would you like to come?"

"I don't know. I'm just getting settled, and—"

"Come on. We're a lot more fun than a book." Rachel smiled broadly, staring Maggie down.

Rachel was delighted when she accepted. The party that weekend was a riot. Seven young women met to eat far too much, compare notes on the boys they were meeting across the campus, and pick the sorority socialites they were destined to despise throughout the year.

Rachel listened while Maggie told the story of her role as the feminine part of a friendly trio—Mark, Jonathan, and her. Over the following months Rachel had observed Maggie's efforts to introduce Mark to each of her girlfriends but without success.

*   *   *   *   *

Maggie and Rachel met at the small sidewalk café just down the street from Jonathan's apartment. The two women built their friendship largely on their contrasting characteristics. Both were attractive, but their features could not have been less similar. Maggie was fair skinned with reddish-blond hair, delicate features and deep blue eyes. Her voice was soft and her mannerisms elegant.

Rachel had shoulder-length black hair. Her eyes were dark pools that could drill holes through solid brick. Her lips were more prominent than Maggie's, and her personality was abrasive and confrontational.

"This is nice," Rachel said scooting up to the table.

The small cluster of tables was nestled between the store front and the narrow street bordered by the park to the west. A large planter encompassed the southern end of the dining area and provided a buffer from what little traffic moved slowly past on the street.

"Jonny and I love it, especially in the evening. And this is our favorite table."

"I can see why." Rachel smiled and scanned the park across the street. She leaned back in her chair casting a skeptical eye on Maggie. "Okay, you got me here. Tell me about this man you think is so perfect."

"Mark? Oh, he is something special," she answered, smiling broadly. "He has been Jonny's best friend since they were boys. He's smart and about as hot as men get around here."

"Yeah, but how does he treat women? I won't spend my time on some rude, self-centered jerk," Rachel challenged. "How does he treat his mother?"

"Well, that's a touchy subject. His folks aren't so great, but he made himself a part of Jonny's family and treated Jonny's mom like a queen. He almost showed more respect toward her than Jonny did."

"I don't know if that tells me more about this Mark guy, or something distasteful about Jonathan," Rachel said with a snarky smile. She looked over Maggie's shoulder as the boyish waiter approached. *Oh my, fresh from the farm,* she thought.

"Hi Philip," Maggie said. "Today I'm introducing my friend to your wonderful café. This is Rachel Armstrong."

"Good to meet you, Rachel. I always say having two beautiful women to serve is better that none," Philip replied with a modest bow. "Me? I'm just looking for a good time, and a nice tip."

"That's good, because we're a couple of girls looking for a nice lunch," said Rachel smartly.

"Well, we're all in the right place. I'm having fun, and you are going to get the finest food and service money can buy," he said. He slowly slid a menu in front of each woman. Then he winked a Rachel.

After the women ordered, Philip whisked himself off to the kitchen. Both women watched him go, and then giggled at his flirtatious nature.

"Okay, to matters of major importance. What can we do to draw this *smokin' hot* man into our web?"

"Philip? Oh, my goodness no, too young," Maggie teased. "Now, if you want to talk about Mark, I'm ready. What would you think about a dinner date with Jonny and me?"

"I would consider that. The question remains: should we invite Mark to join us?"

"That's a good question. The second is whether I can drag Jonny out of his lab for an evening of fun and entertainment."

"Is that a problem? Is Jonathan not calling you?" Rachel was suddenly serious and her face darkened.

"I don't know. I mean during school we saw each other every day, practically every hour. We never let a day pass without meeting up somewhere. He would call and interrupt my studies for the silliest reasons. Or he would text me in the middle of a lecture on purpose. I guess we had a lot of fun, and I miss it."

"Have you said anything to him about it? Personally, I'd ask him straight up if something was wrong. If a man isn't going to be serious and focused on me, I certainly wouldn't want to waste my time on him."

Maggie smiled weakly. Philip arrived with the sandwiches and salads and slid them before the women with flair.

"Here you are, Maggie and," he paused, "Rachel? Right?"

"Well done, Philip," Rachel said reflecting his smile. "You've demonstrated the first half of your promise to us. The service is fine, and now to the taste test."

Philip took one step back from the table, slowly bowed his head and said, "But of course." Then he flashed a big smile and said, "Gotta go. More customers!" The women laughed as he left the table to greet other diners.

"You have to know Jonny," Maggie said after Philip left. "He's great most of the time, but he has a temper."

"Not me. I wouldn't put up with it for a minute. If a man treats me like dirt, he's done. I mean gone." Rachel took a bite of her sandwich.

"I know, but . . . there are parts of him that are just great. He's fun and smart. Those things seem to cover his flaws, I guess."

"I admire your patience," Rachel said looking directly into Maggie's eyes. It was more than a look, almost more like a stare. "But I would be very careful about allowing a man's weaknesses to drag me into his pit."

Maggie caught her breath. *Is that what I'm doing?* She had refused to believe the anger she had seen in Jonathan as a darkness that could overcome him. She decided to let it pass.

"Let's plan a dinner," she said. "Then you can meet Jonny and get to know him, and Mark too. I think you'll find them both very nice, and *smokin' hot*."

"Better yet, why don't you give me some background information on this Mark you want me to meet, and I'll see what I can dig up. Then we can talk about a dinner date. What do you think?"

"We can do that," Maggie said

"I know you have all sorts of information about Mark and what sort of man he really is," Rachel said. "We can do this."

"All right, instead of *Pride and Prejudice* we'll call it *Surveillance and Compromise*. We could be a Private Eye firm in our spare time and dig up the dirt on this guy." They both laughed then spent the rest of their lunch discussing how to improve the décor of the café.

*   *   *   *   *

Waiting is hard. I ache. Did I sleep? Gray is all around me, not dark, but . . . it is.

What is that? I hear the sound! Is it coming toward me or going away? I watch straining my eyes in the gray. It comes fast. I am watching now. Waiting.

I cannot tell where it is coming from. Here? No, wait. Wait. There!

It is always a blur I cannot catch. But I see it when it goes by. It will be much slower when it comes back. That is when I will catch it. But I must wait.

I hope it comes soon. I will rest. When it comes back, I must be strong. Stronger than it is. Faster.

*   *   *   *   *

Mark Vaughn was not a difficult man to follow. His life was routine and his habits quite consistent. His work in artificial intelligence focused on voice recognition. The simple task required in a cell phone to translate voice to text is one thing, but for software to properly hear *phospholipid bilayer* and comprehend it as the same meaning as *cell membrane* a far greater challenge. Simple language was not a problem for AI. However, scientific speech or jargon was a problem, and it was Mark's arena of expertise.

The hospital at Stephens University became a research facility in the late 1990s as robotics grew in popularity. The early focus was on creating machines that could mimic the delicate movements of a master surgeon's hands from a remote location. They had succeeded, but on a limited scale. The hope remained that someday a physician on one continent would be able to operate on a patient in the remotest part of

Africa using the devices and programs developed at Stephens University.

Over the years their success brought recognition to the departments of robotics and artificial intelligence. Scientists and scholars from across the country applied to become part of the research program. Mark Vaughn's scholastic interest and ambitions in prep school drew him into AI and robotic design, providing him the opportunity to return to his home town. A generous gift from his parents insured his spot to develop and hone his skills and knowledge studying at the university.

Unaware that he was the target of the clandestine efforts of two young women, Mark moved through his routine with accuracy and precision. Had he known he was being watched, nothing would have changed. He was a creature of habit, a focus of stability and comfort for him. The women watched, and timed his work schedule, lunch breaks, when he arrived home, and, on two evenings, when the lights went out in his apartment.

"Now *that* was some bit of skull-drudgery!" Rachel exclaimed when Mark's apartment went dark.

"What did we get? Did we fill out the entire day?" Maggie asked.

"I think we have it all. We just need to watch a couple more days to see how close he sticks to his pattern."

Maggie giggled. "He is a busy man! I don't know if he'll have time for you Rachel."

Rachel struck a sexy pose and twirled her car keys on her finger. "Sweetheart, when I arrive on his scene he will *make* time for me." They both laughed.

With every new bit of information Rachel became more interested in this quiet, handsome scientist. As she gathered more information, more questions rose in her mind. Finally, it was decided. She wanted to meet him.

*   *   *   *   *

"Good morning, handsome," Alice said propping herself up on one elbow. "How in the world did a homely old maid like me catch such a charming fellow?" She ran her finger down his cheek and brushed it across his lips.

Martin wasn't quite awake, but he smiled anyway. Just the sound of her voice warmed his heart. Her touch comforted his spirit.

"I'm sorry, my dear, but I just can't pull myself out of sleep. You'll have to wait until my magnificence is fully awake for a coherent reply."

"That's not a problem. I've never listened to you anyway."

They both laughed. Alice had always teased him. She openly admitted she did not understand his babblings of higher mathematics. But right now, she was clearly awake, and he wasn't. It was her turn to play.

"So this afternoon you will probably have time for some baseball in the backyard with Jonny?" She jabbed him in the ribs. He flinched and smiled.

"Yes, my dear. Of course, I will. Whatever you want," he mumbled.

She ran her hand up the other side of his face and twirled her finger through the thinning hair on his head.

"And then we can put a new roof on the garage," she continued.

"I will be happy to do that," he said smiling, his eyes closed and his mind still mostly numb with sleep.

"And there's a church picnic this evening, so I won't need to cook dinner."

"I know . . . I know. That's fine with me."

"And you won't have any problem working all this into your busy schedule?" she cooed softly into his ear.

"No, my love. Whatever I can do to help, I'll do my best." Martin smiled and lingered at the edge of slumber.

"Too bad you didn't have time like this before I was dead."

Martin Walsh lunged awake. He sat upright in his bed. Alice was not at his side. His entire body tingled. Confusion engulfed his mind.

She was here. Right here. Beside me. It was real. I could feel her touch. I heard her voice.

3

Psychotropic drugs can be very dangerous even in the hands of a trained professional. The effects can be generalized but only to a certain point. Specific results from patient to patient often require dosage adjustments and close monitoring of the individual's attitude and personality.

These powerful medications were a significant part of Dr. Jonathan Walsh's scientific studies. Medically, these drugs are little more than an escape—a way for one to stand at the perimeters of normal human life with a slim hope that over time research would provide a cure for an affliction or disorder.

Individually, the drugs provide treatments for psychotic episodes, depression, or simple sleep disorders. Jonathan's work entailed finite mixing of psychotic agents such as amitriptyline, ziprasidone, and chlordiazepoxide. Balanced, the three drug cocktail induced a manageable coma; out of balance, instant death.

Jonathan locked himself away for hours experimenting with different combinations of medications. His studies in graduate school gave him direction to his goal but the application of his discoveries had required the grant money. With the funds he could make genuine headway. The drugs were very expensive.

A knock at the door jolted his thinking. He glanced toward the door but forced himself to concentrate and finish his thought. Another knock interrupted.

"Just a minute!" he yelled. "I'm working."

"Sorry." The voice was small and soft. Maggie. Jonathan leaped from his desk and bolted across the room.

He opened the door swiftly startling her. "I—I'm sorry, honey."

She smiled meekly. "I just hadn't seen you all week . . . I was wondering if you remembered our dinner . . . Do you have time for dinner?"

"Oh, my gosh. What time is it?" Jonathan said, running his fingers through his hair. He patted his trouser pockets for his phone to check the time. It wasn't there. He hurried to his desk. The piles of papers and lab results buried the top of his desk.

"Jonny . . . it's seven-thirty. Are you hungry?"

"Uh, well not really . . . but no—no I *am*. Just let me write something down." He looked at her, paused, and raised his eyebrows. Maggie raised her eyebrows in response, cocked her head to the side and smiled.

"It'll just take a second. Okay?"

"I can wait." She slowly walked around the corner of his desk dragging her finger along the edge. She stopped, leaning slightly against the arm of his chair.

"There. I'm done," Jonathan said smiling at her.

"Done? You're finished?" Maggie teased.

"Well, not *finished* finished," he paused, glanced away, then back to her. "For right now, I can take a break."

"I know, silly," she said grabbing his arm and pulling him to her. "You need fresh air, some good food, and whoa, a clean shirt!"

"I'm sorry. I can change."

"I'm kidding. Relax," she smiled. "I've just missed picking on you." Maggie playfully poked him in the ribs driving him toward the office door.

"Ow! Where are we going? I can't be gone too long. I still have a lot I need to do."

"Jonny, all you do is work. Let's go have some fun. At least a little, okay?" Maggie added playfully. "Besides, we have friends waiting."

"Friends?"

"Yeah, you remember. People you like to be with, laugh with, have fun. You remember fun, don't you?" Maggie laughed as she dragged Jonny down the hallway.

"Alright! I surrender!" Jonathan smiled and allowed her to haul him from the building onto the sidewalk. They laughed as she forced him to move, greatly exaggerating her efforts.

*   *   *   *   *

"Mark! Wow, what a surprise," Jonathan exclaimed as he entered the restaurant.

Dr. Mark Vaughn sat at the table in the company of a stunning young woman with jet black hair. Jonathan stopped, shocked.

Maggie pulled him toward the table by his arm. She smiled with the biggest grin she'd had in weeks. Mark stood and extended his hand.

"Jonny-boy! Man, it's good to see you." The two men gripped each other's hand warmly and embraced. "Where have you been hiding yourself?"

"Well, I haven't really been hiding, just busy."

"*Too* busy if you ask me," Maggie added, teasing him, and squeezing his arm tightly.

"I see *you* haven't been too busy." Jonathan nodded at the young woman sitting at the table.

"It has taken me months to get them together, but I think they are catching on," Maggie bragged.

"Oh, I'm sorry. Jonathan, this is Rachel Armstrong," Mark said. "She's an administrative assistant at the university library. Rachel, this is Jonathan Walsh."

"I've heard about you, Jonathan Walsh," Rachel said extending her hand. Her eyes locked on his in an icy stare. "It's very nice to finally meet the real article."

"It's good to meet you," Jonathan responded. "But you really have to be careful about what you hear from this guy," he said nodding at Mark.

"Wait," Mark protested with a Shakespearian air. "I have spun not a single tale of your exploits. I am innocent!"

"And I will readily admit that I have spun numerous examples of your many talents and good graces," Maggie volunteered sliding her arms around Jonathan's neck and kissing his cheek.

"Then it all has to be true," Jonathan answered and turned to look into Maggie's eyes. "I have no defense."

"But yet, there are many stories that should, and must be told. Why not now?" Mark continued in character, "The tales of your darker and more dangerous side."

So began an evening of friendly banter, stories from the men's childhood, and the foibles and fantasies of young, eager college students. Jonathan and Mark laughed harder than they had in weeks. It was just like the old days to Jonathan. They played off each other's slightly stretched tales and extended them to the limits of rational belief.

Their laughter was too loud, but the men were glad to see each other. It was a happy evening, especially so for Jonathan. His long days locked away in his lab deprived him of his best friends. He was losing weight. But he loved his work. That was most important for now. He was confident Maggie knew he loved her.

The dinner was excellent. Mark continued his tales, or at least his rendition of the events, between courses and bottles of wine. Rachel watched him intently and laughed at Jonathan's protests when the truth was stretched too far. Maggie kept both men honest, having witnessed many of the events firsthand. Finally, the time came for the wind-down from too much fun and good food.

"My face actually hurts. Way too much smiling," Mark jested.

Jonathan chuckled and leaned back in his chair as the waiter began clearing the dishes.

"So, Dr. Walsh," Rachel asked leaning toward Jonathan with an inquisitor's look. "What is this secret study you're involved in? I would love to hear about it."

"You would prefer to hear about my thrillingly uneventful life rather than the intellectual heroic acts of this brilliant scientist?" Jonathan said, gesturing toward Mark.

"I've heard all of his malarkey. Now, I want to hear yours," Rachel replied.

Jonathan didn't like to talk about his work. It was private. It was science that most people wouldn't be interested in or care to hear about.

"Yeah, Jonny, you have been way too secretive about all this stuff. Fill us in, buddy," Mark insisted. His cheeks were flush, and his eyes sparkled from a little too much wine. "Come on. What are you doing?"

"Well," Jonathan faltered a feeble beginning, "I—I don't normally talk about my work. I'm not sure it's all that exciting . . . or even interesting. You see, it's all very technical."

"Oh, Jonny, give us a thrill with your science talk," Maggie said leaning close. "We would love to know what you're up to."

"All the secrecy makes it sound very intriguing, Dr. Walsh," Rachel pressed. "Do tell." She smiled and swished the wine in her glass, dangling it between her fingers. She tilted her head, raised one eyebrow and pursed her lips, begging an answer.

"First, cut the Dr. Walsh crap. Please call me Jonathan." He swallowed hard. "Where to start? How can I make this interesting and not so technical?"

"You can do it, Jonny-boy," Mark said grinning from ear to ear though he was barely able to keep his chin off the table.

"Okay. Let me lay some ground work first. Is that all right?" he asked.

Approvals were given all around the small table, some more slurred than others. They were ready to launch into an impossible tale of intellectual jargon and scientific slang that was sure to generate a laugh.

"First, we have to establish the fact that what we see and know today is probably not all there is, right?" He looked around the table hoping for a little focus. There wasn't much. "I mean, one hundred and fifty years ago people thought if a human being traveled over seventy-five miles per hour the skin would rip right off his face."

"And wouldn't that be a mess," Mark chided as he downed another glass of port.

"Yes, but the perception of what they thought to be real actually wasn't," Jonathan said. "In the same way, some things we believe to be real now are very likely not at all real. Right?"

"Dr. . . . I mean Jonathan," Rachel began rolling her eyes around the room. "Are you implying that although we believe we are sitting in a restaurant drinking this wonderful wine, you are telling us we might actually be at Burger King swilling down soda-pop?" She popped her lips loudly on her last syllable and turned a strong gaze toward Jonathan.

Mark thought it was hilarious and collapsed on the table. Maggie chuckled and attempted to help Mark to an upright sitting position.

"Well, in a sense, that's correct," Jonathan answered with a faint grin. "You see, for centuries we have been steadily reaching beyond the limits of our perceptions with either new machines, innovative methods of discovery, or creative mathematics that has *proven* possible what was once believed impossible.

"Simple mechanized flight is a good example. Men don't have wings, so they can't fly. The Wright brothers shot that theory to pieces in their bicycle shop, for crying out loud. They didn't have a huge laboratory or federal backing. All they had was an idea, and the mechanical skills to make it work.

"I mean, look at Thomas Edison, Eli Whitney, Steve Jobs, dozens and dozens of people over the last hundred years have proven the impossible is actually achievable. Space flight is another impossibility that was brought into reality. And now, we have robots walking around all over the solar system. Who would have imagined thirty years ago that a robot could be sent to Mars, then have it blast a rock with a laser, and from the explosion we could determine the composition of that rock back on Earth?

"Impossible stuff, right? The stuff of science fiction, religion, mysticism. Things that can be believed, but that no one can actually do. Right?"

"Are you going to start making *Star Trek* episodes again?" Mark snickered. His eyes were blurry and Jonathan knew he had reached an end of his explanation.

"No, buddy," Jonathan said smiling. "But I think we need to get you home. You're about done for the night."

"Yeah," Mark slurred. "And I don't care where I fall asleep. I can sleep right on this table, or over on those people's tables—"

"Uh, yup, we're done here, come on big fella," Rachel said dragging his gaze back to the present.

"Oh, hi there pretty lady, do you want to see my etchings?"

"Okay, Mr. Sunshine, this evening is at an end," Rachel said drawing his face to hers with her hands. "Mark, I have really enjoyed being with you tonight, but sweetie you're a little over the edge. You're cute as a button and drunk as a skunk. It's time to get you home."

He thought she was hilarious.

Rachel stood and hoisted one of Mark's arms over her shoulder. Maggie took the other arm and lifted him. He sagged heavily against their effort.

"Hold on. Let me help," Jonathan offered as he stood.

It wasn't a pretty sight. The distinguished young doctor was lugged from the restaurant by his small entourage of friends. In the midst of the disturbance they were creating, Mark's jovial mood amused many in the restaurant.

"I can take him from here," Rachel offered once Mark was in the passenger seat of her car.

"No," Maggie said. "I'll go with you and help you get him home. I really don't mind." She looked at Jonathan. "Jonny, you had more work to finish tonight, isn't that what you said?"

"Well, yes I do. Are you sure it's okay?" Then he smiled. "I mean, I don't want you two to be stuck with this drunk. It might damage your reputations."

His joke affected the ladies' smiles and both beamed at him. They looked at each other then shook their heads.

"Nah! We have no reputations to defend," Maggie said, and they both broke into laughter. "We'll be fine, Jonny. Call me tomorrow, will you?"

"Sure." He took a step toward her and kissed her cheek. Then he paused as the girls struggled with their fumbling charge. "Thanks for dragging me out of my den. This was a wonderful night. I'll call."

Jonathan's mind instantly returned to his experiment. There was much work to be done. He had stopped in the middle of his most complex calculation and was eager to finish. His strides were long. He started to a jog when he got to the campus.

Inside the building he took three steps at a time. Yes, there was work to do. And while his mind was alert, he was ready to complete it.

*   *   *   *   *

A large, dark form is moving through the smoke. It is coming toward me. I must be still. I must not move. I am terrified by the large, dark creatures. They make no sound as they move through the gray smoke. I will not speak to them. I must not be seen by them.

This one stopped. It is just standing nearby. I can barely breathe.

Slowly, it is turning its head.

Toward me.

It looks directly at me. No. I press back into the dense smoke behind me. No. It must not see me. It must not find me.

It is leaning down looking at me. Quick! Push into the gray, into the smoke.

In the dark part of the gray, I cannot see. The smoke around me is too dense. I see nothing but the gray in front of my face.

The large creature is making a loud, deep noise. Is it speaking? The noise rolls like waves of thunder. It increases in volume then rumbles away. I do not understand. I do not like the large creatures. I will hide in the gray.

It will leave soon. I hope it will leave soon. I must hide.

4

Jonathan's "method" was unorthodox at best. At worst, well, it wasn't really sacrilege, but some might call it so. Subcutaneously injected drugs were a very important part of his method. Numerous psychotropic chemicals can create out-of-body experiences in some patients, while the same drug could bring others from their delusional fantasies to a sense of near reality. The balance and mix was crucial.

His experiments over the past several weeks left many of his test subjects dead. Fortunately, those subjects were lab rats, but the more recent combinations of drugs seemed to have a better result. He had expected the rats to suffer erratic behavior after they were injected, and wasn't surprised when they fell onto their sides convulsing and then lay still for several minutes. He was greatly relieved, however, when the first rat roused from a drug-induced "nap" and resumed normal rat activities.

Jonathan's greatest curiosity was what might be going on in the rat's brain during the period of unconsciousness. Did brain activity continue normally as a rat, or a person for that matter, experienced the drug-induced sleep? Was there a significant difference in the brain's responses under the influence of the drugs?

In his study he incorporated real-time monitoring of three key brain neurochemical classes in conscious, living rats. Each rodent was monitored with implantable amperometric electrodes, interfaced to a biotelemetric device.

The mobile device was coupled with a platinum-based biosensor and carbon-based micro sensors to detect three vital chemicals. The three chemicals were ascorbic acid, oxygen, and glucose. Their presence is the clearest evidence that the striatum, or the inside, frontal part of the brain, is still living. It is in the subcortial striatum that information fed to the brain is deciphered in both rats and humans.

Ascorbic acid, closely related to vitamin C, indicates that the process of digesting and distributing nutrients to the brain is occurring in the test subject. The need for oxygen is self-evident as is the presence of glucose, the fuel that actually feeds the brain. As long as ascorbic acid, oxygen and glucose were detectable, the subject was living and was expected to recover.

The small devices consisted of a miniaturized data transmitter, a single-supply sensor device, a current-to-voltage converter, and a microcontroller. The currents were digitized using an analog-to-digital converter integrated in a peripheral interface controller, then sent to a laptop through a miniaturized AM transmitter.

The miniaturized system had been used in clinical tests for several years monitoring lab rats. The findings advanced the science of the human brain functions tremendously. The science had introduced new treatments for Alzheimer's, as well as a dozen other conditions of dementia. Sensors became valuable tools to find answers to brain diseases in humans.

Jonathan was among the first to consider the direct application to the human brain. His purpose was not to heal a diseased or damaged brain, but rather to provide super strength to the human brain in an effort to reach beyond the known limits of knowledge, power, and experience.

His work did not stop there, however. The incorporation of elements of transcendental meditation was one of the links for his project. For centuries, spiritualists had claimed they accomplished astral flying. In effect, it was the mind-manipulated exit of the body, while maintaining full consciousness and control of one's motions and activities. He hoped for a true out-of-body experience enabling one to move from place to place, or theoretically, from dimension to dimension.

Jonathan knew it was still a little down the road. If his calculations were correct, his goal was possible. He felt he was close to achieving the results he wanted with the rats. Then, someday soon, he would take the journey himself.

*   *   *   *   *

Maggie and Rachel had planned to meet for brunch the next morning. Maggie was eager to hear more of Rachel's impression of Mark, at least her impression before the last bottle of port. Rachel and Mark had met for lunch two weeks earlier and it had not gone well. Rachel had confided in Maggie that they had both felt awkward. Their second meeting was better, but the dinner with Maggie and Jonathan had been different. The combination of the two couples brought out the best in each of them, and the clumsiness of Mark and Rachel's first encounter vanished.

Maggie waited for Rachel at her favorite table by the planter in the small café near Jonathan's apartment. Maggie loved the park across the street. She watched two boys tossing a Frisbee. They were obviously beginners. She smiled at their antics and clumsy efforts to mimic the more skillful throws they must have seen accomplished by older boys.

It was at that moment she saw him on the hill by one of the large trees. He was tall and thin, much like Jonathan. He was too far away to see his facial features clearly, but his movements were like him. Still, he seemed uncertain, not confident like Jonathan would be. Jonny loved the park and was comfortable in it. This man seemed awkward like he didn't really belong there. The whole thing puzzled her.

"Hey, what's got you looking so serious and strained?" Rachel said coming up behind her. Maggie spun quickly to see her, and then smiled.

"Oh, nothing. I was just watching those boys over there, and I thought . . ." Maggie glanced back to the park. The boys were still playing, but the man was gone. An odd look passed over her face; Rachel noticed.

"Are you okay?" she asked as she sat and pulled her chair to the table.

"I'm fine," Maggie replied and shrugged her shoulders. "Just, you know . . . stuff."

"I have a bachelor's degree in stuff," Rachel replied. "I know stuff."

"Well, forget all that. What did you think about Mark?"

"Mark the drunk, or Mark the gentleman?"

"Whichever is most favorable. I've known both of them for years."

"I have to admit, when we had lunch last week I thought he was boring and a little too intellectual for my taste. I mean, I love to read, but I have no interest in a relationship with a living textbook."

"Was it really all that bad?"

"No, of course not. Just a little comic relief to lighten your mood."

"Okay, fine, but what about last night?"

"I can't remember the last time I laughed that hard. Before you and Jonathan arrived, Mark and I talked about the most interesting things. And he really is funny."

"Oh, good!" Maggie was elated. Her eyes sparkled with excitement.

"Don't get too eager, now. It's still early." Rachel set a more sober tone. "Deep inside, I am very impressed with Mark, more than I'd like to admit. He's hot. He is a gentleman, and I thought he was very kind last night in particular."

"He is, isn't he. I'm just very happy you like him. He's a wonderful guy."

"There you go selling him again. You don't need to do that Maggie. I like him." Rachel smiled and Maggie beamed back at her.

"We have time for other things to develop," Maggie said. "Lots of time." From the corner of her eye she saw someone enter Jonathan's apartment staircase. She gasped and drew her hand to her lips.

"Are you all right?"

"No . . . I mean yes, I'm fine. I just thought I saw something," Maggie replied. "I'm sure it was nothing." She glanced back toward Jonathan's building. She saw the door close and a chill ran up her spine.

*   *   *   *   *

"Honey, I wish you would take some time to be with Jonny. He works so hard trying to hit that stupid ball all by himself. I can tell he's terribly frustrated," Alice said from behind the island in the kitchen.

"It's good for him. Somehow he has to learn to conquer the impossible. Otherwise, I would wonder if he was really my son." Martin chuckled at his own joke, but it was lost on Alice. She didn't smile.

"You almost sound like you don't care, Martin. Is that how you really feel, that you don't care?"

"Alice, I could spend every waking moment with the boy and do everything for him, but how would he ever learn to do things on his own? He's fine. It builds character." Martin turned the page in his newspaper.

Suddenly, the paper was ripped in two and torn from his hands. Alice stood over him. Fury burned in her eyes. Her teeth clenched, and her fists crushed the pieces of his paper.

"Listen to me, you coward," Alice said with a quivering voice. "I'm dead, and I can't do a thing about that, but Jonny needs you!"

Martin jerked awake. He was in his recliner with his paper in his lap. He looked around the family room and into the kitchen. Alice was nowhere to be seen.

He held up his newspaper. It was still one piece; it had not been torn. His heart raced and his breath was short. *It was a dream, that's all. It was a dream.*

Martin sat quietly, hoping his imagination would calm down. Serious, fearful thoughts haunted his mind. The dream was so real. He felt everything so vividly, even Alice's anger toward him. Was there something more to it?

The doorbell rang.

"Hi, Dad," Maggie said smiling as she came through the door. "I hope I didn't interrupt anything, did I? Is this a good time?"

"You didn't interrupt a thing. And if you did, how could I refuse to spend time with a beautiful young woman—especially you?" he replied as they embraced. "Would you care for some tea?"

"Yes, I would love a cup." Her answer was warm and appreciative, but Martin Walsh knew her well enough to know she was troubled. She wasn't the sparkling Maggie he was used to seeing. Something was wrong. Martin could tell at a glance that Maggie wasn't feeling well. She was upset. He decided fatherly compassion and care might help.

"Have you discovered any hopeful job prospects?" he asked.

"There are a couple of them I'm interested in," she replied. "Of course, after I graduate." She smiled as he handed her a steaming cup of tea.

"Don't burn yourself. I certainly hope none of them carry you far from here. I don't know what Jonathan or I would do without you."

"That's one reason I wanted to see you."

"About Jonathan, or leaving town?"

"Jonny. Then again, maybe both. I don't know, I thought we were really together in this, you know? Working together, getting married, making a life. It all seemed to make sense."

Maggie burst into tears. She buried her face in her hands and turned away from him. Martin had never seen her so distraught.

She faced him. "I mean, we used to talk every day, sometimes two or three times. We ran into each other all over campus, downtown, even when I was out with a bunch of girls, we'd see him, and he would wave and run to meet us. It just isn't like that anymore. Do you know what I mean?"

"Yes," Martin replied locking his eyes on the floor before him. He remembered many times he had behaved in that way. Unkindly, selfishly. He felt the guilt of abandoning his wife and young son far too many times for work that seemed important at the time. None of them were as important to him now as having one more evening with his wife Alice, or making the time to actually play catch with a nine-year-old boy. He quickly brushed away the melancholy.

"I'm at a loss," Maggie continued. "I haven't heard from him, or seen him in over a week. He doesn't call me anymore, and when I call him, even when I leave a message he doesn't call me back. I don't know what to do. Is it something I did or said?"

"No, Maggie, it isn't you, or anything you did. I did the same thing, and I was wrong. I would lock myself away in my thoughts and theories about mathematics, and ignore both Jonny and Alice. It was wrong then, and it is wrong now." His eyes were heavy with a deep sadness. He leaned toward her and his voice cracked as he spoke. "But I don't know what to tell you that will change things. I know I was wrong when I did this very thing to Alice . . . and Jonny. But how to change him? I don't know. I really don't."

"But I want to *see* him. I want to spend time with him, to laugh and smile like we did so many times. Why does he do this?"

"I don't know why, I really don't. Maybe you should just go get him!" Martin urged. "If you can, drag him out of that den of an office of his. Pull him out into the sunshine. That could work. Maggie, when I behaved like this I didn't see the damage I was doing to my marriage, and my son. I kept Alice exiled from my work and it haunts me to this day, and my son is just like me."

Maggie sighed. "I went by his office, but the door was locked." She blotted her tears. "I even knocked, but there was no answer."

"Have you been back?" Martin asked.

"Twice, but still no one answered. I'm worried about him. Why won't he open the dang door?"

An idea flashed into Martin's mind. "Maggie, we can fix this. I'll get a key from maintenance, and we'll get in. Come with me." He took her hand and led her to his car.

*   *   *   *   *

I have waited longer than before. I chased the last one, but I couldn't catch it. I lost it in the smoke. It was hard to get back here where it comes and goes.

I have thought about following it. I think I could go through the thick fog and find where it goes, or perhaps where it comes from. I could do that. Should I? Would I find my way back?

Where does it come from? Is there more smoke beyond here? Why does it come this way? I am not going to sit and wait all the time. I must follow it.

Maybe if I just press into the smoke a little. Wait, I feel something. It is something thick, but I can push on it . . . and then into it.

I pull my hand back. It is warm. The thick smoke is warmer than here.

Is there thick smoke where it goes? I walk to the other side, where it goes out and comes back. Again, I push my hand into the smoke, deeper and deeper. I feel it! Something thicker, but it is cold, too cold. I do not like the cold.

When it comes again I will go to the warm side. I will see where it comes from. Maybe then I will know why it comes here.

5

The test results with the newest combination of drugs were excellent. Jonathan was excited to see a different pattern in the rat's brain under the new drugs than when the rodents slept. It was new in each of the subjects, and the patterns were identical in all of them.

When his subjects experienced normal sleep, the brain activity was distinct and reflected normal respiration, detectable patterns of dream-like brain pulses common in rats, as well as the vital three detectable measurements of ascorbic acid, oxygen, and glucose.

For the last three days the results under psychotropic drugs were successful and produced identical responses in each rat. They all displayed muscle spasms for the first fifteen seconds after injection. When the spasms ceased, they became still, almost frozen.

Now at the end of the three day test, Jonathan was able to detect the slightest evidence of a pulse through the miniaturized devices on the rats. Respiration, however, was not detectable. The only evidence of respiration was in the oxygen levels shown on his laptop computer from the implanted sensors in each of the subjects.

The presence of ascorbic acid confirmed to him the brain was alive. It disturbed him that he could find no measurable brain activity. There was none whatsoever. The brain seemed suspended, nonfunctioning, but it was *not* dead. Glucose measured at near normal levels confirmed the rats' brains continued to live.

"It has got to be *suspended animation*," he spoke aloud. "All major functions are present except those *in the brain*."

Even more astonishing was the fact that each rodent "woke up" precisely three minutes and thirty seconds after going into a comatose state.

Jonathan spent part of the late afternoon constructing a device that could provide three simultaneous injections in three test subjects. He placed three cages side-by-side and prepared each rat for the test.

At the moment of injection the three rats responded identically. A smile spread across his face and he chuckled. *Almost like a chorus line, fellas.* The suspended or frozen state ended the choreographed convulsions and the trio remained absolutely still for three and a half minutes. At the precise same moment the three rodents revived.

Yes! You did it! Jonathan threw his hands in the air, jumped from his chair, and danced his own choreography. He pumped his fists and shuffled around his work station in celebration. The casual observer would conclude he had gone mad. But in his mind, Jonathan was exploding fireworks and dancing to a full orchestra.

He was certain he had come to the proper combinations of drugs that would prove his theory that the mind could be successfully separated from its host and reunited without measurable harmful effect. The math was too precise; the pharmaceuticals were too consistent for him to have any doubt. He had proven his case.

It worked.

*   *   *   *   *

The building was deserted and darkened in shadows as the trio entered. Evening swept over the spent day veiling well known paths into canyons darkness. Maggie headed to Jonathan's lab, along with Martin and the head of maintenance. She felt she was walking into some foreboding lair rather than into a building of classrooms. The ceilings seemed higher, almost out of sight in the gloom.

She wondered what kept Jonathan from seeing her. Was his work really that demanding? Was it so important that it kept them apart? Was there someone else and he was afraid to tell her? Her emotions were wearing thin, and questions seemed the greatest part of their relationship. She longed for their times together and did not fully understand his absence.

She could see the concern etched into Martin's face. She knew he worried for his son. Jonathan was repeating the mistakes his father had made decades ago. How could he relate the story of his own neglect without seeming accusatory? What was the best way to help his son avoid repeating the worst errors of his life? She sensed Martin felt trapped. Could he really not say what he felt? Did he realize that in saying nothing he risked condemning his own son to a lifetime of regret?

The threesome arrived at Jonathan's locked office door. Maggie shivered. The maintenance man slipped the key into the lock and twisted it. The lock made a sharp snapping sound as it released and sprang open. He slowly pushed the door inward into the darkened room.

* * * * *

Jonathan sat hunched over a pile of papers. The formulas that filled the pages documented his journey as he searched for the best adaptation of his research. How much of each drug would he need to duplicate the effects he had witnessed in his test subjects? What was the differential in mass and weight between a lab rat and a human being?

Two days previously Jonathan had started documenting his research on video. The results were remarkable. Each rat went through the convulsions and became completely stiff. The rodents all woke up exactly three and a half minutes later. Multiple videos showed the same results occur simultaneously on two rats injected at the same time, then three, and finally four different subjects. Finally, there it was, the conclusion he had pursued for months: a formula designed to produce, in a human subject, the results he had seen in his lab rats.

"That's it," he said out loud to an empty office. His voice croaked. It had been hours since he had last spoken, perhaps days. Any conversation in the lab was limited to Jonathan's thoughts.

Jonathan spun his desk chair around to his laptop and clicked to open the video of two rats going through what he had come to call "the process." The process included convulsions, the frozen stage he called lockdown, and, after three and a half minutes, revival. He clicked on the video file and leaned toward the screen.

He smiled as he watched each rat rummaging through their respective cages. He could see his own hand in the background preparing to initiate the injection. It came. Both rats stopped at the same instant and suddenly fell to their sides convulsing. He expected it, it was normal, it happened every time. Then they froze as was normal.

Then there was a flash.

"What was that?" he exclaimed aloud. "I haven't seen that before." There was a flash on the video he had not noticed earlier. It was a small, but very clear flash in both views, and not much more than a flicker. He stared at the computer screen. "What was that?" he said again.

He stopped the video and backed up to a frame just before the convulsions stopped. He moved forward in single-frame slow motion. Perhaps it was the shadows of the evening that revealed the previously unseen flash, although it was hardly more than a glimmer. Maybe he was just watching closely for the first time. For thirty frames, a full second in real time, the rats lay frozen on the screen.

Jonathan stared at the screen. He jumped back when he saw it. A single frame. He drew close. It showed a dim glow rising from each rat. The next frame caught a ball of light only centimeters from each rodent. In the third frame the soft glowing sphere streaked toward the lower left corner of each cage. A chill curled up his spine.

He stopped the video and fell back into his chair astonished. *What was that? Was it real? Am I finally going mad?* He replayed the video again and watched one frame at a time. It was real. Every time, he saw the light rise, form into a ball, and flash away. In one tenth of a second, a barely noticeable measure of time, a very mysterious event had occurred.

Jonathan focused intently on his computer screen. The room was shadowed in twilight, dark, veiled in mystery. The lock on the door snapped. He jumped at the sound. Three silhouetted figures stood peering into the darkened office. His mind raced. *Who's there? Why now? What?* Nearing panic, he stood without knowing what to do—run? Run where? He needed to—

The lights flashed on flooding the office in brightness. He shielded his eyes. Slowly, his eyes adjusted to the change from near total darkness to the full brightness of the room. The three figures moved slowly toward him. They approached him cautiously.

Then, a woman's voice penetrated the darkness, "Jonny?"

*   *   *   *   *

It has been a very long time. My gut is killing me. It must come soon. It has to be soon. It went through there. Right . . . there. I watched it. I marked the spot. That is where it will come back. It always comes back through the same place it goes. That is how I catch them. But if I don't wait, I will miss it. I will wait. I hate waiting.

I do not like hurting like this. I am angry that I must wait so long. When it comes I will show it how angry I am. I will pour my rage on this foolish thing. It will suffer more pain than I endure.

What was that? The noise.

Yes, that's it. That's the noise it makes. It's coming. Wait for it. There! Get it! Get it! "Oh, you are afraid. You should be afraid. Don't look at me like that. I have you. I HAVE YOU!"

Kill it! Kill it! Kill it! Kill it!

Yes. Be still. It is warm.

Now, eat.

*   *   *   *   *

"Jonny, are you all right?" Maggie asked putting her hand on his shoulder and sliding into the chair beside him. "Oh, Jonny, you look terrible. Have you eaten?"

He stared blankly at her before answering.

"No, I think I'm fine, Maggie," he spoke with a dry scratchy voice. "No, it was just the other day when we met with Mark and that girl, Rachel. Remember, you took Mark home because he was drunk?"

"Sweetheart," she said as tears formed in her eyes. "Jonny, that was more than a week ago."

She saw the shock in his face as if her words had hit him like a brick.

"More than a week ago? No, just the day before . . . was it yesterday? The day before?" he asked. She could see the confusion on his face, and was alarmed at how he stammered.

"W—was that . . . more than a week ago?" He was speechless.

"Honey, you need a break, you need to stop and eat, and," she paused, "take a bath every now and then."

"Oh, yeah, I got a pizza. It's over there," he said pointing to the dried remains of a supreme pizza, long past edible. "I did have some crackers and Cokes in the cooler. I did eat something."

Maggie gazed around the office. Two partially empty bottles of cola sat open, warm, and by now, certainly flat to the taste. Concern etched deep furrows in her brow. She brushed her fingers through his tangled hair and shook her head.

"Jonny, what are you doing to yourself in here?" she asked as her face reflected fear and concern. "Why haven't you called or come to your dad's house? You've been locked in here all this time?"

"I—I guess I have. I've been very busy, and I must have simply lost track. I'm sorry." He smiled weakly. "I don't know what to say. I mean . . . I was just watching this video . . . there was this . . . thing. And I—"

"Son, I want you to come home and rest for a few days. Please?" his father asked gently. "I think you'll feel better."

It took a moment.

"Jonny, you need to come home." Maggie felt she was pulling a victim from a car wreck. She coaxed him gently while she stroked his shoulders and cheek.

He looked at her. "Wow, I've actually been in here a week?" He shook his head and half laughed. "I didn't think that was possible."

"It's true, son," his father said softly. "Why don't we take you home and get some food in you. Then, you need to rest."

Jonathan nodded.

"You're right. I am beat. And I'm hungry, too." He smiled and looked at the concerned pair next to him. "I really am tired."

"You'd better come with me, buster," Maggie said hoisting his arm over her shoulder. He didn't argue but slowly stood to his feet. The threesome made their way from the stuffy lab, down the hall, and into the crisp night air.

*   *   *   *   *

One of the large shadows made a noise that woke me. I move to the edge of the thick gray smoke to be hidden. I can see just enough. The large creature is passing by my hiding place. Now it is gone. Slowly I emerge from the thick smoke. What are they? Why do they come here?

I feel much better after I catch the smaller ones. I am much stronger. I have decided I am going through the smoke to the warm side. I made the decision when I woke, after the creature passed. I will go through. But I will not go through where it comes from. I will go through further down. I don't want to run into it.

That is what I will call it. I will call it *It*. It never tells me a name. It does not speak to me. It does not see me. Does It know about me?

I run down the side of the smoke to a different place. This will be better if It comes. I will not run into It. I am going through to see where It comes from. I press into the smoke. I feel the thick smoke ahead of me. I push against it, harder and harder. Suddenly, I am through and on the other side.

It is dark here. Many things are around me, touching me, but not grabbing me. The things are soft. I reach to the side. The side is hard. I cannot push through it like the smoke. I reach to the other side. It is hard as well. I reach forward.

I touch something hard there also. I push on it. It moves. Bright! The light is very bright, so bright that I hide my eyes. It hurts my eyes. It is getting better. Not too bright.

Again, I push against what is before me. It moves again. It swings further away and I crawl toward the brightness. The soft things brush against my bare back. I stumble over other things cluttering the floor.

I look out into the brightness. I see things that I do not know. Things here are different than in the smoke. I feel the warmth and I like it. I enter the space. It is a box, a box with holes and openings.

Something is familiar about this place. I have never been here, but I know it.

A small part of one wall has an opening. I walk to it and pull it open. It leads down to a lower level. Yes, these are called stairs. I walk down them. I know this, but I do not know how I know it.

Something is not right. I go back up the stairs. I am naked and to be here I should not be naked. I am not sure why, but I know I must not be naked. I search in the soft things that brushed against me. In the light I can see they are garments that I can put on and wear.

I cover my legs and my arms. The flat circles fit through the small holes in the front of the garment. Buttons, these are buttons. I am no longer naked.

I go down the stairs and outside. It is very bright. It is not smoky or foggy. I can see clearly for a great distance. I walk across the hard surface to the cool, green grass. Yes, this is grass. It is chilly on my bare feet.

I walk to the top of the hill. Perhaps I will see the smoke from there. Perhaps I will see It.

Two small ones are throwing a round object back and forth to each other. Why do they do that? Does this make them bigger, or strong? It makes nothing for them to eat, I can see that. Why should they do it again and again?

Someone is looking at me. I can feel it. Who? Where are they? Oh, that one, the one with the golden hair. I can tell which one it is. I can tell. It is the one sitting across from me, the other side of the hard surface. Why is that one watching me? Did I do something wrong? Now there are two together. I must go back. I must not be seen.

I hide behind a tree and wait. When I see that the one with golden hair is not looking at me, I will go back. Move slowly. Stay out of sight. Get back. Get back to the smoke. I must move quickly through the grass, up the stairs, into the smoke. I am home.

6

The next few days were wonderful. Jonathan ate mounds of food that was not only tasty but reminded him of his mom's cooking. He felt his strength returning.

"Maggie, this is fabulous. I don't think Mom could have made it any better."

"I happen to know that she did," she replied and popped him on the nose with her serving spoon. "She cooked by the way she felt. I just happen to have taken very careful notes."

"Well, I have no complaints here. It's great."

"And you're *looking* a lot better," she said with a playful smile. She leaned across the table and kissed him.

"Whoa! Don't mean to break up the party," Martin said entering the kitchen.

Jonathan and Maggie laughed.

"Hey, Dad. I can't remember ever being so pampered or well fed."

Martin stopped and grabbed the sides of his stomach with both hands. "Now you can understand why I have *this* problem."

Jonny hadn't laughed in much too long. His recovery was evident to all three of them. He was vibrant, alive, and especially enjoyed spending time with Maggie.

Still, the shadow of his research hung quietly in the background. Something very unusual had occurred. The scientist in him hungered to know more. He would still slip into periods of quiet, and his thoughts would drift to his lab.

Later that afternoon, Maggie called to him. "Jonny." He did not respond.

Could the sphere actually be the spirit of a living creature? Do rats have a spirit? Or more of a life-force than . . .

"Jonny," she said again.

" . . . but do animals have souls? Surely not, but there is a common force in all living things that cause them—"

"Jonny!" Maggie said firmly.

He abruptly turned to face her.

"What?" His eyes were wide with surprise. "I'm sorry," he said taking her hand in his. "I was lost in my thoughts again. Honey, I'm sorry."

She was stern, almost fierce. "Do you mean it?"

"I want to."

Maggie's gaze softened. "Okay, I know you're working through not being at your lab, but somehow you need to stay connected to the real world. I think we need to get out and do something. What do you think?"

"Going out would be great. I feel much better. My head is clear, I feel rested and I think I'm ready. What do you have in mind . . . nurse?" His whimsical smile calmed her. He was okay. It was time to play.

Maggie smiled at him flirtingly and made the most of her soft southern inflection. "Oh, doctor, I'm sure nothing I could ever imagine would match your ability to design an evening that would sweep a poor, simple girl like me off her feet."

"I see," he replied leaning back and fumbled into a feeble impersonation of the cartoon character Foghorn Leghorn. "I say, I understand how difficult it might be for a girl like you to encounter the ways of the world without proper guidance. I imagine I could plan a special evening for the two of us."

"Sir," Maggie replied coyly, "are you propositioning little old me?"

"Absolutely. And if you don't say yes, I just might have to whisk you away unwittingly."

"My, but you are so forceful," she said walking her fingers up his arm, "and strong."

Sliding her hand around his neck, she slipped into his lap and kissed him, really kissed him.

Jonathan was breathless and stunned. Not at her, but at the rush of emotion he felt. It seemed he was a dead man brought to life by her lips. It was as if his life that had gone to sleep was awakened by a kiss.

"Holy crap," he said looking into her eyes. In the moment, Jonathan was speechless. His own eyes were wide with wonder. Hers were languid pools of passion longing for more.

"Yes, we need to go out," she said popping to her feet and striding toward the kitchen. "Friday work for you?" she asked over her shoulder.

Jonathan swallowed hard and watched her walk away. *Friday? Yeah, Friday.*

Realizing he hadn't spoken, he cleared his throat and said, "Right, sure. Friday is just fine. It's good."

Friday would be very good, indeed.

*   *   *   *   *

"I'm glad you picked a different restaurant," Jonathan said. As he climbed out of his sports car, he saw Mark and Rachel who were already at the restaurant door. "Hey, you two."

Mark turned and walked toward them smiling. "Hey, back at ya." The two friends embraced. Reunion for old acquaintances was a special treat. They hadn't seen each other for over two weeks, and for boys who had been together every day, it was all the more reason to celebrate.

"You met Rachel, right?" Mark asked placing his arm around her shoulder. "Wait, oh that's right, you were there *that* night, the one I don't remember. Hmm, that's embarrassing."

"Well, I *do* remember, and I *was* there," Jonathan said. Everyone laughed. Jonathan greeted Rachel and kissed her cheek. "Yes, Mark, even a mad scientist doesn't forget a beautiful woman."

"You better not," Maggie giggled pulling him away from Rachel.

"Maggie, what did it take to break this guy out of prison like you did? I mean, Jonathan, we didn't see you or hear from you for what, two weeks?" Mark's jab was well-intentioned, and it was received that way, but it bored a deep ache into Jonathan's heart and thoughts.

"I know," Jonathan replied. "I cannot tell you how embarrassed *I* am for being so focused on myself and *my* ambition. I'm really sorry."

Mark took him by the shoulders and shook him. "It's okay, buddy, just don't do that again. We missed you and your jokes." The two men's eyes met. "I mean that. We were very concerned."

"I don't deserve good friends like you," Jonathan said.

"Yes you do," Maggie chimed in grabbing his arm pulling him toward the restaurant door. "It took a case of dynamite and the secret key to unlock the door. Then, we freed him from his Dungeon of Isolation and Despair. Of course, it took three days to scrub the stench off him once he was out."

Mark gasped. "You mean you scrubbed him? Maggie, you gave him a *bath*? Oh, for the love of God, our dear Maggie has gone beyond all limits of modesty and propriety."

"No, you goofball," she complained swatting Mark's arm. "He showered himself . . . alone! I just kept sending him back."

The concierge greeted the rowdy group as they entered the waiting area. He quietly took their registration and ushered them to a corner booth out of the mainstream of the dining area.

"Okay, Einstein, clue us in on your work. What is it that captivated you?" Mark asked once they were seated.

Jonathan looked at his friend. Mark was smiling.

"Now hold on there," Jonathan said. "This is not going to be Three Stooges material. I know you, and you're most likely expecting some farcical fable of scientific exploits. My work just isn't that. It's not anything silly."

"If it was silly you couldn't help but blab it everywhere and keep us all in stitches," Maggie said. "You've been pretty quiet about it."

"Because it *is* serious," he said gently touching his index finger to her nose. She smiled.

"So spin your tale, doctor," Mark said downing another glass of wine.

Rachel took his glass from his lips and returned it to the table. "You'd better slow down buster or you're going to have the whole room spinning."

In reality, Jonathan's research was deep and trending toward dark. The darkness both intrigued and frightened him. His curiosity had driven him to overcome his fears, but it was also what had trapped him.

Perhaps a light discussion among friends would help him focus his perspective. He smiled and leaned toward Mark.

"I've been studying brain functions in rats."

Mark burst into a laugh.

"I've been doing the same thing, but they all end up back in Washington DC anyway. What's with that?" Those around the table erupted in laughter. "I'm sorry Jonny-boy, I couldn't resist."

"No problem." Jonathan had always loved Mark's wit and in some ways envied it. "Actually, and seriously, I've discovered something that I cannot fully explain. The transmitters I've placed on my test subjects—"

"Transmitters? What do you mean?" Rachel asked. "I work in the library, so I'm sorta out of the brain research loop. What do you mean by transmitters?"

"They're very tiny packets of instruments that measure vital chemicals in the brain. They've been used in Alzheimer's studies for years. When certain essential chemicals are not present, the subject dies. As long as the chemicals can be measured, there is a good chance the life process is continuing."

"Should I be monitoring those same functions in Mark?" Rachel asked demurely.

"One might question if there is any brain function to monitor," Mark jested by rolling his eyes and sticking his tongue out the corner of his mouth.

Jonathan smiled and watched Rachel and Mark kiss. Maggie took his hand and encouraged him to continue with his explanation. He took her cue.

"You see, I have developed a sophisticated cocktail of psychotropic drugs that induce a trance or even near death-like state. It has taken over two years of research while I was in grad school to lay the foundation in finding the suitable drugs and to arrive at the starting point of my research."

"Jonny, are you using the same drugs you wrote about in your grant application? You're talking about some pretty powerful, even dangerous drugs here like you're mixing iced tea and lemonade. Is it really so casual?" Maggie asked.

"No, it isn't at all casual. I know it can sound like that, but I have gone to great lengths to make sure I'm being careful."

"So you monitor the brain functions during the time they are under the influence of the cocktail?" Mark asked leaning forward on the table.

"Yes, as well as before and after. But you must understand this is years of research condensed into a brief explanation. The full scope of what I have accomplished is much more."

"I would imagine it is," Rachel said. "Are you going to hire a lab assistant or is your super-secret work all done in your clandestine laboratory?"

Jonathan smiled. He liked Rachel.

"No research assistant at this point," he answered. "Maybe down the road a bit. I want to keep as much of this under wraps as I can until I am able to gain ownership of the process. Until then, it's just me working with my patients."

"I assume by patients you mean rats, right?" Rachel asked.

"Yes, rats. And they are my only patients. The formula is much more precise than even two weeks ago. I think I'm very close. In more than fifty treatments my subjects have responded to the process, and then resumed normal activity afterward."

"No side-effects?" Mark asked.

"None. They act like rats," Jonathan said. "Of course, early on I lost a lot of them in the testing process."

Mark leaned back in his chair brandishing an imaginary cigar. "So, doctor, how many of your patients have died under your care?"

"Just over two hundred."

"Wait. You mean locked away in your lab you have *killed* over two hundred lab rats? *Two hundred?*" Maggie asked.

"Yes, but that's why we use rats in research. It happens all the time. Things don't always work properly, even if the science is exactly right."

The waiter arrived and took their orders, and when he left, Jonathan said, "I started videoing my subjects. I inject the rats and watch very carefully how they react each time. In each case, the rat goes into fairly violent convulsions for precisely fifteen seconds. Then it falls over and looks totally dead. I can't measure a pulse or respiration, but the brain continues to function normally."

"They're dead, just not brain dead," Mark added.

"In a sense, yes, they do appear as dead, but they're not. And exactly, and I mean at the precise micro-second, in every case they wake up three minutes and thirty seconds after they become motionless. Every single time." Smiling, Jonathan looked around the table at three blank faces.

"So," Rachel leaned toward him on her elbows, "it seems you have affected the proper treatment to give a three and a half minute nap to a rat. What's the objective in that?" Rachel asked with a sardonic smile.

Jonathan caught her humor and smiled. "The goal is not the nap. The goal is a separation."

"Separation? What do you mean by separation?" Maggie asked.

Jonathan knew this was the point where his work departed from common, rational thought. He glanced at the table then quickly at the faces of his three friends and knew even an honest answer could mean trouble.

"Yes, Jonathan," Mark asked. "What are you separating?"

"The goal is the separation of the life force from the life host." His words crashed like cannonballs on the table. Maggie froze. Rachel leaned back in her chair never taking her eyes off him. Mark's jaw dropped. They were stunned to silence.

Jonathan felt their glares as much as he saw them. His mind fumbled his next thought, and he searched for what he should say next. After a very uncomfortable pause Maggie broke the silence.

"Jonny, you're not serious, are you?" Maggie wasn't smiling. She sat still for a second glaring at the table. "I don't know how to say this, but do you know how crazy that sounds?"

"Strange perhaps, but not crazy," he protested gently. "Numerous events occur every year with people who *die*, float above their body on the hospital gurney, and then for some strange reason, reunite with their human mass, and continue to live."

"But Jonny-boy, that's simply cheating death," Mark said.

"No, I'm convinced it's *more* than that. The intelligence and the personality are both living, and they are aware they are outside the body. The patients remember it. They come back to it. Dozens of books are published every year where someone tells about their death and their trip to heaven, or wherever. All I'm doing is investigating that kind of phenomenon."

"Jonny, those people actually die. Isn't it pretty dangerous to play around with something that is such a high risk?" Maggie asked.

"Play around? Now you understand why my father thinks I am a blithering idiot."

"No, Jonathan, you're not an idiot," Mark said. "It's just . . . well, we've just never heard of anything like this. *I—I've* never heard anything like this, and I'm a *scientist*. I mean, *wow*. I mean, my head is spinning with the impact of what you're saying."

"It is a bit *out there*, I admit."

"You said you found something you can't explain. What's the part you don't understand, Jonathan? I mean I don't understand any of it, but what don't *you* get?" Rachel pressed.

Jonathan took a deep breath. He knew he was far past credible in their minds. They had not worked through all the initial investigation. How could they possibly understand what he was just beginning to see? He continued.

"Well, I have videoed all my experiments. Just the other night—the night you and Dad rescued me, and I guess it was because it was dark . . . I noticed a flash in one of my videos." He looked at his friends. He felt like he was telling a ghost story, and his audience was awestruck.

"I hadn't seen it before, so I went back and watched frame-by-frame through the experiment. Immediately after the convulsions stop, in just a three frame sequence, a glowing, kind of smoky ball of light rises from the rat's body and then flashes away. The whole thing takes one-tenth of a second." Every eye around the table was locked on him. Every jaw was slack. Silence hung over their table like a shroud muting the noise around them, and sealing the four friends in a bubble of astonished isolation.

"Then, after three minutes and thirty seconds, *exactly*, it comes back. The rat revives and starts acting like a rat again."

"What do you think the light is?" Maggie asked. Fear was in her eyes.

"I don't know."

"I know. Or at least I think I have an idea," Rachel said.

"What? What do you think it is?" Mark asked.

"Like I said, I work at the library," she began. "I know library science isn't like your studies in science, but it fascinates me. So, I read a lot. This light you said that comes from the rats' bodies, what does it look like? I mean what color? What shape?"

"Well, it's very faint," Jonathan said. "In the first frame it's a simple streak, almost smoke-like. In the second frame it seems to come together into a translucent ball, and then in the third it streaks away. It always exits the video in the same direction, but each frame is only one-thirtieth of a second."

"It forms into a ball, an orb. Is that correct?" Rachel asked.

"Yeah, an orb."

Rachel continued, "Many who research the paranormal claim to have seen the presence of 'life forces,' or spirits, as orbs of light. Some have produced pictures of light orbs they cannot account for. Back home in southwest Missouri, there is this particular road where the spirit light appears. Folks have known about it for years, gone out to see it for decades, but it's still unexplained. No one knows what causes it.

"It could be that you have accomplished your goal, Jonathan. Maybe you have separated that life force from its host." Rachel stopped. Mark and Maggie were speechless.

The waiter arrived with dinner, and the silence was broken. He placed the plates filled with hot delicacies from tray to table with elegant precision. The aromas filled the corner booth.

"I think I'm going to be sick," Maggie said staring at her food. Her face was pale and her eyes swam with confusion.

Jonathan slid his arm around her and moved to her side. "Honey, it is only research."

"I don't know, I just don't think I can eat. Jonathan, this is very serious."

"I'm not doing anything but studying effects, possibilities, and asking questions."

"No. What you're saying, what you're considering, what you're *doing* terrifies me. I can't imagine why you want to do this. What's the purpose?"

"I want to find answers, that all. That's what research is, right Mark?"

He looked to his friend for help, but Mark's face did not reflect much sympathy. His eyes were etched in concern.

"Generally, yes, but you're talking about stuff that goes way beyond *generally*. I mean there are some very bizarre things happening in my field of artificial intelligence. But what I just heard breaches the limits of reason." Mark was stone-faced.

Jonathan sat up straight. "Breaches the limits of reason? Really?"

"Yeah," Mark said. "I read three articles just this week about work in AI to mimic human thought and there has been such a backlash that some very good scientists are getting their funding pulled. And these are people simply *talking* about fringe science, not actually *doing* it."

Jonathan's voice rose. "And I'm not *doing* anything either. I'm just . . . looking." His face flushed.

"It's one thing to create . . . or imitate what occurs naturally using scientific methods, but Jonny-boy . . . this takes a huge leap toward weird." Mark leaned back and looked at Jonathan with one eyebrow slightly raised.

Jonathan knew the look.

"Look, I know it sounds strange," Jonathan said. "And I know it is difficult to grasp. I understand that. We have always been curious about weird things. Remember the comic books we read? Those far-out stories of traveling to a different dimension, wormholes, time travel. We loved that stuff. I'm just asking questions."

"Wormholes, time travel!" Maggie exclaimed. "Jonathan Walsh, what in the world are you thinking? Are you serious?"

"Sweetheart, no, I'm not building a time machine or anything like that," Jonathan said laughing it off in an attempt to console her.

"Don't you laugh at me, Jonathan Walsh."

"No, honey, I'm not. It's just research—seeking to discover, asking questions. Please, settle down."

"Settle down? You're talking about sending rats off to God knows where. What's next? Are *you* going to want to know where *where* really is? Are you going to do something to yourself as a human-rat to see if you can find a *wormhole*?"

"No, I'm not going to—"

"Don't tell me you haven't thought about that. Your mind loves that sort of junk. You daydream about it. I've *watched* you sit lost in some world or other. And I'm supposed to be calm?"

"You watched me?"

"Oh, Jonny, yes. You have been sitting staring off into space a lot this past week. Just the other day I had to call your name three or four times to talk about coming out tonight. Your mind wasn't even in the room when I called you. I don't know, maybe your thoughts were back in your lab, or someplace *worse*."

"I know, but please calm down, we can talk—"

"Jonathan, what am I supposed to be calm about? I love you. I do *not* want you doing something to yourself that goes wrong. I cannot settle down when you talk like that. Jonny, these psychotropic drugs are dangerous."

"I'm not going to do anything to myself. Maggie, I'm only asking questions, that's all." Inside he knew she would join ranks with his father. It would be two against one. He was the only one who really understood what he was doing. "Don't worry about this honey, please. I'm simply looking into something that fascinates me, like books fascinate you. I've thought about these things for my entire life; they're things I want to know."

"Jonny, there are things I want to know as well, but none of them sound anything like this craziness. You scare me. You cannot possibly be saying or thinking these things and not be a serious danger to yourself. None of your grant application said *anything* about stuff like this. You *never* indicated an interest in soul-separation or time travel. I went through your papers and application in *great* detail, *nothing* was written about finding your *orb* or anything like that. You just cannot be serious." Maggie's eyes brimmed with tears.

"I am not some wet-behind-the-ears chemistry student. I have worked for years and studied the effects these chemicals, their properties, even the effects one drug might have on another. In the proper amounts the drugs do not present a risk of causing damage to humans. Trust me I'm a doctor, for cryin' out loud."

"Jonathan, I know you are a meticulous research scientist," Mark said. "But do you think it might be a good idea to bring another pair or two of eyes into your work? I mean, what could it hurt? Maybe another researcher would add credibility to your work, or they could see something you may have missed?"

"Damn it, nothing has been missed!" Jonathan's frustration was beginning to show. He felt exactly like he did when his Dad cross-examined him as a kid. "Believe me, this is a fascinating and ground-breaking research program I have started. Soon, when everything is well documented, I will bring in an assistant."

He took a breath but everyone else was silent, except Maggie.

"I gotta go. Get up, Jonny. Let me out."

"Okay, just forget about it. Let's have dinner and go do something fun and forget all this junk," he said in frustration.

"Get out of my way. I want out."

"All right, I'm sorry," he said as he scooted to the edge of the bench. "But you guys asked."

"Just let me out. Please." Jonathan stood and Maggie bolted from the booth toward the restaurant door. He looked at Mark and Rachel for some idea of what he should do. They said nothing. Then Mark gave him a *go-after-her* nod and he ran for the door.

"Wait, Maggie," he called after her. He raced outside and ran after her. He caught up with her at the far end of the parking lot. "Wait Maggie, please."

"No! There is nothing to discuss." She didn't break her stride.

"Come on, honey," he protested, running after her. "I'm only doing—"

Maggie stopped abruptly and turned to him.

"Jonathan Walsh, there is nothing to talk about. Nothing! Until you are *done* with this crazy idea of yours, I'm done with *you*." Immediately, she turned and ran down the sidewalk.

Jonathan stood alone in the night air. The woman he loved had just rejected him. The work he loved had betrayed him. He felt numb.

*   *   *   *   *

I do not understand why It comes here. When I went to the place It comes from, I thought it was very pleasant. Why would It leave a wonderful place and come into the smoke just so I would kill It? That makes no sense to me.

Perhaps something frightens It like the large creatures frighten me. Is It running from a great terror, or a horrible enemy? Does It fear its home? Why should It pass through the smoke?

I will go again to the warm side through the smoke. I will be very careful and try to discover why It comes. I will not be afraid as I am of the large creatures. Very soon I will go. First, I must wait for It to return one more time. I am hungry.

7

"Dad, I really don't know why it set her off. All I was trying to do is explain my research." Jonathan sat slumped on the living room couch. His dad puffed on his favorite pipe with serious eyes fixed on his young son.

"You may not believe me, but I do understand. Your mother wanted me to be at home more than I was. I could always find more work . . . and I did. I can't say that we ever succeeded in settling the issue. I don't know the answer, son. Wish I could be more help."

The two men sat in silence. The elder longed for the opportunity to fix mistakes in his past, the younger was confounded by errors in judgment made in the present. Jonathan was struck by the odd circumstance. Father and son, constantly at odds, found common ground in their failure to communicate with the women they loved most.

"She thinks I'm insane. And I know you think I'm nuts for the work I'm doing," Jonathan began. "But I have worked very hard and the numbers, the calculations always work out as I imagined they might. Oh, there have been surprises, but those unexpected turns opened new avenues to consider."

"Son, I've chased numbers for many, many years. They have always fascinated me, too. Scalar and vector functions, polynomials, canonical forms of matrices, quadratics, things of serious math just make my juices flow, but I could never begin to explain them to your mother."

"Believe me, I know, Dad. I can't imagine how to help Maggie understand Grundy-Sprague."

"Is that your basis point? Is that where you begin?"

"No, it's not the beginning point, but I got there pretty quick. I mean I'm running two sets of postulations that come to a point of conflict that neither math nor any science I'm aware of has ever clearly addressed. The first is based in biological data whose positions are largely indexed by natural numbers, but very quickly advance to successive heap-sized nims. The second is more ethereal and depends on factors beyond ordinal numbers to simply calculate the size of a single heap equivalent."

"I see where you're going . . . but . . . game theory?"

"I felt it was the most applicable for attempting to bring two such different sequences together. I mean, both are vastly random, and Grundy-Sprague seemed to make sense. After all, isn't life pretty much a game?"

"In a sense, but I'm not sure it's a game with which one should play. No, sorry. That's the wrong word to use."

"You're right. It is not play, Dad." The edge was back. Jonathan's eyes darkened and he glared at his father.

"Of course not, I know your work is not play. I really am sorry. What I meant was can we cross unimagined limits in our work that might have unknown consequences?"

"Like splitting the atom? They didn't know what might happen when the first atom split. I know, what we don't know could be the thing that destroys all of us once we find it. Or, the one that saves us. Maybe . . . but if we never look, we'll never see it either, will we?" Jonathan shrugged and smiled at his dad.

"I guess someone must peek over the edge of the impossible every once in a while." Martin leaned over the arm of his chair toward Jonathan. "Look, we're not going to settle our differences in a single night. All I know is that I spent a lot of time away from you and your mother that, at this point in my life, I would like to have back. There is more to life than numbers, son, much more."

"You're right, Dad," he said nodding. He couldn't be angry at him for the things he regretted. He remembered the times of disappointment when his father failed to show at a ballgame or school play because he was working. He looked at his dad. His father's aged face was tight lipped, and his eyes were softened with quiet sorrow. Jonathan stood up and embraced him. "I need to keep that in mind. Any recommendations on how I could explain it to Maggie?"

"Right now? No. Give it some time, a day or two. Maybe you'll find the right words."

"Thanks, Dad." Jonathan stood preparing to leave. "You know, this was good tonight. We just finished a conversation about research and there was no yelling. Wow. Who would ever think *that* could happen?"

Martin chuckled and grinned at his son. "They say miracles do still happen. We should see each other again, real soon." Jonathan walked slowly to the door.

"Yeah. I think Mom would have enjoyed tonight."

"I believe she would have, son."

"Good night, Dad."

"Night."

Jonathan stepped outside and stood for a moment on the porch. Trying to track Maggie down and make things right was not going to happen on that evening. It would take a while. She would forgive him at some point.

He ambled down the walk and out the gate. He had a choice to make: go home and to bed or spend a little time in his lab; to the right, or to the left? It only took an instant. The lab won, and he took off at a jog toward the campus.

*   *   *   *   *

Maggie didn't call or come around for days. Or was it weeks? Jonathan kept losing track of the time and day, buried deep in his work. Rachel's explanation of the flashing orbs further enticed his curiosity for what might actually be happening in his experiments, intended or unintended. Could the orbs be the actual life force coming out of the rats' bodies? Was he actually witnessing the separation?

The questions drove him deeper. He ordered higher resolution cameras so he could document the events in super-slow motion. The Phantom Miro 310 camera allowed him to record 3.2 gigapixel vids at thirty-two hundred frames per second, more than one hundred times the rate of his original videos. The difference was astonishing.

In the high-definition frame the orbs became crystal clear rather than the smoky blob he had witnessed originally. Every orb was distinct, different from every other orb. The orbs were distinct to the individual subject and unique from the orb of every other rat.

The orbs consisted of a smoky outer layer encasing many constantly changing forms inside. The colors were different as well. Some orbs seemed to contain more of one color than another, more red than green, but another more blue or even yellowish tinges. They were much like a fingerprint or a voiceprint, unique to each subject.

The images held him in near trance. His eyes burned reminding him to blink.

The orbs would exit the body of the lab subject in the shape of a comet. The leading ball that contained the colorful shapes pressed upward a few centimeters dragging a trail of light behind. The tail wrapped itself into the orb as the entire mass slowly spun around. Then, in a flash barely caught by the high-speed camera, the orb would elongate and streak out of the frame.

Jonathan was once again lost in his world of discovery. The formula was working perfectly. He made some slight refinements for the rats that responded the quickest, and recovered most rapidly. The adjustments to the serum improved the event at both ends. The convulsions were less violent and shorter, and the rats resumed normal activity almost instantly. There were no visible physical or behavioral effects on the animals even after dozens of treatments, and the orbs left and returned in precisely the same timing and manner.

He didn't remember when the thought first crossed his mind. He should have written it down. An entire series of questions would not be quieted in his thoughts. *What happened to the rat during the event? Where did it go? Did it go anywhere? Was there pain? Was there fear?* They cycled through his mind again and again, and somewhere in it all . . . the line was crossed.

*   *   *   *   *

The calculations weren't all that difficult. He used a mass/density procedure to assure the medications were measured to the proper amounts. The first test was on a very large rat, then a guinea pig. The calculations were spot on. The adjusted formulas were perfect for the mass of the larger rodents and their heavier weights as well as the pattern was replicated perfectly.

Jonathan got up from his desk and walked across his lab to retrieve data from an earlier experiment. That was when he saw his reflection in the glass door of the book case. He stopped and stared. A shiver ran down his spine as he realized he had completely lost track of time. All time. He knew he had eaten, but he wasn't sure when he had actually eaten a meal.

In a panic he shut down his equipment, made sure his subjects were watered and fed, then grabbed his jacket. Jonathan fled from his lab. But he could feel his research haunting him, following him, and reaching toward him with ghostly talons to drag him back. He felt fear, a terror he must escape. He ran.

Jonathan dashed down the darkened hallway. Outside, his pulse pounded in his ears as he leaped down the steps. Those vaporous claws of unknown evil closed in on him, pursuing him to wrench him from this world, and imprison him in darkness. Perspiration stung his eye and his feet pounded the sidewalk beneath him. His lungs burned and his mouth was parched.

Sprinting toward the parking lot, he swung around the stone pylon marking the campus edge and stumbled as he nearly toppled two young women walking down the sidewalk. He steadied himself and regained his footing.

"Jonny?"

It can't be, he thought. "Maggie?"

Maggie and Rachel stared at him.

I must look like a wild man. I'm a mess; I haven't shaved and I'm covered with sweat. And I bet I smell bad. Jonathan realized he only thinking, not speaking. "I—I, uh . . . my work . . . there was—"

"Jonny?" Maggie said again. "Oh, Jonny, you look awful."

"Oh, yeah," he smiled and glanced toward his building with terror in his eyes. "Sorry, it's been an unusual—"

"Forget it," Maggie said coldly. She grabbed Rachel's arm, turned her, and walked briskly down the walk. Rachel glanced back as they left. Her gaze lingered only a second but spoke volumes of anger and disgust before she turned away.

Jonathan stood still. Words did not come to his lips. His thoughts spun in his head but not a single one was clear enough to enable coherent speech. He was sure he mumbled something, but it was unclear, even to him.

The fear caught up with him and reasserted its threat. The only word that entered his mind was *no*. It echoed in his thoughts, *No, No, No*. He turned and ran, hoping to find his car and flee the wretched advance of the terror pursuing him.

* * * * *

When Jonathan awoke, his apartment was quiet. Sunlight poured through the window and across his bed warming him. He fought off slumber to fully awaken. Exhaustion weighed him down.

The horror that drove him from his office and laboratory had dissipated in his heavy sleep. He could not remember dreaming. Actually, he didn't remember returning home or getting into bed. He did recall the fear, but could not imagine why it seemed so real and threatening. He was relieved it was gone.

He rolled to his side and looked around his bedroom. It was a mess. The closet door stood open with dirty clothes hanging on both knobs, a pair of jeans tossed over the top of the door itself. Dirty socks and underwear were scattered in the direction of the hamper, some partially in the open lid. Shoes, papers, more shirts, and other articles of clothing were scattered everywhere.

Jonathan sighed and glanced at the clock on the bedside table. It was almost eleven in the morning. His stomach gnawed at him, but he forced himself to crawl from his bed. But before he ate anything, he would pick up and shower. He could barely stand being around himself. *No wonder Maggie walked away*, he thought.

He was unable to force himself to move quickly. Collecting his soiled clothing was a slow process. Weakness weighed him down. Normal life was little more than a memory and his greatest accomplishment seemed to be alienating the person for whom he cared the most. Maggie's look of disgust was burned into his memory. He was losing her. That thought alone depressed him.

The clutter around his room was finally gathered into the laundry basket. Jonathan stripped himself and trudged into the shower. The hot water burned him, and at the same time seemed to wash a great weight from his back and shoulders. He did not feel energized, but he did feel clean. He decided that alone was a step forward.

He toweled off and dressed. Gina's Laundromat was around the corner and a block to the south. He lugged the overflowing basket down the stairs and across the narrow street. A sense of normalcy gradually returned to him.

The neighborhood was an older one. His building held four apartments, all small and plain. The stairs creaked when he ascended and echoed with clunking thuds in the descent. He loved the old building. It was simple and uninspiring. It was just right for him.

The plainness that surrounded him would never distract him from his thoughts. Jonathan's mind had always carried his imagination to extremes. He didn't care if his living quarters were fancy, well decorated, or even clean. The less attention his surroundings attracted him, the more he could allow his mind to probe the deep mysteries that seduced his thoughts.

To Jonathan Walsh, beauty was found in numbers, in the vast expanses of a finite science that through its exercise revealed new layers of discovery. Math was music in his mind, digits working in harmony, rhythmically pushing his thoughts forward in an unheard melody of reason. His imagination soared with numbers.

Mozart was criticized for using too many notes in his music. Picasso was too bold, too angular with his paintings. The founder of the Motorola Corporation was soundly criticized at his suggestion of putting a radio in an automobile. Critics abound when true creativity and imagination speak. Jonathan Walsh was not going to allow critics, people, society, or even his best friends to interfere with his work—his art.

The neighborhood was far enough from the campus to avoid any aimless drifters who might wander in looking for a good party. The noise level was tolerable, and for being in town, nearly non-existent. Besides Gina's, there was a small grocery store, a sidewalk café that was a great treat on a nice day, a good bookstore, and a small, wonderfully upscale restaurant.

Across the street to the west was the reserve that had been set aside by the city fathers as a park, and a low, stone wall defined the perimeter. Their intent had not been to establish a playground, but rather an open area of grass, trees, and flowering bushes to brighten a city encased in a tired, perpetual gray. Although the benches were hard and designed without much consideration for the human form or comfort, Jonathan loved to sit on them and allow his mind to drift.

Once the laundry machine was running, Jonathan ambled toward the sidewalk café. The small café sandwiched between the park and the community was his favorite spot. His apartment, the park and the café had become his haven during grad school. The trio provided him rest, green grass, and good food when he needed a respite from his studies. He was well known by the waiters. Many of them were students that had attended classes he taught while finishing his PhD.

"Good morning, Dr. Walsh," Philip said as he approached carrying a menu. "Haven't seen much of you lately. Everything going okay?"

"You know how it can get. All work and no play," Jonathan replied. He half smiled as he took the menu from the younger man. His eyes scanned the pages without reading a word. He had known what he wanted before he seated himself. Only one item on the menu was of interest to him on this day.

"Philip," he said as the waiter walked away. "I would like the biscuits and gravy with a side of hash browns if it isn't too late."

"It will take a little longer," he replied. "Gary has started lunch preps, but I'll do my best to convince him for you." He smiled and ducked through the double doors to the kitchen.

Jonathan muttered a *thank you* to him but he was out of earshot. He reached for a newspaper on the table next to his and scanned the headlines.

"War, wars, and rumors of war," he mumbled. The news from Iraq and Afghanistan listed details of a conflict he didn't understand, and he was pretty sure no one else did either—not completely. Then again, what was complete understanding of anything?

Philip arrived with a steaming cup of tea. It was Jonathan's favorite and as close as anything could get to the herbal brew his mom had made. He breathed in the aroma as he sipped the tea. If he closed his eyes he could almost hear her clattering in the kitchen as breakfast had come from stove to table.

"Gary will have your order out in just a minute. Would you like some eggs with your biscuits?" The interruption brought Jonathan back to the present in a snap.

"Sure. Yeah, that sounds healthy, I guess," Farm fresh scrambled eggs with a pile of biscuits and gravy sounded delicious, although it was far from what either Maggie or his mom would have declared healthy. Jonathan figured he had missed enough meals over the last several days that an excessive indulgence of fat and starch wouldn't hurt him.

He sat warming himself in the sun and felt a pleasant comfort settle over him. The terror from the night before was gone. The grogginess and sluggish feeling he struggled under only a few minutes earlier was fading. He liked this life. He loved the café. Everything was good. Everything was good but one thing, that is.

He missed Maggie.

*   *   *   *   *

Hunger gnaws in my gut. I am not interested in catching It. I just want to kill It. I do not like Its pitiful cries when I try to rest. I do not like the noises It makes. I can kill It when It becomes quiet or falls asleep. I will kill It if I find It. Sometimes It runs far into the smoke. I don't want to go there to find It, so I wait.

Why does It keep coming? It comes again and again. I must learn more about It, but where do I begin? I went into the smoke on the warm side but I am confused about what I saw. I do not understand.

I could go into the warm side again and be very quiet. I could watch. I could listen. Would It hurt me if It found me on the warm side?

Would I need to kill It there to be left alone? Do I want to stay in the smoke?

The pain is very strong and I feel angry. I will go back to the warm side. I will watch It. I will understand why It comes here.

8

Jonathan spent the rest of that spring day in the park. The light breeze stirred the budding leaves, played across the grass, and cooled his face from the bright sun. He listened to the birds and watched them in their endless pursuit of survival. He marveled at how different they were, how unique their cries and songs were from each other. They seemed to busy themselves searching for seeds or small insects, never really working but always on the hunt. It struck him that for all the birds, all of differing kinds and species, there seemed to be enough. They all found food and made their homes in the trees without an ounce of labor.

How different they are than men, he thought. Jonathan tried to imagine mankind living by simply eating what they found growing naturally around them. *How could that possibly work?* he asked himself. *Of course, seeds and insects don't do much to arouse my appetite. Mankind would not be satisfied with simple survival. We lust for too much satisfaction. Our demand for abundance would deny any pursuit of a meager life. We crave for more, to create more, develop something better, and make a profit. In the end, greed will always win.*

Jonathan stood and stretched. He didn't want to waste the entire day contemplating birds and their habits. He rubbed the back of his neck and stretched first to the left, and then to the right. That was when he saw her. Was that Maggie?

The woman had crossed the street just a block from where he stood. She looked in his direction and stopped. Was she looking *at* him? Was it really Maggie? He drew his breath to call her name. Just as quickly, the woman turned and crossed the street, striding from his view. Should he follow?

If it wasn't Maggie it would be fruitless to chase her down. If it was Maggie, and she had recognized him, it was clear she didn't want to see him. His heart sank a little. Jonathan breathed a deep breath almost sighing as he let it out. The time wasn't yet right for him to see her.

He looked at the ground beneath his feet. He kicked against the hard-packed soil with the toe of his shoe. Small clumps of dirt and small rocks scattered in front of him. A melancholy smile played over his lips and he chuckled softly. Again, his thoughts turned to the simplicity of nature surrounding him.

"As easy as that, I can break up the packed ground, so a bird might find a pebble for its gizzard or maybe a little bug for dinner. Why can't my life be that simple?"

He stood by the bench with his hands deep in his pockets and looked in the direction he had seen the woman. Maggie. She hadn't returned. The café across the street was busy with afternoon coffee drinkers. He stood silently watching mothers with small children as they hurried in and out of the grocery store, then to their cars. He wondered if they were hurrying to pick up other children from school or simply rushing home to start the evening meal.

He was alone. No one was coming home to see him. No one waited for him. Jonathan felt a twinge of self-pity, and immediately brushed it off. *People make choices,* he told himself. *They choose the life they want . . . and with whom they want to share it.*

His clothes were most likely dry and ready to be folded. He would take them home, check around his small apartment, and drive to his lab. No, this time he would walk. He would take his time, enjoy the afternoon, and maybe run into some friends along the way. Maybe.

Still, he was alone.

*　　*　　*　　*　　*

When Jonathan arrived at his office he checked his mail and glanced at his answering machine. No calls. His lab, more of the L-shaped extension of his office, was as he left it with everything in its place awaiting his next set of experiments.

Afternoon sun strayed through the blinds casting an amber hue. The instruments and stacks of files waited unanimated, quiet. The menace, or whatever terror that drove him from the building the night before seemed distant, almost forgotten.

He walked to the cages where he kept his subjects. The rats scurried back and forth pushing paper bedding or hiding a morsel of food deep in a corner of their cage. Their repetitive motions and constantly quivering noses brought a smile to his face. *Rats doing rat stuff*, he thought. He chuckled to himself.

Few words were spoken in Dr. Jonathan Walsh's office and laboratory, but the conversation was loud and constant in his mind. The volume of his thoughts, their individual shouts and exclamations were enough. The quiet was, however, frequently shattered by declarations of discovery and questions of wonder.

Jonathan walked to his video equipment and flipped the switch. The electronics whirred to life, screens flickered, and the images of his last experiment on a guinea pig appeared. He watched carefully as the animal passed through the brief period of convulsion, flopped to its side, and remained motionless.

The orb flashed. He rewound the video and played it in super-slow motion. He watched intently as the orb rose. The colors were different than those that rose from the rats. More purple. Sparks flashed like micro lightening strikes inside the smoky ball that reminded him of cloud-to-cloud flashes in a spring thunderstorm.

How much difference existed between animal life and the Earth as a living entity? Were the storms he watched with marvel and wonder as a boy, the life-expression of our planet as these orbs held life itself?

His intensity deepened. He was watching something never before seen in a laboratory, something of great significance. But he was only watching.

As the brightness of the afternoon faded outside his office window, gloom descended on Jonathan Walsh. He was at the brink preparing to step over the edge. An abyss of the unknown yawned before him, an experience never recorded by mankind. He faced an experiment that had never been accomplished throughout millennia of mankind's scientific discovery.

He turned to his computer and began calculating and entering weights, body mass calculations, chemical profiles, hydration levels, muscle and bone density. The scientific measurements were not taken from a lab rat or a guinea pig. They were not from an animal at all. The measurements and data were from a human; they were his.

It was time. It was *his* time.

*   *   *   *   *

Maggie plopped herself heavily into the restaurant chair. Mark and Rachel had been waiting for her. The joy-filled faces of previous dinners were now drawn and grave.

"I saw him," she said flatly. Her eyes shifted between her two friends. She neither expected nor found hope or encouragement. "He was sitting in the park across from his apartment. Just sitting."

"Did you talk to him?" Mark asked. Maggie could tell he felt a loss in his friendship with Jonathan. She could see the hurt in his eyes. But he was with Rachel, and it was very clear to her that Rachel loved him. Maggie was alone.

"No. I turned and ran back the way I'd come. I didn't want to see him, or talk to him, or anything him."

"But he wasn't in his lab, and he *was* outside," Rachel said. "That's at least different, maybe even better." Her hopeful words fell on Maggie's skepticism with little benefit.

"But Rachel, after we saw him running off campus like a wild man, I don't know, I can't bring myself to go to him. You remember how scary he looked."

Rachel snorted her disgust. "My heart nearly stopped when he ran into us. I'm just saying if you never make the effort, what you guys had will certainly wither away."

"I know," Maggie replied softly. "Sometimes I want to go to him, put my arms around him and *beg* him to come home with me. Then I just want to *slap* him as hard as I can. I want to *be* with him, but I can't stand the *thought* of him." She wrestled the conflict, not allowing herself to accept the fact that the ringmaster of her battle was his betrayal.

"I didn't see him, but Rachel's description was enough for me," Mark said. "I just don't get it. What can he be up to?"

"He's buried himself and is taken over by his work!" Several heads turned their way. She blushed and lowered her voice. "He locks himself in his office. I don't hear from him. I don't see him. And when I do, he looks and acts insane."

"I don't know what else we can do at this point, Maggie," Rachel said casting a glance toward Mark. "Somehow he needs to get through this. We can *hope* he'll get through it anyway." Rachel's attempt at encouragement failed to raise hope. Maggie looked at the table cloth and picked at the fabric design. Tears pooled in her eyes and clung to her lashes.

"Look," Mark began with a smile. "We're here and are going to have a lovely evening and a fantastic meal. We all love Jonathan, and we all wish he was with us, only like the old Jonathan. We simply cannot have that at the moment. Let's do with what we have, friends."

He raised his glass in toast to their friendship. Maggie's face brightened with a smile and they toasted their friendship. However, a sense of melancholy hung in the air much like after a funeral of a loved one. The food even lacked its customary richness, and the wine brought tiredness rather than lifted spirits. Things were not as they had been. It would take a miracle to bring Jonny back.

*   *   *   *   *

As evening faded into night Jonathan walked up the steps to his apartment. Long, dark shadows traced his steps and seemed to follow him to his rooms. Closing the door behind him, he flipped the switch on a small lamp beside his bed. The light cast highlighted shadows with harsh, angular exaggerations.

Jonathan felt out of sorts. He no longer pondered the beautiful afternoon or the simplistic existence of nature he had observed. During the last few hours he had locked his thoughts into mathematics and the combinations of pharmaceuticals in volumes he'd not previously imagined.

Cautiously, he drew the syringe from his jacket pocket. It looked huge to him. The injections he'd given to the rats averaged two to three milliliter doses. This injection was twelve times that size. It was huge.

Jonathan took off his shoes and tossed them toward the closet. He left the door to the closet swinging. He had never been one for neatness. It simply didn't matter to him. He loosened the collar of his shirt and eased back on his bed.

So, you're the rat after all. Inwardly, he chuckled at the double meaning as he thought of Maggie. She deserved better. If his calculations were incorrect, he wouldn't survive. Maggie would suffer his loss for a while and go on with her life. She would eventually be fine.

But if he was successful, he would be known as a genius. Then she would see and understand his behavior. She would forgive him, and they would be together as they had planned.

He smiled when he considered a lifetime with Maggie. He would prove himself to her. He would prove himself to his father. Everyone would see the revolutionary concept he had developed and applaud his efforts.

He sat on the edge of his bed and quieted himself. Transcendental meditation was a simple exercise for him. An exercise he felt he had ignored much too long. The demands of his work fought against inner peace. The pressure of discovery carried his thinking to distant realms of thought, but denied him rest.

For the first time in a long while, peace settled over him. The repetition of his mantra soothed him.

"Ommm . . . eye'nggggg namahhh . . ." His voice resonated in his chest and face. Breathing in slowly he repeated the mantra. "Ommm . . . eye'nggggg namahhh . . ."

Again and again he hummed the words in monotone. His thoughts became quiet. He could feel the world lifting from him.

Jonathan lay down on his bed. He looked at the ceiling wondering what the next three or four minutes would bring. Fear and excitement surged through him. If it was ever going to happen, now was the time. He looked at the clock by his bed. It was 7:35 p.m.

He pinched his abdomen between his forefinger and thumb, and carefully inserted the syringe needle into his skin. This was it. He put his head back on the pillow and closed his eyes. Then, he pushed in the plunger.

*   *   *   *   *

I wait all the time. That is all I do. It is hard to wait, and it is hard to kill It when the time is right. I must kill. I do not like the pain.

What was that? I saw something move in the smoke. Whatever it was, it didn't move quickly, it just walked. There! I saw it again. Whatever it is, it is much smaller than the large creatures. Wait, I know that. I know what that is. It is a man. He does not move quickly like It does. He is not slow and lumbering like the creatures. It would be easy. I could catch him.

He is looking at me, directly at me. Why is he here? It surprises me that I am not afraid. I am not angry. I have no feeling that I should run. I have no need to kill him. I can tell that he is not afraid of me. But why is he looking at me?

Now he is gone. The Man left simply walking through the smoke. I will pay attention and watch for him. Maybe the Man can help me understand.

9

Jonathan could sense the convulsions before they began. He relaxed and measured his breathing. The mantra he had rehearsed for months flowed from his lips allowing him to be drawn into the shaking. He did not resist. When the convulsions hit him with full force he feared his joints might separate. His legs thrashed and kicked throwing him from side-to-side, lifting his body from the bed, crashing back again, twisting in exhausting heaves and spasms. The contortions jerked him about like a flag in a gusty wind, bending, stretching, and flattening him only to repeat it again and again.

Then, it happened.

Jonathan felt a great swelling from his face and chest, as if he was some kind of bubble. The pressure was tremendous. His eyes and nose ached, and then it popped. He was thrust forward at light speed through flashes of color, blinding brightness, then through shades of grays and blacks, and back to colors.

It could not have been more than a second . . . or was it? Jonathan sensed unmeasured time, an awareness of him being but a dream—not in a dream—but the dream itself. Flashes of every hue from the spectrum and brightness surrounded him. Flashes of color seemed to penetrate him. Or did they? It all happened in this moment that seemed a lifetime.

Suddenly, he stumbled forward landing on his feet. He staggered and caught his balance. He straightened himself. He stood in his room. Moments before, he had laid himself on his bed and taken the shot. He reached for his stomach but there was no mark from the injection. No needle prick in the skin. No mark whatsoever.

That was when he realized he was naked. He smiled and laughed a little. In all his calculations and experiments he had not considered clothing. Why was he naked? He was dressed when he injected himself, but why not now?

"Arrived" seemed a strange word all of a sudden. He remembered the injection and the experience of the convulsions. His rats had always flopped to their sides and appeared dead. But he was very much alive. The rats had remained still. How was it he could move so easily? *Is this a different place? A different room? If so, how did I get here? Where is here? Where am I?*

Jonathan had arrived in what appeared to be his own room, yet it was different. He looked to where his dresser stood. A dresser was there but it wasn't his. He walked to the dresser and opened the top drawer, where he kept his underwear and socks. It was filled with new, neatly folded briefs. The socks were from-the-store bundles of the kind he preferred. Everything was new. He began dressing.

The second drawer held some pullover shirts. He pulled one on. It fit. In the third drawer he found four pairs of new blue jeans. He slipped on a pair. They fit perfectly.

He noted how clean the room was. It was spotless. Everything was in place, and everything was new. He hadn't purchased clothes in the months since he received his grant, yet everything in the spotlessly clean room was new.

Jonathan looked around the room for some shoes. He found three pairs in boxes just inside the closet on the floor. He never put his shoes in the closet and certainly not in boxes. The shoes also fit exactly right.

As he prepared to leave the room to begin his investigation, he noticed money and a watch on the nightstand next to the bed. He picked them up and examined them carefully. He slipped the watch on his arm. The time said 7:35. It was evening.

The bills were not crisp and looked as if they had been in circulation for several years, at a minimum. He looked closely at the date on the bills. 2025. *But these are old bills, old money,* he thought to himself. His mind spun. What had happened? Where was he . . . no, not where, *when*?

He slipped the cash into his pocket, descended the stairs, and onto the sidewalk. It wasn't the same. Then again, it was. The sidewalk was flatter, not buckled and uneven by years of exposure to the heat and cold. The concrete wasn't pocked and chipped, but fresh and even. Even the buildings looked fresher. They were the same shape but almost every one had a new exterior, or a brighter color.

The streets appeared the same. He turned and looked at his building. It looked much better, fresher, and newer. *Had someone tuck-pointed the brick?* It just looked cleaner.

The park seemed as it had been earlier in the day, but it too was different. The landscape was fuller. The bushes and trees were larger. A couple of the trees were missing. He assumed they had been removed due to their age. Some of the playground equipment looked newer, but the park was still the park.

His eyes scanned the wooded area and open field of neatly trimmed grass. Two men stood talking silhouetted against the background evening sky. Their silhouettes were darkened against the amber haze. A group of small children clumsily played a game of Frisbee as their mothers watched with amusement.

As he crossed the street, Jonathan looked for Gina's Laundromat where he had washed his clothes that morning. The building was the same, but Skip's Bike Shop filled the space.

He looked further down the block and saw tables and chairs. *The café.* He jogged toward the familiar café and was surprised at how agile he felt. He picked a table and chair near the planter, his favorite spot. Both the table and chair were new.

"What can I do you for today?" a voice said from behind him. It was familiar. He turned toward the waiter approaching him. Could it be? This couldn't be.

A man in his late forties carrying a pad and wearing a waiter's apron walked toward him.

"Philip?" he asked in astonishment.

The waiter stopped dead in his tracks. He looked at Jonathan with an unusual expression on his face. His head canted to one side and he squinted. "Do I know you? You look very familiar."

"Uh, well, no . . . why do you ask?"

"I don't know. You look a lot like a grad student instructor I knew some years back." He looked even harder at Jonathan.

Jonathan was suddenly unsure how much about himself he should reveal. *Could too many questions create a problem?* The thought had not occurred to him until that moment. He had no identification, no way to prove who he was.

"Really?" Jonathan said feigning wonder. "Have you been here long?"

"Kinda got stuck here, I guess," Philip replied. "After I graduated from college, the economy was so bad I couldn't find work. Then the old man that owned this place had a heart attack and died. I was either going to be unemployed or become a business owner. His widow worked with me to get started, and I've been here ever since."

"So how long is *ever since*?" Jonathan asked slowly.

"Oh, I guess almost thirty years. Why?"

Thirty years! What has happened? This can't be real. Jonathan did his best to conceal his shock and looked around at the tables. A newspaper had been left on a table two tables away. He stood abruptly, but caught himself, and stepped to the table. The headlines meant nothing to him, but his eyes widened when he saw the date.

"April 27, 2037," he read out loud. He glanced back at the waiter. The look on Philip's face had changed. His warm smile had melted into confusion, almost fear. Jonathan froze. Even a question, or worse, the truth about his presence in 2037 would be dangerous for him.

"Do you want a menu or not?"

Jonathan sneaked a look at his watch. It read 7:42. Seven minutes had lapsed since he found himself standing naked in his bedroom. His heart skipped a beat. Did he really have a three and a half minute window? Had he missed it? The rats were gone for exactly three and a half minutes. He'd gotten distracted and stayed too long. Terror gripped him as he realized he might miss his opportunity and not be able to return to his life.

"Uh, no. Sorry!" Jonathan said and bolted down the street toward his building. He leaped up the stairs three at a time and burst into his room. He hadn't been there more than a second when he felt as if something grabbed him and threw him into his closet.

The bright lights flashed all around him; he swept through the grays and blacks, followed by more flashing and color. Jonathan sprung awake with a gasp. He was on his bed, fully clothed. He looked at his clock. It read 7:38. Three minutes had passed.

*   *   *   *   *

I press through the smoke again and into the closet. I dress myself. The clothes smell different. I didn't notice this smell the first time. I pull on a light shirt over my head. A pair of jeans is hung on the doorknob. They fit me very well. The shoes slip on my feet with ease.

I walk carefully down the stairs to the outside door. Bright sunlight streaks long shadows into the stairway as I slowly open the door. I move quickly out and across the street to the park. This is a safe place.

From the hill in the park I can see all around me. If a creature was here, I would see it long before it came near me. If It appeared, I could deal with it. I would kill It.

I am most curious about the others. What do they do? I do not see any of them hunting for food. I do not see any killing. It appears these soft creatures, people, simply walk from place to place. Sometimes they ride large machines that move. I am puzzled about the purpose the people have. Are they necessary?

I sit on the ground by a large tree and watch. This is not a bad place. Why would anyone leave here? I have seen enough. This is quiet and very pretty. I like it.

I don't know how long I have been here. Shadows are stretched across the park and the street. It is time to leave. I walk toward the door and the stairway and slowly take each step. I open the door at the top of the stairs and walk into the small room.

I gasp when I see it. *No!—No! It can't be.* I stumble away from it. *On the bed—on the bed . . . I—I see It.* My skin prickles and a shiver runs up my neck. It is lying on the bed fully clothed and completely still. *It looks dead. It might be dead! I must not stay.*

I pull off the clothes and leave them on the floor. I run into the closet and press through the smoke. A new sensation floods me. *I have to get away; I have to run. It is behind me and I must get away from It!*

I stumble into the smoke from the thick gray. Home.

Suddenly, the terrifying noise begins. The noise It makes when It goes or comes back. In a flash It stands before me. It is confused, It is naked as always. I pounce before It has a chance to run. I catch It. Then, I kill It.

*   *   *   *   *

Jonathan could not stop shaking. He lay on his bed for more than half an hour. The trembling washed over him in short bursts. He was sure they were not caused by the drugs. It had to be excitement. *Had it really happened? Or, was it all a dream, a hallucination?* How could he prove he had actually traveled thirty years into the future? The questions were endless.

Finally, he stood and paced back and forth in his small room. How could he explain to his friends what he had experienced? How could he explain it to himself? Why was he wearing clothes at the start, in the present, and not wearing anything when he got . . . wherever it was he went? Had it been the same *dimension,* or a different one? Was it only a hallucination?

He knew the calculations that he had made were right. Each psychotropic drug included in the cocktail was very specific. But how did it *work*? How had he moved and gone where he had gone? Again, did he *go* somewhere or was it imagined? What? What? What?

The camera. He needed to do it again. He could record it and then watch the event as he had with the lab rats. Yes, that was it. He could prove his departure with the recording the same as the rats and guinea pigs. He wanted to observe his orb, his life force rise from his body. Certainly a similar event would be observed with him. It had to be.

But how could he prove that he had really gone to the future? How could he prove that on this date, April 27, 2007, he had advanced thirty years into the future?

"I can't take anything with me . . . not even my clothes! Can I bring something back?" Jonathan quickly discarded the idea. He didn't understand how *he* got back, much less anything of substance.

The answer came like the dawn of the day—slowly. It rose as certain as the warmth of the sun. *My mind! I remember what I saw . . . what I did!*

He gasped. *I can use history. I need something that can be confirmed only by actually seeing it happen.* Something that would prove he had been in the future.

But what? News about politics, a war? No, too much of that. It had to be something ordinary, not a disaster or anything like that; something that many people would see; something that no one would fear or find threatening. Something cool. An event everyone would remember.

He had to go back.

Jonathan pulled on his shoes and charged down the stairs. He needed to bring a high-def camera from his lab to his apartment, and to do it all again. His heart pounded in his chest. He jumped into his car and raced toward the campus and his office.

Nothing like this had happened in all of recorded history. No one had ever written about doing what he had just experienced. Suddenly, the excitement froze in his mind. He slowed the car and stopped.

What if someone else had gone to the future? What if something had gone wrong? What if they actually failed at some point and didn't want to admit their failure? What if they weren't able to admit they had failed? What if . . .

The car behind him honked. It startled Jonathan. Emerging from his daze he realized he was stopped in the middle of the street. He pressed on the accelerator angrily and zoomed toward the campus. The tires squealed as he swung into his parking spot. He was barely able to think.

Jonathan slammed the door of his car and ran toward his building. He dashed through the door and leaped up the steps to his floor. Sliding to a stop, he placed his key in the lock and twisted it. The lock popped, and the door opened.

Jonathan quickly went about unhooking the best camera and gathering everything he needed to make a quality recording. Just as he headed to the door, he remembered he would need to mix the formula.

Slowly, he placed the video gear on his desk. He turned to the equipment he used to mix the cocktail of drugs. Now he forced himself to slow down. He could not afford a sloppy concoction of powerful psychotropic and hallucinogenic drugs. He needed to be very careful.

He sat at his workbench and began assembling the chemicals based on his calculations and notes from the previous day. His hands shook. His mouth was dry, and his vision slightly blurry. He stopped.

Jonathan rested his arms on the edge of the table, lowered his head, and closed his eyes. He took a deep breath, then another. He had to settle down. He was so excited he could be a danger to himself if he were not very attentive to what he was doing. He took another long, deep breath.

When he opened his eyes he felt better. His hands weren't shaking. The jitteriness subsided in his chest. He breathed in again and began mixing the formula. This would work. This time he would have the proof.

*   *   *   *   *

Maggie, Mark, and Rachel walked out of the restaurant into the cool evening. The women bristled against the chill, but Mark embraced it and breathed it in.

"I love the spring chill, that lingering sentiment of winter. Ah, like an emersion in a babbling brook of mountain spring water."

"Oh, shut up," Rachel snipped, grinning. "Besides, I thought the mountainspringwaterthing was a beer ad on TV."

"Fine with me," Mark responded. "Anybody want a beer?" He pulled the door into the restaurant open again and waved the ladies to enter.

"Mark, you're drunk. Enough already," Maggie gasped in mock despair. "I couldn't eat or drink anything more. And my face is so tired of smiling."

"Well, there certainly has not been enough of that in the last three weeks, my lady," Mark teased with a sweeping bow. He briefly lost his balance but caught himself.

"Okay, sir prince, let's get you to your apartment. I think you've had enough," Rachel said taking Mark's arm.

"Unhand me, woman," he protested pulling himself upright. "I am clear as a bell and twinkling like fairy dust."

Maggie laughed out loud at his antics. Both Rachel and Mark reflected her joy as the three fell into an embrace. It was like the old times with laughter, warmth, and friends. Maggie felt her soul had been nourished and refreshed. It made her glad.

"Alright, you two. I need to get home," she said pulling herself away. "You guys have a wonderful evening, but I do need to go."

"Did you hear that, my love?" Mark jested playfully. "The lady wishes us a wonderful evening. Shall we pursue a *wonderful* evening?" Rachel blushed and pushed him away.

"See what you've done to him, Maggie? You've corrupted him. He's a monster!"

"I'll leave him for you to figure out," Maggie said over her shoulder. "I have to go."

Maggie hopped into her car, started the engine, and glanced back at her friends. Mark was holding Rachel in his arms and they were kissing.

Maggie's heart soared and sank at the same time. She was happy for Mark, that he had found someone very special, but sad that her special someone was lost to her. She pulled from the parking lot and turned in the only direction she could; she drove toward the campus.

The trip was short. Maggie steered her car into the parking lot at Jonathan's building. She saw his car and noted it was parked like the driver was either drunk or on drugs. *He really is crazy.* Then, she saw the lights in his office. Anger swelled in her stomach; her face burned. She heard herself utter a growl deep inside. A fresh bitterness, tinged with envy, overwhelmed her. Jealous bile rose in her throat. Maggie tromped the accelerator and sped from the parking lot.

10

Assembling the concoction of powerful chemicals took less time than he expected. The process was fresh in his mind from having completed the task earlier that evening. The excitement he felt as he put the drugs together was empowering. Jonathan knew he was on the crest of greatness. His work would change the world.

The timer went off, and the NOAH HD 125 mixer slowed to a stop. Jonathan smiled. Someday he would be mixing his formula in liters rather than single injections. *This will be worth millions*, he thought. He imagined endless possibilities.

Advertising companies could travel ahead to see what works and return to better target their advertising dollars. Military planners might seek new advantages over potential enemies. Investors could look back at market results from the future. That thought popped into his mind and stopped him in his tracks. *I could*, he thought. *I could do that.*

He needed to get home and do it all again. He tucked the syringe neatly into his shirt pocket, and he gathered the video equipment under his arm. When he entered the hall, he realized he had failed to turn off the lights. The door clicked shut before he could turn and catch it. *I'll be back.*

Jonathan pushed open the outside door of the building just as a familiar looking car squealed its tires and sped from the parking lot. *Was that Maggie?* "Maggie!" She was gone. He let out a sigh.

He held on to the confidence that someday Maggie would understand what he was doing. *I refuse to believe she is that narrow in her thinking. She isn't that dumb. I will not give up hope, even if it is only a faint hope.*

Jonathan packed the equipment into his convertible and drove toward his apartment. During the trip his imagination was inundated with anticipation. *This is just the beginning. Who knows what I'll discover? I know I can do this.*

As the wind blew through his hair his self assurance seemed to blow away in it. Doubt edged into his mind uprooting the position he held firmly only moments before.

Has my confidence gone too far? Is this confidence in my training and abilities or just arrogance? He knew what Maggie thought, that was clear. *Mark and Rachel probably think I'm nuts, too . . . and Dad. Probably everyone.*

Jonathan immediately took hold of his emotions. He shook off the feeling. *Memories and emotions get in the way of good science. They will understand later. Everyone will understand. I'll show them.*

Back in his apartment the equipment required little set up. He checked the data links and the batteries. The last thing he wanted was power failure in the middle of his experiment. The data transfer by an infrared link worked perfectly. It was easy.

Once everything was in place, Jonathan pulled the syringe from his shirt pocket. He checked the dosage to make sure nothing had leaked during transit and set up. Everything looked fine.

Jonathan's pulse hammered in his eardrums from the excitement. He forced himself to focus and then began his mantra. *What if the military really wants this stuff? It could be worth millions! Is there a better mix that would reduce the convulsions? What happens after several uses? Could I get to a point that I wouldn't need the drugs?*

He had to stop. Jonathan stood and walked slowly around his small room doing breathing exercises to calm himself, focus himself. After several minutes he felt relaxed.

Once again he sat on the edge of his bed and began his mantra. *This is more like it.* This time he felt a quiet peace cover him like a blanket. He slowed his breathing and rested.

He lay on his bed and checked the time. The clock showed 8:52 p.m. He then pulled up his shirt and pinched his abdomen and gave himself the injection on the opposite side of his stomach from the one a few hours earlier.

The effect of the drugs was almost instantaneous. The next thing he knew he stumbled into his bedroom, naked. He chuckled. Actually, he giggled. This was too amazing. It was exactly as before. The difference was that this time he knew what to expect and was not surprised at what lay before him.

He dressed quickly and checked the time on his clock by the bed. The time also read 8:52 p.m. The clock was newer than the one at home, and he wondered who had placed it there. He slipped on the shoes from the closet and dashed out the door.

He intended to run to his car before he realized he didn't own a car in the future—at least, not yet. Again, he chuckled at himself and broke into a run toward the campus and the Stephens University Library. Running felt as it had when he was a kid. His muscles were lean and tight. His legs felt like there were springs in them. Running was as easy as he ever imagined, almost dream-like.

Jonathan entered the library and walked directly to the reference section. He scanned the shelves of books looking for old newspapers. He didn't find a single bound copy of old newsprint anywhere. He knew that as early as 2002, media had begun moving to electronic methods of distribution. He chuckled remembering the report he saw of first experiments with electronic media in the early 1980s. The computer screen was small and the text consisted of green pixel letters.

But what about 2037? Were there no more newspapers? He had seen a paper at the café, so there *had* to be newspapers. But there were none in the library.

He crossed the room to the computer stations. Surely he could find a paper online. Jonathan sat in one of the cubicles. Immediately in front of him was a flat, black screen. He looked for a keyboard, checked under the desk top for a pull-out tray holding the keyboard. None were in sight.

His face must have reflected his bewilderment. A very attractive young woman about his age, a library employee, approached him with a smile, no, a smirk on her face. He assumed she thought he was some ignorant country bumpkin who didn't know his way around a computer. Then, he realized that's exactly what he was. He knew all about technology in 2007, but that was so far out of date, so behind the times. He blushed at the thought.

"Need some help?" the woman said with a smile. It was more than a smile. She was checking him out. Her eyes worked him over head to heel with neither shame nor tact. He almost felt violated, and definitely ogled.

"Uh, well yes. I was looking for a keyboard. Do I need to check one out or something?" he asked haltingly.

Her smile stretched into a full grin. Her teeth were perfectly straight and gleaming white. He knew she was toying with him. He hated ridicule. He could not stand women who were forward. He considered them cheap, even trampy.

"You're not from around here, are you?" she said leaning over his cubicle.

"Well, yes, and no, not really." Jonathan was becoming very uneasy and this woman was getting a little too friendly. She was being much too helpful, and not in any way that interested him. "I just need to know how to make this thing work." He swallowed hard.

She leaned in closer, all the while looking into Jonathan's eyes and smiling. He froze with no idea what to do next. He didn't notice her hand reaching behind the computer screen.

"It's as easy as pie, honey," she said inches from his face. He could smell her perfume, and her minty breath. She was almost on top of him. "Just put on the earpiece."

Immediately, she stood up straight and held a small device toward him that would clip around his ear. The earpiece did not fit into the ear but rather behind the ear against the skull.

"Oh," Jonathan said awkwardly. He slipped the piece over and behind his ear. Instantly the computer screen came to life.

"There," the young woman said softly. "Easy as pie. Do you need anything else? Anything?"

"No, no thank you," he replied averting his eyes to the screen. *Please go away*, he thought to himself.

Another voice spoke into his ear.

"Why should I do that? You just got here."

"What?" Jonathan blurted out. The volume of his own voice surprised him and brought the pretty librarian back.

"Is something wrong, sir?" she asked softly, moving in very close once again.

"No, not wrong, just . . . different."

"Yes, at this university we talk with our computers. Have you never talked with a computer before?" Her question was riddled with sarcasm and bordered on disdain. Now he was certain he looked like a hillbilly.

"Yes, I—I understand voice recognition. I've just . . . never had one *read* what I was thinking," he stammered.

"And what were you thinking?" she asked seductively.

"Nothing of importance I assure you. Now, if you'll please excuse me . . ."

"Just remember one thing, and I'm telling you this because I like you. Be careful what you think about while you're here. Not everything is proper these days, you know." She didn't move.

Jonathan looked at her. She really made him nervous, and now the fear of what he might think made him all the more anxious. He glanced away from her boring eyes. He felt as if she were trying to read his thoughts as well.

"Okay, I think I have a handle on this. I simply think about my interests and talk with the computerized voice, and it will lead me to the information I need. Is that correct enough to make the program work?"

"That should do it. Just remember to think pure thoughts, and you won't get into any trouble," she said without moving. "Oh, my name's Marcia. If you need me just ask the computer to call Marcia. It'll let me know, all right?"

"Sure. Hi, I'm Jonathan." He held out his hand to greet her, but she just looked at him and smiled.

"How quaint. I don't remember the last time I shook someone's hand." She snickered a little then shook his hand.

"Really?" he responded. "Is that something people don't do around here?"

"Not for a long time," she said. "You know, germs and all that."

"Right. Well, thank you for your help, and I'll tell what's-his-name if I need you," he said gesturing to the computer. He relaxed a little. But just a little. He couldn't let anyone know exactly where he was from.

"So, where are you from?" the voice asked in his ear. Jonathan didn't jump quite as high as before, but he did jump.

"That's not important. Disregard. Now, I need information on something significant that occurred around or shortly after April 28, 2007."

"Politics, the economy, faith-based, education, or sports?" the voice asked in his ear.

"Sports," he replied whimsically.

The screen never even blinked, but began showing video of a baseball game. It was a game between the Colorado Rockies against the Atlanta Braves. His jaw dropped at the clarity as he watched the video. *It's almost 3-D! And of a game that hasn't happened yet.*

"This is perfect. Perfect!" he said a little too loudly. He saw Marcia glance his direction, so he waved to her and nodded he understood he needed to be quiet. He made some notes—seventh inning, second base, Troy Tulowitzki. A grin spread across his face.

"Now, computer, I want you to—"

"My name is Connie."

"You have a *name*?"

"Yes, I do. My name is Connie."

"All right then, Connie, I need a list of the IPOs in the years 2007 and 2008 that posted the fastest growth and paid the highest returns over the following ten years."

The screen simply clicked from the baseball video to a completed list of companies. He picked three that looked the best and committed the information to memory. He had a start. He would simply go home, and tomorrow he would look up those companies and make an investment.

Jonathan grinned with satisfaction and said, "Connie, I'm finished. You can go help someone else now."

"Thank you, Jonathan. Be careful going home," it replied. He rocked back a bit. He had not told his name to Connie. *How did she know?* he thought.

"I was listening while you spoke with Marcia, Jonathan. That's where I learned your name. Is that all right with you?"

Wow. A computer with manners, he thought.

"Why, thank you, Jonathan."

"You're welcome, Connie." He shook his head as he removed the earpiece and hung it behind the screen. This was going to take some getting used to.

*   *   *   *   *

I have never gone to the cold side—only into the smoke. Leaving the warm side does not make sense. Why would someone leave a perfectly nice place for the gray and the smoke? I do not like cold. I have decided I like the sunshine. It is warm on my face. Why does It go into the cold?

I hear the thunderous roar of a large creature. The noise startles me. Carefully I move toward the thick smoke near the gray. The sound comes closer and I move deeper into the smoke, into thicker smoke. The creature lumbers into my view. I try to stay hidden in the smoke.

The creature turns toward me and is standing still. I do not move. It leans closer. Suddenly the dark monstrous form lurches at me and roars with such a deafening thunder I am knocked off my feet.

I scurry into the deep gray and sit very still. My heart pounds in my chest and I shiver from the terror of the creature's voice. I do not understand fear. I do not like fear. I will wait for a while longer in the gray.

*   *   *   *   *

"Have you thought about how you will be able to help him if this doesn't work?" Alice was slightly more indignant than normal. The tone in her voice cut a little bit.

"I don't really think we have anything to worry about. He's just doing research on some very outlandish theories. I don't give it much concern," Martin said turning the page in his book.

"Honey, you never gave him much concern," she answered with a softer tone. "In many ways, he's still the same little boy needing your attention and affection. He's just . . . tall, and he shaves."

Martin laughed. He loved her sense of humor. He loved talking with her. He loved her.

"How would you suggest I help him, my dear?" he said smiling toward the kitchen. He closed the book and waited for her reply.

"I'm not sure he's the one that needs attention right now," she said looking right at him. "Have you thought that your inability to help him might have something to do with the mess in your own life?"

"Me! My life is a mess? That's simply preposterous. I have an excellent job, a good retirement, and a wonderful home. If anything, my life is ideal."

"Dear husband," Alice said as she shifted her weight and put her hand on her hip. "You have no idea how empty all those words sound. Job, house, retirement could all be gone in an instant. Then what would you have?"

"Sweetheart, I'll always have you."

"Really. Did you forget that I died three years ago?"

Martin jerked awake. He lurched forward. His fingers gripped the padded leather on the arms of his recliner. He gasped, followed by several quick breaths.

It was just another dream, nothing to be afraid of. And something she said made sense. He leaned back and put his head against the pillow on his recliner.

"Something she said made sense," he said out loud. *What was it?* he asked himself. *What did she say?*

"It could all be gone in an instant. Then what would you have?" Her words echoed deep into his mind. *What would I have? What did she have that I don't?*

She had found something he had missed. He needed to find it for himself.

11

Jonathan had the proof. All he had to do was contact his friends and convince them to meet with him the following day to watch the baseball game. Simple.

He hadn't felt this fresh and excited since he was a kid. It was almost like Christmas but with a slightly smug edge, which he knew he could not allow himself to show. Maggie was not pleased with him. Perhaps she would be willing to forgive him, acknowledge his success, and be ready to move on with their life plan, or so he hoped.

In the meantime, Jonathan wanted to make a couple of investments. His savings wasn't huge, but it would be enough. It was the remainder of what his mother had left to him in her will. She hadn't been fabulously wealthy, but the sixty thousand dollars from her savings and life insurance had come in very handy during graduate school. The remaining half of the original sum could go into some investments.

The call to a broker, a friend from high school, was brief. A meeting time was set for later that afternoon.

After a refreshing shower, Jonathan set out to see where he stood with Maggie. The safest place to start was the university library. He knew he could find Rachel hard at work among the many shelves of volumes and books.

He pulled into a parking slot and strolled to the front of the building. As he reached to open the door, he realized they were the very same doors he had opened last night, only thirty years in the future.

He suddenly felt very odd. Yes, he had really done it. He had actually traveled through time. They were the same doors. The heavy metal handles were the same, but more clearly defined, not worn smooth. He stepped back. The same ivy grew up the stone sides of the entrance, not as high, nor as full as in the future. It was weird.

Once inside he began scanning the large room for Rachel. She wasn't at the main desk, so he walked along the edge of the stacks checking down each row. He expected she would be placing books back on their proper shelves.

Finally, he spotted her. He approached her with a smile. Her greeting wasn't quite as warm as his.

"Well, look what the cat drug in," she said without smiling.

"I was hoping for a warmer reception, but it's fine, I understand." Jonathan smiled before he realized Rachel was ignoring him. He waited a moment to speak. "Do you think there is any chance Maggie will see me?"

"And we're right to the point. No, *hi there, Rachel, how have you been?*" she said turning to face him. Her eyes glared at him with a dismissive, cold stare. She folded her arms across her chest. He stopped, looked at the floor in front of his feet, and sighed heavily.

"You're right. I am sorry. I did this all wrong, and I'm sorry. Please, forgive me. I just don't know how to go about doing this. I don't know where I stand or how anyone feels about me and the things I've done."

"I can tell you that no one has changed their feelings since they were last expressed to you, if that gives you some clarity on the matter," Rachel said with an icy stare. "Me, I'm easy and would have appreciated a respectable *hello*. Mark is pretty upset, for his own reasons. And Maggie," she paused and looked him over. "She is still very angry at you. Does that help?" Her tone was sharp and deep regret pierced Jonathan.

"Maybe I deserve that," he said folding his arms across his chest, and again his gaze turned down.

"No *maybe* about it, Jonathan. You *are* a jerk." Rachel slammed a book into its place.

"You're right. I've been a jerk. But I need to talk to Maggie. I need to apologize and I need to tell her some things. Do you think she'll let me spend some time with her?"

"Not alone, that's for sure," Rachel said coldly. She turned to face him once more. "As a matter of fact *if* she meets with you at all, there will be two more people with her, and on her side, if it matters."

"No, that's fine . . . and fair," he replied. He looked at the floor, searching in his mind for the right words. "I know I owe both you and Mark the same apologies. I would like for you to be there."

"Just a minute," she replied. She glanced at him with contempt as she turned and disappeared behind the next row of books. Jonathan heard her talking softly behind the large stack of history books. Then, he heard another voice, a woman's voice.

"Maggie?" he called out much too loudly. "Maggie, is that you?"

Rachel stepped from behind the shelf glaring at him. "Keep your voice down. You're in a library. And stay where you are." She slowly stepped again from his view, and the muffled voices continued.

"Are you talking to Maggie?" he whispered, but his question remained unanswered. The cart stacked high with books blocked him from following Rachel.

He could hear the two women speaking softly, but he could not discern the words. Suddenly, the conversation became very rapid between them, almost harsh, yet it remained too quiet to hear.

Rachel came around the end of the bookshelf and walked toward Jonathan. Her demeanor was the same. Her eyes were cold, and her lips drawn tight.

"Okay, she'll meet with you but on her terms," she said sternly.

"Fine, wonderful, whatever. What do I need to do?"

"Maggie's apartment, tomorrow afternoon. No food. No booze. Mark will be there too, I can you promise that." She stood with her arms folded. Her face displayed no friendship or kindness. It was tolerance, and just barely that.

"That's excellent. Can we watch the ballgame?" After he said it, he realized how calloused it sounded. Rachel's face reflected the offense. "I know that didn't come out right, but there is a reason for all this. Please, help me a little here."

Rachel moved toward him. She came right up to him only inches from his face.

"I've helped you more than you deserve, buster. But fine, we can watch the game if you need to."

Jonathan had looked at Rachel many times, but never this close. When she was literally in his face, he realized there was something familiar about her. Like he had just seen someone that reminded him of her, but who? It hit him like a lightning bolt and he flinched. *Marcia, the librarian!*

Rachel saw his reaction, misinterpreted it, and took further offense. "Listen, if you don't want this deal, then fine. You're on your own." She turned to walk away.

"Rachel, no, it was something else. It was nothing to do with this, right now. I'm sorry."

She turned to face him.

"All right, tomorrow, at her apartment after lunch." Rachel turned back to her books and ignored him.

Jonathan ran to the end of the shelf and looked down the row where Rachel had spoken to Maggie.

"She's gone," Rachel said without breaking her pace shelving books.

He glanced down the empty aisle. She was gone. He returned to the row where Rachel was working.

"Thank you," he said gratefully.

"Don't mention it, please, *don't,*" she replied as she turned the cart and walked away from him.

He had made contact, not direct contact, but the time was set. He knew he had a long way to go to regain Maggie's favor. He doubted that Rachel would ever forgive him. Even Mark's acceptance was in question. Nonetheless, it was a start.

*   *   *   *   *

Jonathan hurried to his lab and set up his video equipment to view the recording of his trip on the large monitor. He forwarded through the preliminary footage of him setting the shot, the lighting, focus, and then checking the amount of memory available on his camera. Finally, Jonathan watched himself lie down on his bed and prepare for the injection.

He was surprised at how long he took to give himself the shot. Even though it was the second trip, the hesitation was very clear. Then, it was done. Jonathan was surprised at the violent, even inhuman contortions his body made. As he watched he wasn't sure he could bend his arms and legs in the same way if he tried. He had known the convulsions would come, but it was still hard for him to watch. He would never allow Maggie to watch this part of the experiment.

His body on the video suddenly stopped convulsing. He switched the playback to super-slow motion and began the wait. Rushing through at this point could allow something to go unnoticed. He wanted to see it all.

After several minutes of frames clicking by, the orb ascended from his chest and face. It was not a tiny ball of light like those that rose from the lab rats or guinea pigs. Jonathan was awestruck. The orb, his personal life force, was the size of a basketball. His mouth hung slack. He could not take his eyes from the screen.

The orb that slowly left Jonathan's body was brilliant. Colors of every hue and magnitude of the light spectrum flashed from within the orb. Every imaginable color moved and swirled in the smoky ball. Was it simply electrical charges? Was he watching intelligence carried in a ball of smoke? Or was he seeing his spirit?

It was simply stunning.

He leaned toward the screen. The orb exited the frame moving down and to the left of the screen. Jonathan sat upright. *Down and to the left*, he thought. From where he had placed the camera the only thing that was to the left was his closet.

After meeting Marcia at the library, he recalled running back and entering his room. He remembered he had been grabbed and practically thrown into the closet. The next thing he was aware of was waking up on his bed.

"Wow," he wondered out loud. "Did this process make my closet a time portal?" That seemed very strange to him. He dismissed the thought. Portal or not, the experiment was a success.

Jonathan moved the dial on his playback machine to fast forward. He watched the counter and stopped the video three minutes and twenty-five seconds after his "launch." He wanted to observe the return.

He ran the video at regular slow motion until he saw the flash then backed up and moved to super-slow motion. The orb entered from the direction it had departed, the lower left corner of the screen, and without a pause it re-entered him.

The motion was almost like a slam dunk of a basketball. The orb moved directly over him and *POW,* slammed into his chest. Jonathan's reaction on the video was as if he were hit by ten thousand volts of electricity. He watched himself shoot to a sitting position, just as he remembered.

Now that he had seen everything, he rewound the video to the departure of the orb. When the sphere was at its highest position over his body and milliseconds before it left the screen, he hit pause. He then zoomed in on the smoky globe and centered it on his large monitor.

The essence of human life hung suspended in time. Slowly moving the video from frame-to-frame, back and forth, he sat in astonishment, mesmerized by the pulsing of light and color. He watched the force that gave him breath, thought, imagination, and the capacity to love hover in silence.

What could science learn by observing these orbs? Would science be able to determine future health risks or find evidence of pre-criminal activity? Could goodness or evil be determined by watching and measuring the lights and colors? What did they mean, what could they possibly tell us about life, about the universe?

"Someday, Maggie, you're going to have to see this. This is incredible." Jonathan stopped. He was talking to Maggie in an empty room. Madness pressed on him. Jonathan pulled back from the screen. He was alone, alone with his imagination, his thoughts, his orb. *Is it arrogance that drives me? Do I care so little for the people who are precious in my life that I would sacrifice it all to see this "orb"? Do I? Is that what this is all about?*

Suddenly, his mind was divided, torn between opposing loyalties. All of it seemed astonishingly foolish. He flushed with embarrassment, and anger washed over him. He loved Maggie. He ached to start a life with her, to share laughter and to brave the difficult times. He missed her.

But my work is ground-breaking. I am bridging new horizons of science. My discoveries are huge. No one in the history of mankind had witnessed this amazing moment. I must press on and prove to everyone—

"No!" He pushed himself back from his desk. He felt divided inside. Schizophrenic. Two individual lives battling for supremacy. Two wills at war in his mind. "And yes." He breathed out heavily, and then said softly, "I must carry this to the end. They will see."

He shut down the video equipment. Still the thought that he had carried it too far hammered at his conscience. His only hope was that she would come around, that she would forgive him and finally understand. It was all he could do. The experiment was a success. Surely she wouldn't remain angry when she learned he was fine. Tomorrow would present his first and perhaps his only opportunity to make his case and win her back. It had to work.

*   *   *   *   *

The Man is here again. Like the last time, he is standing still and looking at me. I am not afraid of him. I stand to face him. He is coming toward me. Still, I am not afraid of him.

"What is your name?" he said.

"I am One."

"And so you are. Are the others still around?"

"I have not caught all of them. I hear them cry. Should I go kill them?" I want to know if killing is expected of me.

"No," he said. "You have learned to go through and buy food, have you not done that?"

"I did not know I could go through to the cold side like It does." I am surprised. "Do I not need to remain here?"

"No. You may go through the same place he does. You can find food there and you will not need to kill the others."

"The cold side is too cold for me. I do not like it."

"Once you are through, it will be warmer than it feels from here," the Man said. His eyes seem, I do not know, happy. He is not afraid of me. Nor does he seem angry with me. "Once you get through, you can get dressed, use the money you find, and buy something to eat."

This is a new idea for me to consider. The Man explains how I can buy things. I think on this. I like the idea. When I turn back to the Man to ask a question, he is already walking into the mist. I will ask more questions the next time I see him. I will ask many more questions.

12

Sunday morning Jonathan paid an impromptu visit to his father. He was surprised to find him dressed and wearing a tie.

"Hey, Dad," Jonathan said. "You're looking pretty spiffed up for a weekend."

"Thanks," his father replied with a chuckle. "It's more like putting icing on a turnip, if you ask me."

Jonathan smiled. He had loved the warm banter they had enjoyed when Mom was alive. He missed it. She had been a tiny woman, but managed to command her husband and son with majestic authority. He marveled at the way she had always made him smile, even when he was in real trouble. When Mom ruled the kitchen, there had been a lot of smiling. That was deeply missed.

"No, Jonny-boy, I went to church this morning." That little bit of news threw Jonathan completely off balance.

"You went to church?"

"Yep. Your mother was after me all her life to go with her. I could manage a Christmas or Easter every now and then, but just couldn't bring myself to go with her regularly."

"So, why start now?"

Martin Walsh stopped his salad preparation and leaned against the counter. He sighed and pursed his lips as he contemplated his response.

"Jonny, your mother was a wonderful woman. I loved her and still love her beyond anything I have ever known or imagined. She was a good woman, and I miss her. But she was a good person, too. There was something about her. You know, you and I would get into terrible fights, but she would always clear the decks and set things right again. How did she do that?

"I have yet to figure out where she found her solace, how she would suddenly be so wise and discerning when we were blinded with rage. Then it came to me. The one thing I refused to do was go to church with her. I've decided if I want to discover what she knew, I might look at what she did."

"You don't think she was so together because of the free time she had?" Jonathan asked as he plucked a chunk of lettuce from the mixing bowl. "I mean, she had all the time in the world to analyze us and our behavior. She didn't need to work. Maybe she just had the time to think things through?"

"That's a good point. But she was spot-on pretty much all the time. If something happened between us, let's say, and she had the afternoon to consider it, you might be right. And I'm not saying that didn't happen. It's the times when things blew between you and me that she was able to step into the middle of it and make it stop. She could do it on the fly, like an improvisation."

"Yeah, she did that," Jonathan said as he sat on one of the stools. "Now that I think about it, she amazed me. Remember the limerick?"

"The one about making notes?"

"Yeah, how'd it go?" Jonathan's eyes scanned the counter top as he remembered. "There once was a fellow who thought, very little, but thought it a lot."

"At long last he knew," Martin added, "What he wanted to do . . ."

"But before he began, he forgot. *Write it down!*" they said in unison. The two men laughed. It was classic Alice. A teaching moment wrapped in humor and wisdom. They were quiet for a moment, each trapped by a warm memory.

"Jonny, I need to find what *I* have forgotten . . . or missed. Being part of her church was important to her, and something I never considered. Did she learn or discover something there? I don't know. At this point I figure it's a good place to start."

Jonathan nodded. Of course, he wasn't interested in anything like that. Religion was a trap for the weak, a crutch for the intellectually impaired. He was fine. Maybe when he was old he would share his father's emotions and check it out.

"Good for you, Dad. That's good." He smiled as he realized they had just spent five minutes in conversation without an argument.

"Stay for some chicken and tossed salad?" Martin asked as he returned to his chopping.

"Thanks, but no. I'm meeting Rachel and Mark at Maggie's apartment to watch the ballgame. We'll probably eat a ton of junk." It was a brighter picture than Jonathan really expected, but it kept the conversation light and away from his work.

"I understand. You're welcome anytime, you know. Swing by some evening, and we'll fire up the grill. Summer is on its way, and it will be nice to be outside again."

Jonathan's mood was further lightened by the invitation. "That sounds like an excellent suggestion. And I think I'll be able to find the time in the next few weeks." He braced himself for the question about his work. It never came. The day remained free of argument.

"I'll look forward to that, son." Martin looked up from the salad before him and smiled. Jonathan was glad to see him smile.

"Well, I'd better get moving if I'm going to make the first pitch. I'll call in the next couple of weeks, and we'll spend some time together." For the first time in a very long time, Jonathan hesitated to get up and leave. He was enjoying this time with his father, really enjoying it. But he said he was leaving, so he took a skip toward the door, waved, and was outside.

"Good to see you, Jonathan. Say hi to Maggie," his father's voice trailed after him. Jonathan answered something meaningless over his shoulder as he strode down the walk. Home felt warm like it had when Mom had been there, or like when Maggie had been there.

Maggie.

He sensed he was moving into enemy territory. *It shouldn't be like this*, he thought. *Why is the idea of hanging out with my best friend and the girl I love such a dreadful thing?*

He dropped himself into the seat of his car and let out a heavy breath. This was important. The next few hours could set everything right, or so he hoped. Then again . . . no, there was no *again*. It had to be set right. Jonathan started the engine and shifted the transmission into first. Now was the time.

*   *   *   *   *

"Are you up for this?" Rachel asked. Her expression was dark. "I get angry just thinking about him. You're my best friend, and I hate seeing you suffer because of his stupidity and arrogance."

Maggie looked at her through eyes that had cried too much, and endured loneliness for too long. Then, she grinned. "Be nice, Rachel. I don't know how to be ready or *up* for anything anymore. I am tired of hurting and being by myself."

"You're not . . . by yourself," Mark insisted.

"I know," Maggie said. "I can't imagine facing him without you backing me up."

"Do you know why he wanted to talk to you?" Rachel asked.

"No. But I imagine he wants to convince us that he is doing something grand for the cause of humanity and all that rot." Maggie sighed and shook her head. "I don't know if he's capable of understanding how selfish all that heady stuff is. I mean, we had something really wonderful going . . ." She turned away.

The doorbell rang. Mark looked at Rachel. "I promise I won't punch him in the face." He walked to the door and opened it.

Jonathan stood on the porch holding a bag of snacks and treats for the game. The bag surprised Mark who furrowed his brow at the sight. Jonathan smiled like a school boy on his first date.

"Hi Mark," Jonathan said. "It's good to see you."

"We'll see how long that lasts. Come on in, but I'm not sure you have a clue what you're up against." Mark stepped aside and opened the door for him.

Jonathan entered the apartment with a broad smile on his face. He jumped a little inside as the door closed firmly behind him. "Hi ladies, I brought some snacks for the game," he offered.

"Don't know that anyone feels much like snacking with you around," Rachel snipped.

"Oh, you two, please stop." Maggie walked toward Jonathan and hugged him. "It's good to see you, Jonny. I've missed you."

"I've missed you, too, Maggie." He thought she looked different. She looked tired and frail, worn-out. He was surprised how deeply it showed in Maggie.

"Let's sit down, okay?" Maggie said taking him by the hand and leading him to the living room. The arrangement of who sat where was awkward at first. Maggie moved to a winged-back chair beside the fireplace, Rachel and Mark immediately took the love seat, leaving the couch for Jonathan. It was a big couch and he felt alone and isolated as he sat.

"You asked for this, Jonathan. Perhaps you'd better explain yourself a bit," Rachel said as she sat back. "As far as I'm concerned, the only item we have to discuss is whether we lynch you or pummel you to death with ping pong paddles."

"Rachel," Maggie said as she shook her head.

"Thanks for letting me come," he began. "First, I want to apologize for the absolute jerk I have been over the last few months. I have ignored you, Maggie, and I am terribly sorry. I have offended all of you, and I want you to understand that wasn't my intention. It was an unfortunate result of one of my many shortcomings."

Rachel snorted and glanced away from Jonathan, shaking her head and diverting her icy stare out the window. Maggie furrowed her brow at her in silent scolding.

"I'm not asking for anything from you now. I know I don't deserve your forgiveness. I just want you to know that I love all of you. Maggie, I love you beyond words, and I ache at the thought of the suffering and pain I've caused you."

It was a good start. He could see Maggie warming to him, believing him, even a little. He hoped she would be eager to forgive him, but he wanted to move slowly.

"Jonny, I'm not sure you are aware of what you've done. I mean specifically . . . to Maggie," Mark said. He glanced at Rachel.

"I say we string him up."

"Rachel! Please, let's try to be civil," Maggie said nearly coming out of her chair.

Jonathan took a deep breath, and looked at Mark and Rachel before he continued.

"I've had a couple of good talks with my dad that have helped me understand . . . I don't know . . . I guess, my compulsion for my work. Maggie, you know that Dad and I are a lot alike. We are too easily focused on ourselves and what we do . . . and we tend to block out those around us . . . even the ones we care for the most."

"I know that, Jonny. Your dad lost a lot of time with you and your mom. Time he can't get back. Do you see that he doesn't want you to make the same mistakes?" Maggie said. She sat back in her chair and folded her arms across her chest.

Jonathan hung his head. "Yeah, I—I do see that. I feel like I got my father back a couple of days ago. I mean . . . we really connected. Even this morning when I stopped by, it was great. We talked for a whole five minutes without a fight."

"Well, that's encouraging." Mark was still distant. "Jonny, you know my family. They've always been absent. Your family is the only real family life I've ever known. Your family is more important to me than my own. You've got to know that withdrawing from your dad has wounded   him   deeply."

"You're right, Mark. That was one of the things we were able to discuss," Jonathan added. "I am a lot like him. And I know he regrets how he treated my mom and me. You look to him with immense respect . . . and that's great, but I saw the monster in him when I was a boy."

"He's no monster, Jonny," Maggie protested.

"No, he isn't. But he has a temper . . . and when he's disappointed it comes through loud and clear. To a nine year old boy, it—it's monstrous. I've *been* there." Jonathan's eyes scoured the floor at his feet. "And . . . as much as I *hate* that attitude, I—I find myself reacting the same way. Maggie, you saw me at the reception. When Dad mentioned the grant awards I was unreasonable . . . and unfair.

You said as much. And although I hate it . . . it comes out through me just the same." He realized his palms were sweating.

"None of us are perfect, Jonny," Mark said.

"Shut up, Mark," Rachel snapped. He immediately sat back at her reproof.

"Rachel," Maggie scolded. "Dial it back just a bit, please. We're all friends here. We've known each other for a long time, especially you two boys. I just think we need to be patient . . . and calm."

Rachel scowled and glared at Jonathan. Contempt would have been a compliment for what he saw in her eyes.

"Thanks, Maggie." Jonathan ignored Rachel as she rolled her eyes. "Look, I know I messed up. What do I need to do to fix the things I've broken?"

"Have you considered suicide?" Rachel stood and walked toward the kitchen.

"Rachel! Stop it! That was totally uncalled for."

"Not entirely, Maggie," Jonathan said. "Rachel is angry, and I deserve it."

"Okay, we can sit here and spit nails at each other all afternoon, and not get anywhere," Mark interjected sliding to the edge of the love seat. "Jonathan, we know you've made mistakes. Believe me. I want to know what has taken away my best friend and locked him up in that smelly, old laboratory."

"Me too," Maggie added.

"Fair enough," Jonathan agreed. "When we had dinner and everything got a little confused, I didn't make clear enough the extensive precautions I have taken in building my formula. I condensed everything, tried to avoid the technical stuff and present things in a general way. I started my research three years ago on the newest drugs in sedation and psychiatric medicine. Maggie, do you remember all the work we did?"

"Yes," she replied softly. "You worked very hard to eliminate those that presented the remotest possibility of side-effects or nerve damage."

"And we settled on the two antipsychotics and amitriptyline? Remember? They were the safest, the most commonly used, and they had a track record. Right?"

She nodded. Together they had read and discussed dozens of reports and how laboratory rats had responded with no ill effects.

"Would you agree, Maggie, that we were very thorough in our research?"

"Yes, I do agree," she said.

"So, you've seen me work and know that I'm not reckless."

"Yes, for the most part . . . especially, then. I don't know about now."

Jonathan ducked his head and held up both of his hands.

"Fair enough. Most of my formulas were based on findings in the *International Journal of Pharmacology* and the *British Journal of Psychiatry*. We did a lot of digging to find a starting point."

Rachel returned from the kitchen carrying three glasses of iced tea. She gave one to Mark.

"Thanks, babe." Then he said to Jonathan, "What about the math? Did you review all of that with your dad?"

Rachel handed a glass of tea to Maggie.

"I did," Jonathan replied. "We had a long talk the morning after our misunderstanding at the restaurant. Amazingly, we didn't argue. I was shocked. I think that was the first time we had been able to discuss mathematics since Mom died. I think he really grasped at least the basics of what I'm trying to accomplish."

"By that do you mean perfecting the three-minute nap for a rat, or time travel?" Rachel sat beside Mark and sipped her tea.

"Rachel, don't do that," Maggie snapped.

"Sorry," she said. It was clear she didn't mean it.

Jonathan sighed. "No . . . in the math part I elected a theory called Grundy-Sprague, commonly called game theory. The theory advances the chance effects of numerous random events, like in a game of baseball, for example. The speed . . . the vector, and even distance of a baseball is hit from home plate, all of it is a series of outcomes that depend on the speed of the pitch, the spin on the ball, where it strikes the bat, what material the bat is made from, and even if it is a sunny or cloudy day. Game theory allows for those and many more variables in coming to a specific conclusion."

"Still sounds like a huge risk to me," Maggie said.

"Nothing ever totally removes risk," Jonathan answered. "But through repeated experimentation one can minimize risk."

"In spite of the risks, do you really believe these orbs you told us about contain the essence of intelligence and individual will?" Mark asked sitting back.

"I'm not sure, but it seems to be the most obvious conclusion," Jonathan answered sliding to the very edge of the sofa. "I don't know of a method to decipher what constitutes the orb, this sphere of life, or how it works. Guys, this is like the first scientist to view an individual cell. Who was it, Van Leeuwenhoek?"

Mark moved forward on the seat and said, "No, I'm pretty sure it was a British scientist named Robert Hooke . . . in 1665—"

"Exactly, and with what *had* to be a very primitive microscope. That was more than four hundred years ago," Jonathan replied with measured excitement. "Another example: science has known for a *long time* about the important role blood plays in our body's survival. I think the Bible talks about it and that goes back thousands of years."

"They knew there was a connection, but didn't actually *see* it until the 17th century, nearly three thousand years after David wrote his Psalms," Mark added.

"For all the time men have been walking on the face of the earth, no one has ever *seen* what lets us live . . . or makes us the people we are. What I'm doing is that *first viewing*." Jonathan relaxed a little. His mouth was dry, but he felt good about the points he was making. "And depending on where science will take my findings in the next four hundred years, all my equipment and calculations are the primitive beginnings of who knows what—"

"That's all fine, Jonny, but it's not the problem," Maggie jumped in. "I cannot believe it's good for you to lock yourself away like you have. You need to be out *doing* things . . . and going places, you need co-workers, friends and family. Locking yourself away all alone is not a good thing."

"You're right. But I am not doing this to avoid seeing anyone. I don't know why, but I get enthralled by all this, and I—I simply lose track of time. Heck, I lose track of entire days. Honey, you saw it when you and Dad rescued me. I was totally out of it, but at the same time completely absorbed by it—"

"Or completely full of it," Rachel snorted.

"You're *not* a lot of help, Rachel," Jonathan snapped.

"No, Jonny, please don't."

"I'm sorry," he said. And he halfway meant it. "Look, I am not intentionally blocking you out. Some very strange things have happened that I don't understand. Like the night I practically mowed you two down by the parking lot. I realized I had been taken over by something quite frightening. I actually became terrified of my work. I had to stop and give very serious thought to *how* I was working. Dad helped me a lot with a new approach to work."

"You were pretty freaky that night," Maggie said.

"I heard you weren't very graceful," Mark said. "More like an entrance Kramer would make on *Seinfeld*, or some dude on the business end of a stun-gun."

Jonathan fell back on the couch smiling. He rubbed his face with his hands. He was embarrassed. "I can only visualize what I looked like that night. I mean, Kramer? Really?"

"A wilder version of Kramer, if you can imagine," Rachel said with a grin as she snuggled beside Mark. "The look on your face, careening around the corner . . . that was really funny. Terrifying . . . but funny."

The tension lessened.

"How can we help?" Mark asked. "None of us want that to happening again."

"I'm not sure. I don't know . . . maybe force me to be here with you guys like this?" Jonathan leaned toward Maggie. "When all this started, my work and research, we knew it would consume a lot of my time and attention—"

"Yes, Jonny, your time and attention . . . but not *you*."

"Right." He paused. "But I'm *so* close. I'm almost to that point I believe will allow me to back off a little bit."

"So, where are you in your work now, Jonny?" Maggie asked. The mood turned quiet once again. Jonathan looked at the floor. This was it. This was the make or break moment he had dreaded. He raised his eyes to meet hers. He knew he had to risk it all.

"It works."

The silence in the room was palpable.

"Which means . . ." Mark asked slowly.

"Which means it *really* works." Jonathan was smiling weakly.

"Jonny, you didn't use it on yourself?" Maggie whispered, her voice caught in terror.

"I did . . . and I'm fine."

"You did *what*?" Rachel snarled.

"I gave myself an injection of my formula specifically designed for me."

"And you did all the things the rats did in your tests," Mark said flatly.

"Yes."

"Oh, Jonny, you didn't . . ."

"Look, I'm fine. I—I feel great. There are no side effects of any kind," he said, coaxing approval.

Mark leaned forward, "So, you did . . . what?"

"I traveled to the future."

A pin dropping would have crashed like a lab flask shattering on concrete.

"To the future . . ." Mark echoed peering up through his eyebrows.

"Yes."

"And you went there without a time machine or any mechanical device to help you get there."

"Yes."

"Is it that you believe your orb containing your mind and," he shifted uncomfortably, "I guess, your spirit popped out of your body, and went, what? To the future? Is that what you're asking us to believe?"

"I don't think I could have described it any better, Mark."

"When you got there, in the future, how were you walking around? I mean what were you using to go places and do things?"

"I was in a body, my body . . . just me, I guess." Jonathan grinned as he shared his excitement. "It's weird, because after I took the injection I went through some . . . stuff, but in seconds, I'm there. I'm in the future. I'm stark naked, I'm in my room, but I'm . . . there, not here."

"I can do without the naked part, but *where* are you? Really." Rachel asked.

"It's my apartment. It's cleaner, picked up and clothes and shoes are there that fit me. I even found some money. That was my first clue that I actually traveled in time. The bill was dated 2025, and it was old."

"No way—"

"Maybe you just imagined it. I mean you take a crap-load of drugs first, right?" Mark asked. "Could it all be some kind of hallucination?"

"I wondered the same thing. But it was too real." Jonathan looked at Maggie and saw that she wasn't buying it. "Listen, I don't know how it works completely yet, but that's what the next several steps will discover. What makes the transition complete? How is time travel actually accomplished? What is the differential that allows unlimited time in one dimension but limits the current time to three and a half minutes? These are huge questions. I have lots of questions to answer."

"Oh, this is just too much," Rachel said flopping back on the couch. "You actually expect us to believe this cockamamie story?"

"No, Rachel, I don't expect you to believe anything! But I can demonstrate it with a very specific fact, if you care to listen."

Maggie sat motionless and speechless. Rachel huffed indignantly.

"If it's science, I'm all ears," Mark said.

"It is science, the best kind, the provable kind." Jonathan chose his words carefully keeping his eyes on Maggie. "A baseball game is being played right now between the Colorado Rockies and the Atlanta Braves. The Rockies are going to win that game, but something very significant is going to happen in the seventh inning."

"You already know about something in the seventh inning of a game that just started," Rachel scoffed.

"Yes, I do," he replied smiling.

"Okay, I'm game. What's going to happen in the seventh inning?" Mark said.

Jonathan glanced at Maggie. She looked like she was in shock. Her eyes were locked on him.

"While I was *there*, I went to the campus library and looked for something that would happen today, April 29, 2007, that would prove I traveled through time."

Silence surrounded him.

"In this game, in the seventh inning, the second baseman for the Rockies, Troy Tulowitzke, makes an unassisted triple play, the thirteenth unassisted triple play in major league history. He will catch a line drive hit by Chipper Jones, step on second base to catch Kelly Johnson coming back from his lead off, and tag Edgar Renteria as he barrels down the baseline from first. Boom-bitta-bang! Three outs by one player."

"You're kidding," Mark said.

"Not a bit." Jonathan smiled broadly.

Rachel walked to the television, snapped it on and said, "Okay, prove it." She turned her back.

Maggie was frozen. The game came on the screen. It was the bottom of the first inning. The score was zero to zero.

13

I have never seen a place like this. No, I *have* seen this place. I came here first. I remember. This is where I came at the very start.

Here are the clothes. Yes, I got dressed. I remember how to do that. I feel warm in clothes. I like this. Oh, and shoes, and money for food. I remember the food, hot, good food. Not warm. No killing here either.

It is not as cold as I thought it would be. I walk down the stairs and outside to the street. This is much like the warm side, but a little different. I must pay attention and compare it to the warm side the next time I go there.

I do not know where to go. The Man said I could buy food here, but I do not know where. I will look in the buildings along the street. Each one is different.

I enter the first building and notice many small machines with two wheels. Some hang from the ceiling, others are lined-up side by side on the floor. But I do not see anything to eat.

"May I help you?" a voice says behind me.

I turn to see a man I do not recognize. He is smiling and looks friendly. I do not think I will need to fight with him or kill him.

"I am looking for someplace to eat," I say nervously. My eyes dart around the building. Was another man behind me? Would someone attack me? It is all new and I do not understand.

"You probably want to go to the café down the street," the man says, still smiling. "I think they're open."

I have never spoken to another person like this. I glance at him. He seems fine, but I look away to make sure no one is behind me. I am very uncomfortable. I am not sure what to do.

"It's just down the street a ways," he says in a kind voice. "You can't miss it."

I turn and walk out of the building. I want to know what "down the street" means. Nothing is lower than here. The ground is flat except for the hill in the park. I look both directions to make sure everything is on the same level.

I see the café. It is further along the street just past a few more buildings. I walk calmly toward it. Several tables are spread across the sidewalk in front of the café. A wall with plants on the top separates the tables from the sidewalk.

An older woman with golden hair is sitting alone at a table beside the plants reading a book. She looks sad. She looks lonely. As I walk toward a table she looks up at me, directly at me. A look of horror floods her face.

"Oh, no!" she screams. "No! Jonathan?"

Suddenly, I am terribly frightened. Why is she looking at me like that? I do not know what I have done. I did not say anything to her. I did not do anything to her.

"Hey, you!" another man shouts at me. He has just come from inside the café. He looks angrily at me. What did I do? Why is he angry?

I must leave. I turn and begin walking back toward the apartment. I walk quickly along the sidewalk. I hear very unhappy voices behind me.

"Was that Jonathan?" the woman says.

"No, it's all right," the other one says. "He's leaving. You'll be fine."

I do not know what happened. I hurry up the stairs and into the room. I will leave the clothes here and go into the smoke. It is safe in the smoke. I must hurry.

*   *   *   *   *

The game progressed as all baseball games do, from dullness to excitement, to disappointment, bad calls, and great plays. Some of the time it seemed like old times to Jonathan. Almost. Maggie was quiet. She smiled at the jokes Mark and Jonathan made, twice she booed the refs. Then, the seventh inning began.

It was exactly as Jonathan had told them. Boom-bitta-bang.

The rest of the game played to a room of silent spectators. No one spoke. Jonathan was confused. He was certain his evidence would convince his friends of the validity of his research. He thought they would be overwhelmed with joy for his success. He expected Maggie to be thrilled and run to his arms. But nothing happened.

The Rockies beat the Braves nine to seven. It was just as Jonathan said.

"You traveled to the future using your drugs," Maggie said flatly.

"Yes," he replied.

"Jonny, there is something very wrong in this. I—I don't know what it is, but it is wrong." She looked upset, angry, frightened.

"I have to admit the baseball thing is a very good trick," Rachel said.

"It's not a *trick*," Jonathan replied with anger in his voice. "This is a result of good science. It's safe science. And now . . . it's *proven* science." He said each sentence with more emphasis than the one preceding it. His face became slightly flushed.

"Keep it cool there, Jonny-boy," Mark said. "You have to admit it's a pretty big load to swallow without digging through the science ourselves."

"I know it is. That's why I've been trying to explain the research I've been working on for over four years. It's very hard to explain everything I've done in such a short time. Have a little faith in what I've accomplished here. Come on."

"Jonny, it's not faith in you or your ability that bothers me," Maggie said. "It's what all this work is doing to you. I'm afraid for you."

"Honey, I have worked the formulas time and time again. The science is good, it's strong, and it works—"

"But the work, it holds you like a hostage. You never come out of your lab; you don't call me; we never laugh or just spend time together. It's changing you."

"Maggie, I'm getting to the end of this. I know it's difficult to wait, I don't like it either. But I have made real progress, *exciting* progress."

"But *we* aren't making any progress. We are falling away from each other. I don't want that to happen. I want to be with you, Jonny."

"I know, and I want to be with you," he said still trying to justify himself. "We knew the initial period of my work would be difficult for us. We knew it would take time. Unfortunately, it's taking more time than I ever imagined. I never dreamed the things I'm discovering would be so exciting. This thing is huge. Imagine if wars could be avoided. What if politicians could go ahead in time, view the effects of their policies? Then they fix their laws and those mistakes would be avoided. What could be greater than that?"

Rachel stood and half-turned away before saying, "I don't know, maybe inventing the ultimate rat nap."

"Now you just shut-up," Jonathan barked at her.

"Hold on there, Jonathan," Mark raised his voice in her defense.

"No! Stop it. It's wrong. *This* . . . is wrong." A single tear streamed down Maggie's cheek. She was trembling. "What is happening right here, right now, is *wrong!* Jonny, what you are doing to yourself and to your friends is *wrong!* You don't see it. You're *blind* to the hurt and pain you're causing. You find it too easy to alienate *me* to loneliness, sitting here day after day, night after night, all by *myself.* If I didn't love you, I—I would *beat* you. I am at the end of what I can stand. All of this is because of *you* and your *blasted experiment!*"

Jonathan had never seen her so angry. He reached for her. She bolted to her feet and screamed, "*No!* Go back to your damn lab. You can *rot* in there for all I care!" Maggie ran from the room.

Jonathan felt the stares from Mark and Rachel. He turned to them. Their expressions were furious. Rachel's eyes spoke directly to him saying *don't you see what you've done?*

He opened his mouth to speak but Mark cut him off.

"Intriguing science, buddy, but I think you just lost your most important vote. It didn't work. You lost me, too."

Jonathan's heart sank. Mark was right. Yes, he had lost. His proof did not sway his friends to understand his research. His temper had just cost him his best friend. The idea of losing Maggie . . . he couldn't finish that thought. As for today, it was over. Finished.

Without saying a word he stood and left Maggie's apartment.

*   *   *   *   *

Next time I will follow It like the Man said. Not right away, but a little while after It goes. I will go where It goes and see what It does.

I have thought about this. This place is empty. Why does It go through here? Where does It go? Now, I will find out. I will follow. I will learn what It does and not be afraid. I do not want to frighten people like the last time.

I hear the sound. It has come many times. I know Its sound. I know what It smells like when It passes. I know what It smells like when It returns.

I need to know many other things. That is why I will follow. I will see this time where It goes.

Yes, that's the sound. It's coming close. There! It goes in an instant. Wait. Now slowly, go through . . . right there.

14

Jonathan burst into his lab. Rejection didn't sit well with him. Maggie's inability or unwillingness, or whatever it was, her failing to accept his proof, was the final straw. He was done with her. Rage asserted itself in his very core.

He slammed the door behind him. The first thing he saw was the stack of papers for his grant that he and Maggie had labored on for months. He grabbed them and threw them into the air.

"Maggie opposes *me*. I will oppose *her*!" He grabbed books stacked on tables and shelves and flung them across the room smashing them into the walls and knocking picture frames at odd angles. Glass tinkled to the floor below.

Jonathan's fury exploded on a stack of research journals that he ripped with his bare hands. He threw his arms wildly crashing into the stands holding test tubes and drip lines in his chemical experiments. Bottles of drugs and chemicals smashed on the floor.

"*Rachel*, you have *poisoned* her against me!" he snarled. "You are now *my* enemy. I'll make you pay, you snide, little . . ." He couldn't finish his sentence. He seethed with hatred. "I will humiliate you at *every* opportunity I find." He knew Mark would take her side, deceived by her manipulative feminine treachery. Jonathan's eyes peered into empty space, focused not on Mark, but on the anger he felt towards him. "She's *your* problem. We'll just see how that goes for you, *ole buddy!*" he growled.

Jonathan fell into his desk chair exhausted. He breathed in huge, dry gulps of air, roaring with every inhaled breath. He had never been so enraged. Anger pulsed in his muscles, his heart thundering in his chest. With fists clenched he leaned forward, resting his elbows on his knees. Jonathan's lungs felt on fire, and they burned with each heaving gasp.

Minutes passed. He did not move. His breathing eased as the storm passed. The muscles in his arms and legs relaxed and his heart slowed its rhythmic pounding. Jonathan raised his head and scanned the nearly destroyed lab. Then he wept.

*   *   *   *   *

Jonathan sat at his desk completely worn out. All energy was drained from him emotionally, physically, mentally. In a state near total collapse he decided the only way to prove his point was to bring the future to the present. Over time he could make more investments, introduce ground breaking ideas, and initiate research that would advance science by decades.

He was done with people. Their small and narrow minds would have to fend for themselves. Now he could, and would make a difference all on his own.

Slowly he stood and began collecting his books, papers and equipment strewn around the lab. He carefully picked up the broken glass and mopped the chemicals spilled on the floor.

Once the room was set in order, he applied great care as he mixed the largest batch of the cocktail he had ever imagined. Rather than a milliliter or two, Jonathan combined the chemicals and drugs for a full liter of formula.

It didn't matter. He would use it all. He would take as many trips as necessary to answer his questions, find new paths of discovery, and make his mark on the world. They would see. Eventually they would understand, even if it was a hundred years after his death. Everyone would see him as the forward thinking scientist of this century.

The mixer beeped. The process was complete. Jonathan gingerly placed the canister in an insulated carrying case. Before he left the office, he straightened his desk and work bench. He didn't plan to return any time soon. Toting the canister under one arm and carrying the video equipment with the other, he opened the door to leave.

He paused as he stood in the doorway. For a reason he didn't understand, he felt he would not return to this office. He shrugged it off. His emotions were not to be trusted. Too much had happened today. The last thing he wanted was emotional attachment . . . to anyone or anything.

He stepped out of the doorway and walked down the hall. The lock snapped shut behind him. The click of the lock echoed down the empty hallway. He ignored it. This part was finished for now, at least for him.

*   *   *   *   *

Three days later Mark knocked gently on the door to Maggie's apartment. No answer. He waited for a few seconds and knocked again, this time a little harder. Behind the door he heard noise but no voices. Someone was in there, so he knocked again, still no answer.

Mark's imagination began working against him. He immediately dismissed the thought that Jonathan had come here ahead of him and might be inside arguing with Maggie. *He wouldn't come here after that confrontation,* he thought.

But, what if it was something else? Didn't bad things happen in threes? What if someone other than Jonathan was in her apartment? Mark tried to quiet his imagination, but it persisted, triggering unreasonable fear.

"Maggie," he yelled as he banged on her door. "Maggie, it's Mark. Open the door." He pounded again. "Maggie!" Adrenalin was pulsing throughout his body. He had to get in. He backed up and prepared to crash through the door.

Suddenly, it swung open. Maggie stood looking at him incredulously. Her hair was ruffled, uncombed, and her baggy sweats made her look frumpy. "Do you think I want *anyone*," her eyes dropped to the floor, "even you, to see me like this?"

Mark realized she was probably right. She looked awful. Still, behind the *awful* he could see Maggie, and she was beautiful.

"Sorry. I had to check on you," he said timidly.

"Oh, it's okay. Come on in," she answered with a wave of her hand as she walked away from the open door.

He followed her in and sat beside her on the couch. The drapes were drawn across the windows casting a gloomy haze over the room. He could tell she was still angry. Mark understood the workings of the mind as a scientist, but the darkness of pain in a woman's heart mystified him. He knew what made intelligence function in the human brain and much of how human senses fed and triggered thought patterns, memories, and even emotions, but the atmosphere in Maggie's apartment terrified him.

Mark knew nothing about women. He knew how he felt about them and how the nice things he did for them often softened their attitudes and feelings toward him. He was good at making a woman comfortable in his presence. But he knew this was out of his league.

"That didn't turn out so well, did it?"

"Honestly, Mark, I had little hope it would be anything different. I mean, I know Jonny will always want to prove his point, or try to justify what he's done. I know him well enough to expect that. I didn't expect him to think he could convince me so easily."

Mark wasn't real sure how to reply. "I don't think he was trying to insult us or make anyone uncomfortable."

"Not to make us uncomfortable," she said. "But he knew exactly what he was doing. I simply didn't buy it, and what's more I will never buy it."

"Help me here, please. What is it you believe he wanted us to *buy*?"

"He wanted us to see the simple fact that this science is the right thing to do. Don't you see that?" she asked.

"As a scientist I consider all science a worthwhile pursuit. In that sense, no, I don't see it as a problem."

"But Mark, this is our friend, the man I love, doing something no one has ever done, and something that may have consequences we cannot imagine, and he's doing it alone. To me that is a problem." Her eyes reflected her words and mirrored her fear.

He thought about comparing Jonathan to people like Edison, or ground-breaking scientists like Madam Curie, or the early scientists who worked on developing x-rays or MRIs. He caught himself. Many of them died as a result of their exposure to radioactivity or dangerous diseases. He was stuck.

"You're right," he said putting his arm around her. "I guess the best I can do is keep checking on you and make sure you're all right."

Maggie lowered her head to his shoulder and rested her hand on his chest. She sighed heavily and leaned against him.

"Every now and then I do need a good hug," she said. "Thank you, Mark." She smiled and patted his chest.

He squeezed her against his side. She sat up, and then kissed him on his cheek. The impulse seized him to kiss her back. He stopped it and excused himself.

"I'd better be going," he said with a tinge of discomfort. "It's laundry day, you know." It wasn't, but he knew he needed to leave.

"Thanks, Mark. I really mean it," she said as she stood. "Just about everything is difficult right now, but I think I'll make it." She smiled a winning smile and blinked the moisture from her eyes. She reached out and hugged him firmly. He wrapped his arms around her and held her.

"Okay, I'd better go." He smiled and walked to the door. "You'll call me if anything comes up, right?"

"Absolutely."

Mark stepped out her door and turned toward the stairs. That was when he saw her. It was Rachel coming to see Maggie. She stopped in her tracks when she saw him.

*   *   *   *   *

It has been said a tiger cannot change his stripes, and a man cannot change his stars. Jonathan had decided that a man could. He was tired of trying to please Maggie at the expense of his science. He now understood why great men and women in both science and industry were known for being poor family members. He also decided there simply wasn't time for her pettiness.

At least, he didn't have time for Maggie's fears. The pursuit of knowledge had carried him to a new dimension of scientific discovery. It was now his duty to make that innovation a workable, useable concept for mankind.

Jonathan climbed the stairs to his apartment and eased himself through the small door so he wouldn't drop his precious cargo. He couldn't imagine the kind of mess a full liter of this new compound would make on hardwood floors, and he certainly didn't want to try it as an experiment.

He placed the video equipment where he had before. He would record and study every event and every return. The study of the human orb that rose from his body fascinated him. He had no idea what he could learn, but the lust of inquiry burned in him.

He placed the canister of formula in his refrigerator and sat at his desk. He began writing a list of questions he wanted to answer in the future. What advances would begin development in the next five or ten years? How would the evolution of computer memory proceed? What inventions in communication would he find? How did the mind-reading computers of the future operate?

Jonathan wrote for an hour, filling pages and pages with questions. He was confident that his memory was among his best assets, and he could rely on it to carry his questions with him and return with remarkable results.

He committed three important topics to memory and sat down on the edge of his bed to prepare his attitude and state of mind. His breathing was deep and slow. He began his mantra slowly and softly.

"Ommm . . . eye'ngggg namahhh . . ." Again and again he repeated the sounds allowing them to resonate in his face and chest. "Ommm . . . eye'ngggg namahhh . . ." Peace settled over him.

Jonathan laid his head on his pillow quietly repeating the soothing words of his mantra. He slowed his breathing and closed his eyes. Without looking, he pinched the skin of his abdomen and carefully inserted the needle.

He barely noticed the injection and convulsions. The next instant he stood naked in his neat and properly cleaned bedroom. He immediately turned to his dresser and began getting dressed.

15

Afternoons in the future didn't appear much different to him. The normal rumble of traffic was more subdued, a background noise. The wind was still, and the leaves on the trees hung in silence, but the cacophony of spring was coming to life as evening blanketed the neighborhood.

Jonathan was reminded why he had chosen this section of town to be his home: partly because of its distance from the campus, but mostly for the park, the café, and the family atmosphere that buzzed from home to home. That had not changed.

The cars were different. They moved silently. He figured they were electric, and that over the last thirty years someone had made advances in cost-effective, durable batteries. He thought that would be something to check out and add to his list of future investments.

Jonathan walked briskly toward the campus library. He considered visiting his old office building but decided his immediate interests were more pressing. Although the library was several blocks from his apartment, he covered the distance quickly.

Again, at the front of the library he noticed the old, heavy wooden doors. Jonathan had never paid much attention to such things. He was young and had been exposed to only a relatively short period of time. However, his ability to move thirty years into the future had broadened his sense of reference. He was struck by the things that had changed. Many of the office buildings, businesses, and homes seemed brighter, fresher, and even newer somehow. Although the trees and shrubs had grown, the landscapes had not changed significantly. People had changed, however.

Philip, the waiter at the café was physically older, of course. But the man inside the aging body was different. The brisk and happy person Jonathan knew in his natural time had been transformed by the passing years into a somewhat more jaded, slightly cynical man. Jonathan's thoughts wandered to his friends.

Where are they now? Did they all survive this long?

Once inside the library, he went directly to the same computer he had used a few nights before. He sat and reached for the earpiece that hung from a small hook on the back of the screen. The response was instant.

"Well, hello, Jonathan, good to see you again."

"Thank you, and how have you been, Connie?"

"I don't get out much."

Jonathan smiled and sat back. *A computer with a sense of humor*, he thought.

"Thank you, Jonathan," Connie replied softly through the earpiece.

"I'm going to have to be careful with you watching my every move," he said in a teasing manner.

"And every thought, you remember."

"Yes, thank you for your clarification."

"How can I help you today, Jonathan? May I call you Jonny?"

A shudder hit him and stopped him cold. He couldn't think. Suddenly he felt someone's eyes on him. He turned quickly from left to right, looking for someone staring at him. He pulled the earpiece from his ear and hung it behind the monitor.

He stood, still looking all around him. His hands trembled and perspiration trickled down his forehead. When he saw her, he gasped.

Marcia stood in the shadow of a large bookcase. Light streamed behind her making her silhouette ghostlike. Her face seemed pale; her eyes were riveted on him. Her eyes terrified him. He told himself it was just the drugs; it wasn't really all that bad. Surely he was imagining the strange look on her face.

He looked at her again. She hadn't moved and continued to glare at him. Then her mouth moved and without hearing a sound he understood perfectly.

Get out of here! she mouthed pointing at the door.

He didn't need to be told twice and moved as rapidly as he could to the door. Her face haunted his mind, and as he approached the door, he distinctly heard a whisper, *Get out of here! Get out of here!*

The identical fear that pursued him across campus the night he almost knocked Maggie and Rachel to the ground seemed to be at his heels. He stumbled out the double wooden doors and onto the sidewalk. He made no pause in his retreat and left the campus at a dead run. The more space he could put between himself and the library the better.

The fear eased and he stopped to catch his breath. He bent over and rested his hands on his knees. *What the heck was that?* He glanced toward the library to assure himself nothing was actually chasing him. The street was empty.

* * * * *

I will go to the warm side again for food and to see what I might learn about It and why It comes to the smoke. Now that I understand moving in the smoke and the gray, it is easy for me to go. I push hard against the dark gray and go through.

I put on clean clothes, ones that do not smell. The clothes are soft and comfortable. I like wearing shoes.

I walk along the street past the buildings and watch the people around me. Fear has no place in this world. I find nothing terrifying. Some things seem unusual and I do not understand them, but I am not afraid.

The sun is setting and the shadows stretch long bands of twilight across the park. I continue to walk as the lights along the roadway come on automatically. My way is easy to see. People stroll past me and are kind and very pleasant. They smile and say good evening to me.

I turn a corner near some houses and a woman approaches me. The closer she gets, the slower she walks. Suddenly, she stops completely. She looks frightened.

"Do you have any idea what you are doing?" she says. I turn to look behind me. Perhaps she is speaking to someone else. I know exactly what I am doing and do not understand why she asks me that question. I look at her, and I am confused.

"You don't look well. You need to stop this, and stay away from me." She turns quickly and runs away from me. Who is this woman? Why is she angry with me?

I do not understand many things in this place. Someday I will know what women mean when they speak to me. I must find food. I am hungry.

*   *   *   *   *

Maggie felt drained and depressed. She was a lost soul. She knew Mark and Rachel wanted to help her and encourage her, but their visits made her tired, so Maggie chose to bury her life in other people's exploits and adventures. Her real friends were the characters who lived between the covers of the hundreds of books that became her refuge. She embraced the character's fears, identifying with Cosette in *Les Miserables* as the lost orphan searching for salvation. Her dreams of romance blossomed in the pages of *Jane Eyre* and carried her to a different land, a different time, one less painful that her own.

Maggie put down her book and looked out her window. It was a beautiful evening, and it seemed a shame to waste it. She took a sweater from the closet and slowly walked to her door. Through the open door Maggie paused and sighed. She would still be alone but she needed the walk. Besides, being outside would feel good. She stepped outside.

The cool evening air was pleasant. It seemed to refresh her, and wash the staleness out. Once she was down the stairs she looked at the sky and saw the first star of the evening. *Is that Venus or Mars?* she asked herself. It really didn't matter. She wasn't much for astronomy. Maybe she would take it up.

Several families walked through the neighborhood, their voices and laughter making the evening more festive. Children skipped ahead of their parents then waited impatiently for Mom and Dad to catch up.

Maggie's own family was a splintered, dysfunctional disaster. Her parents had taken interest in other things early on in their marriage, interests that eventually led to other people, lovers, and finally a bitter divorce. Her only brother Mick, three years her senior, had had enough and left home right after high school graduation leaving no information about where he was going or when he might come back.

With her father out of the picture and her brother in self-imposed exile, she was left to sort out life with her mother. That was difficult for Maggie. Throughout her high school years her classmates talked behind her back. The stories of her mother's loose lifestyle led to rumors and fantasies in the minds of school boys regarding Maggie. None of it carried any truth, but the stigma remained.

She was drawn from her memories by the distant sound of dogs barking. Maggie had always been interested in dogs but had never owned one as a pet. Maybe she should learn more about dogs. She thought about having a pet, the responsibility, the extra food, and the inevitable messes that come with puppies. Maybe dogs were not part of her future.

She came to the end of the block and a man slowly walked around the corner and came toward her. She slowed her pace. *Was it . . . ?* She came to a stop. She could see his form silhouetted by the street light. *It's him.* It was Jonathan. He looked awful. His hair was a mess, and he hadn't shaved in far too long. He stopped several feet from her.

"Do you have any idea what you are doing?" Maggie asked. Her heart began pounding in her chest. She felt extremely uncomfortable and did not want to be near him. He turned and looked behind him. *What sort of foolishness is he up to?* she wondered.

"You don't look well. You need to stop this, and stay away from me," Maggie said. Suddenly, fear gripped her. The peaceful evening descended into gloom and darkness. She turned and ran from him.

*   *   *   *   *

The sun was low in the western sky, and Jonathan felt hunger gnawing his insides. He headed to the café near his apartment. *Would they still be open on a late evening?* he wondered. *Would Philip still be working?*

Much to his delight the café was open. In the old days, Jonathan's time, the café was popular with dormitory students on weekends. Now, the customers were a bit older, perhaps former students, but appeared to be in their mid-thirties.

Still, a few people who could pass for graduate students were sitting at the sidewalk tables. He let out his breath from the fright, the run, and brisk walk, and took a corner table with his back to the planter at the café's south end.

"Welcome back. Are you going to eat this time?" Philip approached him with a menu in his hand and looked very tired.

"Yes," he replied smiling. "I was glad you're open."

"Hardly a day or evening goes by that I'm not open," he said dryly. "At this point, young man, I don't have much else to do, and if I'm closed, I won't have any business at all. Better a little than none."

Jonathan nodded and smiled. Philip was older, slightly hunched in his back, and he moved slower. He was definitely more cynical; *worn down* seemed to be the proper description. Jonathan wondered just how hard the last thirty years had been for him.

"Do you need a minute with the menu, or do you know what you want?"

"Oh, sorry. Of course I know. I understand your potato soup and grilled cheese sandwiches are excellent." In reality they were Jonathan's favorite. The first time he had eaten at the café, before he started grad school, he had stopped in on a whim. It had become his regular spot.

"Yep, we still make them. Do you want the bacon crumbles and cheese on the soup?"

"You bet," Jonathan replied with a broad grin.

Philip smiled and turned toward the kitchen. Then he stopped and pivoted back to Jonathan.

"Are you sure you aren't from around here?" he asked. "You sure remind me of a guy, a teaching assistant who taught one of the classes I took. I think his name was Dr. Walsh. That's it, Jonathan Walsh."

"My uncle."

Philip lit up as if he'd met a long lost friend. "I can see the family resemblance," he replied, and he turned toward the kitchen with a little bounce in his step.

Jonathan leaned back to wait for his meal and try to enjoy the rest of the evening. The sky was streaked with bright yellow stratus clouds, wisps of color against the pink and orange rays painted on the darkening blue. The evening was cool and refreshing.

A few children played in the park across the street, breaking the quiet evening with their squeals of laughter and delight. A single man stood on the top of the hill by a large maple tree, a silhouette against the evening sky. Another man sat on the park bench facing the street and at a slight angle to the café. Something about him was familiar. Jonathan wasn't certain in the soft light of dusk, but he thought the man looked at him.

After what seemed only moments, Philip appeared carrying a tray of steaming soup. The sandwiches were made of toasted, thick-cut sourdough bread housing slabs of melted sharp cheddar cheese. Jonathan's mouth watered at the sight.

He devoured the delicious meal reveling in the treasured blend of taste and aroma. The hot food warmed his belly and helped him relax. He didn't want to think about Marcia and the library. He wanted that memory to be gone. As were, far too soon, the soup and the sandwiches. Jonathan sat back on the chair and gazed into the park.

His eyes fell on the park bench where the man had been sitting. *What was familiar about him? Why did he look at me?* A flurry of questions raced through his mind. He discarded them. Besides, the mysterious old man was gone.

16

Jonathan "awoke" with a jolt, fully dressed and in his own bed. He stood and stretched. His stomach growled with hunger. He turned off the video equipment, and his stomach growled again.

"But I just fed you," he said bending toward his belly. The growling and accompanying cramping continued. "Fine, I'll feed you again." Another order of potato soup and grilled cheese would clear things up. Just the thought made him smile.

In spite of the scare he had had in the library, Jonathan felt light and liberated. He knew his research was valuable and by now the technology was proven to be safe. He went quickly down the stairs, skipped across the street to the café. He took the same seat by the planter he had chosen only a short time before, but thirty years in the future.

"Do you want a menu or just coffee?" A younger version of Philip approached him wearing a broad smile.

"Thanks, but I already know what I want," Jonathan said returning the grin. "I'll take a bowl of your potato soup and a grilled cheese sandwich."

"I like that. Decision already made, as is the soup. Would you like cheddar cheese and bacon crumbles on the soup?"

"Absolutely," he replied. Jonathan leaned back as Philip disappeared into the kitchen. The café was populated with a small

Sunday evening dinner crowd. *Perhaps the college kids ate earlier*, he thought. He delighted in the evening air and the smaller crowd.

While he waited, his eyes scanned the park across the street. The stone wall that surrounded the grassy knoll paralleled the sidewalk and enclosed the verdant three-acre refuge. Jonathan loved the sounds of the birds and the noise of the wind blowing through the leaves in the summer. The gentle breeze soothed him.

His eye stopped on the bench where he had seen the older man who appeared to have looked at him. *Who was that man?* he wondered. *Why would he watch me?* A perfect stranger would not necessarily be friendly to another stranger. Usually they would avoid eye contact or simply look away. This man acted differently. Maybe next time he would try to meet him.

After a few minutes, Philip reappeared with a steaming bowl of soup and a plate of sandwiches. It was almost a replay of his earlier meal. The soup smelled just as wonderful, and the toasted sourdough bread was enticing.

"Here you are, hot and fresh from the grill." Philip swung the plates onto the table in front of Jonathan. The steam from the bowl warmed his face as he breathed in the aroma. He was certainly ready for a meal, even if he had just eaten.

In the back of his mind, he couldn't figure out why he should be hungry again. He decided it would probably require more thought than he was willing to apply at the moment. He discarded his concern and dug in to his second evening feast.

*   *   *   *   *

Maggie pulled hard to open the heavy wooden door as she entered the library. Through the summer it had become a sanctuary to her. It was cool and dark, and a very good place to hide. She was finding solace in literature since Jonny wasn't around to distract her. She had read many of the books before, but returning to them was like visiting old friends. They, the characters in the novels, were always waiting for her, and they never ignored her attentive gaze.

The library had a number of designated areas. Maggie walked past the tables that were for study and research. The heavy wooden chairs were uncomfortable. They awarded students a sense of sacrifice in their pursuit of higher knowledge. The reading areas Maggie loved were furnished with very comfortable wing-backed chairs in which one could bury oneself and become lost in 18th century England or the wispy hillsides of rustic Ireland.

Maggie was careful to not look for Jonny. After the fright of the previous night she wanted nothing to do with him. She was certain he spent most of his time in the lab with his rats. She imagined he was alone in his apartment . . . or in the future. She snorted.

His demonstration with the baseball game had impressed her, but she decided it had to be a trick of some kind. She didn't know if he had really traveled in time, nor did she care. Whatever he was doing, it was wrong. She was convinced of that. Besides, it kept him away from her. It *took* him away from her, and for that she hated whatever it was.

"Penny for your thoughts," Rachel said coming toward her. She smiled as she took a chair to Maggie's right and sat leaning forward, her elbows on her knees.

"Hi, Rachel. I don't think you would appreciate my thoughts just now. I am being very selfish and petty."

"If you were considering either crucifixion or castration, I might find them fascinating, depending on who the subject is." Rachel could snarl through a smile and make the darkest images humorous. Maggie found her very entertaining.

But when she answered, her voice was hollow. "Nothing quite so dire, I'm afraid. I took a walk last night and ran into Jonny. He looked dreadful. This is the only safe place I know outside of my apartment. I just love sitting here and being carried away by a great book."

"I understand. Sweetie, you've got to be lonely. I'm sorry." Rachel was sympathetic, but only for a moment. "I won't say who, but I know exactly who to blame for that." They both chuckled, but that, too, was empty. The laughter simply masked their sadness. "Do you want to go to a movie tomorrow night with Mark and me?"

Maggie sighed and her face pinched a little. "I don't know. I don't want to be a third wheel—you know the tagalong, scorned girlfriend. Pity does not look good on me."

"Not a bit of pity allowed, sister. We're friends. Whether there are three of us, four, or dozens, we go together because of our friendship. We like you. We miss you. Come on, girl, do your thing." Rachel did a little sassy dance in her chair. It made Maggie smile.

"How can I say no to such a provocative proposal?" she replied. "Do you have one picked yet?"

"*Spider-Man 3!*" Rachel replied reaching toward her with clawing fingers. "That's what Mark wants to see anyway. What do you think?"

"I think I'll probably fall asleep. Those action flicks are too much. I don't know why I get so sleepy. I guess I can't keep up with everything, and I lose interest. It used to drive Jonny . . ."

Maggie stopped mid-sentence. She immediately folded her hands in her lap and bowed her head. She had said his name out loud. Hearing herself say his name shocked her. She did everything she could to hold herself together. A tear streaked her cheek.

"Bastard," Rachel muttered.

"No, please, Rachel, don't speak of him like that. He's just confused and making some really poor choices. But, please, don't . . ." Maggie's voice trailed off. Her eyes met Rachel's. Maggie shook her head slightly. Rachel sighed and looked at the floor.

Both women sat without speaking or moving for nearly a full minute.

"You still love him, don't you?" Rachel grimaced. "Damn, girl. After what he has done to you? You surprise me. Then again, maybe someday I'll love someone that much. Maybe even Mark." Rachel bugged her eyes wide and smiled.

Maggie took in a breath and sighed. "A movie sounds like a wonderful idea," she smiled. "And . . . I promise not to mention ole what's-his-face."

Their laughter broke the gloomy spell the mention of Jonathan's name had imposed. Feeling better, Maggie said, "A little laughter works like medicine, doesn't it?"

Rachel reached for Maggie's hand, and looked into her eyes to reassure her. "Okay, tomorrow night at seven. We'll pick you up, all right?"

"I'm looking forward to it."

Rachel stood and left pushing her cart laden with books to be shelved in the stacks.

Maggie was no longer interested in reading. Reality had burst the bubble that isolated her from missing him. She closed her book, stood, and picked up her sweater to leave. Even though her laughter with Rachel had lightened her heart, she was still alone. It was going to be a difficult night.

*   *   *   *   *

After his first trip on April 27, Jonathan had continued to add questions to the list. His original stack of pages filled with questions had more than doubled. He was curious, amazed, even awestruck by what he was learning about everything from kitchen appliances to the new cars, from advances in computers to new farming techniques. He had truly discovered a bold new world.

Jonathan sat at his desk to catch up on the paperwork with clumsy technology of the present day, a notebook. Every trip was recorded on video and electronically stamped with the time and date it occurred. During June and July, he had made many excursions to the future collecting both scientific and financial information.

He didn't fancy himself a bookkeeper, but fastidious records were the hallmark of his career in grad school. In the excitement of encountering so many advances in the future, he had fallen behind. As he considered his neglect of records, he was alarmed at the lack of information he had collected on himself. His notebooks were filled with data on the lab rats he used during development, but very little was recorded on him.

The implants on the rats had detected vital brain and body processes needed to sustain life during the "sleep" periods, or while they were making their trips to the future. They also registered blood pressure, heart rate, and respiration just as if they were a patient in a hospital.

"Why in the world did I not do the same with myself?" he asked out loud. He knew the answer before he asked the question. In his mind he had always hoped that Maggie would be with him to watch and help with data collection. "Well, that idea fell flat."

He knew the process worked. By now he was well acquainted with what happened during the process and confident that nothing would go wrong. After all, he had run the numbers, done the science, and perfected the combination of chemicals and drugs to make it work. He was sure there were no side effects. He was certain of that.

The records needed to be organized and completed, something of which he was acutely aware as a scientist. Jonathan activated the video equipment and began reviewing the first event. He noted the time and date on a spreadsheet on his laptop. He logged the duration of the event, looked closely at the still frames of the orb; he noted the colors, diameter and speed at which it moved.

It was monotonous. Much of the busy work of science is the boring repetition of collecting the same information time and again. This was no different. He marveled at the precision of the departures and returns, every one exactly three minutes and thirty seconds. Inwardly he cursed himself for falling behind. He berated himself for his inattention to good science, muttering that he could have written a program to automate the entire process. That would be next on his list.

The events continued. Jonathan grew increasingly frustrated with himself. He had no idea how many trips he had actually taken. When he passed one hundred and twenty-seven recorded events, his anger began to boil. How could he have been so unprofessional?

"Why have you not been paying attention to this?" he said to himself gruffly. "You are much better than this. This is sloppy and dangerous. Do you have any idea what you might be doing to yourself?" Anger continued to mount in his mind.

The count stopped at one hundred and thirty-nine. One hundred and thirty-nine trips to the future in—how many days was it? Jonathan grabbed his desk calendar to confirm the date of his first experiment. There it was, April 27, 2007. He had entered the data for each event. But anger had muddled his thinking. *What is today's date?*

"August 19," he responded surprised. "One hundred and thirty-nine trips in one hundred and fourteen days?" He crashed his fists against the desktop. His eyes burned with rage. "I recorded one hundred and thirty-nine events and no personal data on *any of them*?"

Rage won. He pounded and pounded the desk. Files fell to the floor.

"Stop this!" he shouted. "This is not you. Get control of yourself." His breath was labored and heavy. He could not believe how poorly he had conducted his work.

He stood and faced himself in the mirror above his dresser. He couldn't remember ever feeling such anger. He stared at his image with a fiery hatred.

"You have got to do a better job," he said through gritted teeth glaring at his reflection. "You cannot expect people to understand if you treat this like a toy. This is serious science. Pay attention to what you are doing."

He was startled to see an image looking back at him that reminded him of his father. A childhood memory flooded his mind. It was a memory of his father angrily rebuking young Jonny for failing to keep water in the dog's dish on a hot summer day. Jonathan flushed at the memory. He looked just like his father. He was acting just like his father.

Jonathan shook his head and turned to his desk. His rampage had left a mess, and his laptop teetered on the edge of his work station. He quickly moved the computer to safety and picked up his files.

The outburst embarrassed him. *Humiliation does have a certain level of cleansing*, he thought. Jonathan knew he had made mistakes. He vowed to correct it. He would do better.

Slowly, another sin rose to accuse him. Maggie. Could that offense be made right? He thought not. It seemed to him some things would remain broken forever.

*   *   *   *   *

"So, have you found it yet?" Alice sat across from him in her chair. The chair that she liked best was smaller than his, and it wasn't very comfortable. She sat erect with excellent posture supported by the straight back and lumbar support built into the piece of furniture. That had always bothered him. He loved to slouch, hunker down, and recline in deeply cushioned comfort.

"Found what yet? What are you talking about?" he replied.

"More than a week ago you told Jonny you were searching for whatever it was that made me the woman that I am. At the time, you were going to check out my church."

"Oh, right. Church." He wrinkled his brow. "I've gone a couple of times, and . . . it's nice. The people are friendly and the choir is pretty good. I was surprised about that. I recognized several people in the choir and had no idea any of them could sing that well."

"That's better, but is that what you were looking for?"

"I'm not sure. Is that what I should be looking for? I mean, you're the one who seemed to have found the secret ingredient, right?" Martin could always answer a question with another question. It was a defense mechanism for the few times he had no answer for what had been proposed.

"Are you asking me what that secret ingredient is?" Alice countered with another question.

"Is there someone else I should be asking?" He looked at her and smiled. It was a game to him. If he could keep the questions coming he knew he would eventually learn something from his adversary. Rarely did this technique actually work with Alice, however.

"Cute." She stared him down with a slight grin on her face. "Martin Walsh, you're playing games aren't you? Don't you remember your games simply do not work with me? You stinker. You haven't found it, have you? And what is worse, you don't have a clue what you are looking for, do you?" Alice read him perfectly.

"No. I don't." He hung his head. Not out of shame or failure, but certainly from consternation and even a little frustration.

Alice smiled. She had him. He was backed into a corner in his own mind and could not imagine his way out. To him, everything was a calculation, a formula that would result in an answer. This was a challenge he would not be able to work out on paper, a chalk board, or with the aid of a computer. He was stumped.

He noticed her smile and took offense. "You're mocking me. Please do not make fun of me."

"Martin, dear man, I love you with an unfathomable love. I do not mock the people that I love," she said leaning forward in that uncomfortable chair. "You will not find what you are seeking by using the same methods you teach your students. In this situation, my dear, you are not the teacher. You are the student."

Martin rolled to his side and woke up.

"I am the student?"

17

Research requires that one collects and confirms data then chronicles the evidence of any effects on the subject during the research. Jonathan had traveled thirty years into the future more than one hundred and thirty times, made several notes of things that might interest him, but failed to chronicle any effects his experiment had on his physical body or his mind.

To him there was only one way to remedy his lack of diligence. He must do it all again. This time, however, the research would have the accompanying data to provide full proof.

Jonathan took the longer route to his office and stopped by his father's home. It had been weeks since his last visit, and this one was long overdue. He walked briskly up the walk, leaped up the porch steps and poked his head inside the front door.

"Dad," he called into the house. "Are you home?"

"As home as I can get." The response came from the kitchen. "Come on in, son. Come on in."

He entered the kitchen to find his father apron-wrapped and standing at the stove. A smile spread across the older man's face. The room was filled with a familiar fragrance that drew Jonathan to the center island and the stove top.

"Is that Mom's—"

"It certainly is," his dad grinned broadly. "Mom's marinated chicken and twice-baked Alfredo potatoes."

Jonathan sat on one of the tall chairs at the counter and inhaled the aromatic mixture. The combination of spices was like none other he had ever encountered. The blending of soy, Worcestershire, and teriyaki sauces coupled with molasses, paprika, brown sugar, and garlic penetrated his senses and succored waves of memories from his childhood.

He closed his eyes and breathed in deeply, absorbing every ounce of memory and each molecule of the culinary bouquet. He knew if he opened his eyes his mom would not be in the room, but in this moment, this memory, she was.

"Amazing, isn't it," his father said interrupting his dream.

"What? Oh, right. I hadn't smelled such a wonderful fragrance in a very long time. I'm glad I stopped by."

"Me too. Stay for dinner?"

The invitation required little consideration. Until he had eaten his fill, it would be impossible for Jonathan to leave, and it would give some time with his dad.

*   *   *   *   *

Mark stood outside Maggie's door. He was nervous. He knew he shouldn't be, but Rachel's reaction to his last visit shadowed his concern for Maggie's wellbeing. He knew he would be pulling her away from some 17th century adventure, but he pressed ahead anyway. He knocked gently on her apartment door.

"Oh, hi, Mark." Maggie's face brightened upon seeing him. "What brings you to my neck of the woods?"

"Hey, Maggie. I just thought I would, you know, stop and check up on you."

"Come on in," she said as she swung the door wide open. "I have some kinda-fresh coffee if you'd like some. Can I get you a cup?"

"Sure," Mark sat on the loveseat. "That would be great." He watched Maggie amble into the kitchen. She was beautiful even in a tee-shirt and sweats. He watched her a little too closely and forced himself to avert his eyes. He knew his concern for her could get him into trouble.

He had a good thing going with Rachel and didn't want to mess that up. Mark had a knack for provoking a woman he was dating to jealousy by showing too much attention to another attractive woman, but he loved Maggie. He always had loved her. It had broken his heart when she had fallen in love with his best friend. He had never stopped loving her. But Rachel had come on the scene at exactly the right time, and Mark was totally taken by her charm and intellect. Almost totally, that is.

"So . . . how's life treating you?" Mark asked as Maggie returned from the kitchen.

"It sucks." She handed him a steaming cup of very dark, strong coffee and sat across from him on the couch. "So, here you are," she said putting her mug on the end table beside her. "What's up?"

"Well, I hadn't seen you around much, and . . . you know, I thought I'd better make sure you were okay." It was a stumbling and clumsy excuse. He was certain she could see right through him. And he was pretty sure he looked foolish.

She smiled and leaned back on the sofa. Her eyes sparkled, and a lock of her hair fell out of place and across the bridge of her nose. She laughed and puffed the lock of hair back where it belonged. Her smile was warm and charming.

"I'm glad you came to see me, Mark," she said softly. "I get carried away in a good book and nearly forget I have real friends that like me and want to spend time with me."

"That's for sure," he replied a bit too quickly. "Rachel and I were saying just the other day we needed to hijack you out of here for some night life."

"It's been a while, hasn't it?"

"Yeah, it has. Is your work schedule and school demanding at the moment? I mean . . . mid-terms are just a few weeks away, and I know you've started on your dissertation. Do you have the time?"

"For friends? Of course I have the time," she said. "And I think it would be fun to go out with you two."

Just as she finished her sentence, Mark's cell phone chirped to life. He looked at the face of the tiny phone then back at Maggie. It was Rachel. He flipped the phone open.

"Hi, Rachel," he said turning away from Maggie. "What's going on?"

Mark suddenly cringed. Maggie smiled.

"Oh, well, I was on my way to the store, and stopped by to say hi to Maggie. I'm at her apartment." The pause was palpable.

He nodded his head in tacit agreement with something Rachel said. Maggie covered her grin with her hand. He pursed his lips and wrinkled his brow.

"Maybe five minutes . . . you know, I don't know . . . just a little bit," he replied, again clumsily.

Mark folded his arms tightly across his chest and continued nodding.

"She's great," he said. "We were just talking about the three of us getting dinner sometime soon."

Mark glanced at Maggie and saw she was enjoying this conversation at his expense. She could barely restrain her laughter.

"Absolutely," he replied. "I was going to see if you ladies would compare your schedules and set a date. I can go about anytime, but I know you both have work and classes and all. Sound good to you?"

He smiled and gave Maggie a quick thumbs-up.

"Will do," he said. "Are you still coming over tonight for a movie?"

He nodded at her response.

"Okay, babe. I'll see you then. . . . Love you." He closed his phone.

Maggie burst out laughing. "You're in trouble, aren't you? Or did you forget something?"

"Oh, yeah, like always," Mark answered. "Why do you ask if I'm in trouble?"

"I don't know, you're just a little flush, and I thought there might be a problem," she said.

"Nah," he said waving off her concern. "I guess it's a little weird being here, just the two of us. In the old days you were the odd-guy-out. I mean, when it was Jonathan and me . . . then you."

"And now it's Rachel and me, and just you," Maggie teased. "You're getting your comeuppance, mister. Us girls need to stick together, you understand that, right?"

"I do," he said. "And I probably have some abuse coming from the two of you. Anyway, Rachel said she would give you a call."

"Good. That will give us time to figure the best way to torment you," Maggie said attempting a wicked smile. To Mark there was nothing wicked about her smile, perhaps a touch of deviousness, but not wicked. She was lovely.

"Which means I'd better scoot," he said taking a final sip of the hot coffee. He stood and headed to the door. She cut him off.

Maggie walked up to him, and threw her arms around his neck and kissed him on the cheek. "That's for being a thoughtful friend. Thank you for coming to see me. I'm just fine."

"I can see that quite well, thank you," Mark said and kissed her cheek. She squeezed him very tight. He wrapped his arms around her and held her, then released her from his embrace and stepped out the door. Once outside Mark exhaled heavily.

Yes, that was the Maggie he loved. She was a real spitfire. Her eyes sparkled as she teased him and he loved it. His mind spun with far too many conflicting thoughts and feelings for him to have stayed longer. He also saw he shouldn't have come to see her in the first place.

That was a hug! he said to himself skipping down the stairs. *That was a real hug!*

*   *   *   *   *

It was difficult for Jonathan to get past his failure to document his accomplishments. He berated himself constantly for the oversight. Of course, it was perfectly understandable. The experiment was an exciting adventure, and it had swept him away. That was his emotional excuse. But there was no excuse for blindly skipping the documentation on the scientific side of things. He had measured everything meticulously with lab rats, but ignored the statistics when it involved his own life. It was inexcusable.

The human-size monitoring equipment was much more affordable than the miniature models for rodents. All the equipment he needed had arrived by overnight courier. The only thing he needed to do was a chemical analysis of the drug cocktail to insure it had not degraded over the past few weeks. He didn't want to inject himself with a flawed batch of psychotropic drugs, especially now that everything would be monitored and recorded.

The chemical analysis took only minutes. He checked the battery packs and the infrared links between the different piece of equipment for recording and collecting his personal data.

When all systems were ready, he reviewed his list of things to investigate in the future. He took two concepts with him every time. Upon his return he wrote detailed notes of everything he could remember. His intention was to pick topics closely related to his own research and initiate the ground work. He would advance science, make a name for himself as a remarkably forward thinking scientist, and maybe, just maybe make a bunch of money. Why not? Ideas are ideas, aren't they? Make the most of the opportunity his research had given to him.

Jonathan turned on the video camera and sat on his bed to address his audience before launching himself thirty years into the future.

"Hello," he began. "My name is Jonathan Walsh, and today is September 21, 2007. The purpose of this video is to monitor my physical body during the time I will experience travel to the future. I have made more than one-hundred and forty trips. Each time, I advance exactly thirty years to the day—to the hour—for that matter. I don't know why it is exactly thirty years, and I have not devised a method of traveling to a particular date or time in the future. This is simply what happens.

"Regardless of how long I stay there, in the future, when I return to the present only three and a half minutes have passed. I have observed this phenomenon two hundred and sixty-eight times with rodents in my laboratory. As I said, I have traveled many times into the future. If I choose to spend the entire afternoon reading and learning about scientific, financial, or even political advances in the future, only three and a half minutes have passed in this present time when I return.

"I am going to inject myself momentarily and fall asleep. You will notice a flash shortly thereafter that is the life force exiting my body and this present time. After three and a half minutes, the flash will occur again as I return. During my absence, my body's respiration rate, heart rate, and brain activity will be displayed along the left side of the monitor.

"As proof that I have indeed visited the future, I will return with news of an event that will occur sometime in the next seventy-two hours. Those events will be recorded with a time and date stamp on the screen and later edited into this video as they occur in real time. So, without further ado, let the experiment begin."

Jonathan lay back on his bed and attached the wires to the monitoring sensors already on his chest and temples. The equipment came to life and reflected his vital signs on the monitor. He repeated his mantra and felt his mind and body move into a calm, restful state.

"I'm all set here. See you in thirty years, or three and a half minutes, whichever comes first." He smiled at his own joke, laid his head on the pillow, and pressed the plunger on the syringe.

Jonathan popped into his bedroom, the future version of his bedroom, and as always, he was stark naked. He dressed quickly, ignoring the nagging question of why he was naked when he arrived in the future. It was something he could study later. For now there were too many things to investigate. He quickly scribbled some notes from memory for the day's excursion. Each trip must not only be recorded and monitored but productive. He tucked the note in his pocket and hurried down the stairs to the street.

*   *   *   *   *

I hear It coming. Yes, that's the sound. It's coming close. There! It goes in an instant. Wait. Now slowly, go through right there. I press against the gray into the dark gray and thick smoke. Follow It. I am through.

I can see It standing by the bed. It is getting dressed. I will wait. I will be very quiet. I will follow It.

What's that? It is going out. I dress myself and creep down the stairway to the outside door. The light is bright. My eyes hurt. What is It doing? Where is It going?

I follow It outside. The air feels warm and good on my face. I cannot let It see me. I will stay behind, but not too far. I pass the store with the small machines. I do not want to go in there.

It looks back. Does It see me? I must be careful. Slowly follow, but do not lose It.

It sits down. I will go in this building and wait. Can I get food here? I have Its money. Yes, I will eat and wait. I will wait.

"May I help you sir?" the young woman behind the counter asks.

I look at her. I must look angry because she is frightened. I try to smile and not sound mean.

"One of those, please," I say pointing to a bread item in the case.

The young woman gives me the pastry and I pay her. I take a bite. I have never tasted anything as wonderful. It is warm and sweet. It smells fresh and inviting. I take another bite and another. Then it is gone. I turn to the young woman to buy another one.

She is definitely frightened. I pay her and hold the second pastry in my hands. I cannot believe how wonderful it is to eat. I look at the surface and the light crispness that is so sweet and marvel at it.

For a moment I have forgotten about It. But I must keep watching It. Carefully I go outside the store and look to where It was. It is sitting at the café eating. How long will It stay there?

I do not think It will be distracted from the food if I cross to the park. I will go to the top of the hill and watch from under a tree. It will not notice me. I will watch.

18

This trip had two objectives. First, Jonathan decided he would investigate transportation, specifically the latest in automobile design and luxury. Americans' love affair with their automobiles would never die, and he couldn't go wrong making an investment on the fascination. The Cadillac dealer was six blocks from his apartment, the opposite direction of the university. That would be a good start. Besides, he'd always liked Caddies.

Afterward, he would visit the university library and sharpen his other investment plans a bit. New 3D printers were gaining traction in the investment world, and oddly enough, a small coffee roasting company in Vermont showed great promise. He knew playing the investment game in reverse was tantamount to cheating, but a little payback for his hard work and sacrifice justified it in his mind. Besides, what's wrong with eliminating a little risk?

He walked down the sidewalk at a fast pace toward the business district. The bright sun reflected sharply off the shop windows. He loved autumn. The air was crisp but not chilled. That would come soon enough. Winter was one season Jonathan could live without.

The cars that drove past were quieter than most of the cars he remembered back home, well, back then. They still looked like cars were supposed to look, maybe a little sleeker.

Suddenly, he noticed the older man he had seen in the park weeks earlier. He was across the street walking toward the park near Jonathan's apartment. The older man saw Jonathan at the same time. Much to his surprise, the older man immediately turned and walked back the way he had come.

"Hey! Sir, wait a minute," he called after him. "Sir, do you have a moment? Wait. Can we talk?"

The older man's pace was faster than Jonathan expected. He didn't want to appear to be chasing the man, so he stopped and decided to drop the matter. Besides, the older man ducked into a building. It was clear he didn't want to talk to him.

Jonathan stood on the street corner. He sighed and continued down the street. He had the odd feeling he was being watched. Was he? Was someone following him? He looked back toward his apartment. Nothing. He looked forward. It was only two more blocks to the dealership. He continued walking, occasionally glancing behind him. Something was different.

Once inside, he was intrigued by the strong lines in the design of the new Cadillac. Even sitting still, the car seemed to be moving. He was enthralled. It was beautiful.

The salesman approached Jonathan with a grin. Jonathan wasn't sure if he was sizing him up as a grad student, a young addition to the faculty, or another salesman with the day off. He was pretty sure he would get the whole sales pitch.

"You picked the right time to check these new babies out. Yes sir."

"Oh, well I don't think I'm really ready to buy today," Jonathan said sheepishly. He was fascinated by the new car. "Tell me about this magnificent machine."

Jonathan could see the salesman stifle his disappointment. After all, no one ever came to a car dealer carrying a bag full of money with the expressed intention of actually buying a car. It was all in the presentation and closing the deal.

"Why sure. This is the new 2038 Cadillac Mirage. An amazing machi—"

"2038? This is 2037, isn't it?"

The salesman looked at Jonathan as if he'd stepped out of the Stone Age, or at least the 1990s. "Well yeah. You know . . . early release. The new models come out every September just like they always have."

"Right," Jonathan said. He should have known that.

"Well, this little marvel is the first generation of a transportation revolution."

"Really, what do you mean?"

"Thorium."

"Thorium?"

"This is the first daily driver powered entirely by a thorium nuclear reactor; the car of the future here today." The salesman popped the hood and raised it, revealing three cobalt gray boxes.

Jonathan drew a breath then bent over the compartment that, in his day, had held a greasy, oil-belching, gasoline-burning internal combustion engine. He was spellbound.

"Yes sir, this is, without a doubt, the next big thing in transportation. The reactor contains less than two ounces of highly refined thorium ore. It's enough to power this car for the next one hundred years, without even an oil change. Why, this car will not only run without gasoline, it is pollution free. No exhaust.

"Zero to sixty in three-point-two seconds, and it corners like a dream. Would you care to sit in the operator's seat?" He opened the left side door and motioned for Jonathan to enter.

Jonathan peered inside. No steering wheel, just an odd little key pad. *They finally did it*, he thought, *cars that drive themselves*. He remembered the work Google had begun in 2004. Over the years the company combined an advanced GPS with their mapping techniques, creating a new system to operate cars more safely than humans.

"No, I don't think so. But wow! One cool car," Jonathan said. His eyes were wide, taking in every detail. "Automatic braking, collision control—that is something!" He scanned a long black band that swept across the dash. "What is that?"

"That's the video bar. It provides information retrieval and data uploads to the cloud, as well as a three-hundred-degree view of everything around you. During the day it repeats what you see anyway, but at night or in fog, the radar imagery lets you see through the weather."

"What's the cloud you mention? Is that what you can see through?"

"No, the data system. You know, where we store all our stuff." The salesman gave him a serious glance. Jonathan felt like a complete idiot.

"Oh yeah, that cloud." It was time for him to leave. His ignorance was beginning to show. "I need to be going. Thank you. I wanted to see this, but today . . . I just can't do anything today. Thanks though. It's a real beauty."

He made his way to the door while the salesman stood beside the open driver's door. Jonathan imagined what was going through the man's mind and thought it would be best to leave. He stepped outside.

Jonathan walked quickly back toward his apartment. Again, he was nagged by the sensation that someone was watching him. *Was it the older man?* He stopped at each street corner and casually looked back the way he had come. Of course, people were walking everywhere. Still, something felt a little strange.

He had two observations to note in his ledger: thorium reactor development and Cadillac stock. Even more importantly, he was eager to analyze his physical data on his return.

The nagging fear continued to press. *Was it something to do with Marcia?* Suddenly the fear swelled to panic. Unreasonable, but real. His hands shook, and he kept looking back. *Someone is following me!*

When his apartment building came into view, Jonathan broke into a run. He sprinted past the café and ran hard to get home. He ducked into the entry way to his apartment and held the door open just a crack. The library would have to wait. He watched. Then he saw him.

"No!" he whispered in shock. "No, it can't be. It can't!" Jonathan turned and ran up the stairs. At the top he heard someone on the steps behind him. *He's coming!*

The instant he stepped into his bedroom, he was whisked into the closet and through the grayish blackness. He popped awake on his bed.

* * * * *

Not so fast! I must follow It. I cannot lose It.

Slow down. Too close. Just stay with It, stay just behind. Why are they looking at me? I am not It. They look and smile at me. Why? What do they mean?

Stay with It. Why is It walking fast? I can keep up. I can walk fast.

It got to the door. Follow It! I don't know the way back. I must see where It goes to get back.

It's running up the stairs! Is It afraid of me? Why is It running? Quick, up the stairs! Quick. Quick. Hurry!

It runs into the closet.

Its clothes are here. I will leave my clothes and run into the closet. Quick.

Run! I burst through the closet into the gray, into the smoke the dark.

There It is! It saw me. It is running away. I cannot catch It this time. Too fast, too far behind.

I will have to find this one. I will find it and kill it.

* * * * *

Ouch, he thought, *that time it hurt a little.* It was more like a cramp or a sore muscle after playing a game of softball on a sunny afternoon. It was nothing of immense concern, just something to note. He removed the sensors from his chest and temples, and then pulled the shunt from his abdomen.

He stood and stretched. It was time to make some detailed notes about what went on while he was in the future. He checked the video camera and noted the customary three and a half minutes had registered between his departure and return. Exactly. He backed the video to the start and watched it to the end.

On the screen he appeared to be sleeping. Jonathan's vital signs were displayed along the left side of the screen. He watched the recorded results. They fell dramatically lower the instant he went to sleep. His respiration dropped by sixty percent, blood pressure to almost nothing. The brain registered only faint activity.

I'm dead, he thought, *just not totally dead*. The thought of his body so near death sent a chill through him. *That's it, I'm mostly dead.* He burst out laughing thinking of Billy Crystal's character in *The Princess Bride* diagnosing Wesley as "mostly dead." Again, he shivered with the thought.

He backed the video to the beginning again and watched frame-by-frame. The convulsions passed in a matter of seconds, the orb rose and vanished, and the vitals plunged to levels far below normal.

Wow. This is what happens each time I leave. Inwardly he kicked himself again for his negligence. Every trip should have had recorded vital signs, every one. He had been sloppy.

The orb returned precisely after three and a half minutes of recording. The vital signs immediately returned to normal, and he watched himself jerk awake in the video. He breathed a sigh of relief. Of course, he knew he was fine, but watching the actual change was always dramatic.

The recordings he had made of the vitals in his lab rats were far less spectacular in their scope than what he had just witnessed. For a moment he was puzzled, and then it dawned on him.

The difference was in the magnitude of the life force of a human being and that of a rat. Certainly the intelligence and life energy of a human would be much greater than that of a rodent. The life factors of longevity, strength, intelligence, even mere size would be greater. The effect of separation of the life force and the host in a more complex being would be more dramatic than in a less developed creature. It made sense to him.

But there was no way to measure his initial experiences. He wondered what his vital signs were months ago when he entered himself as a test subject in his experiment. Jonathan had failed to maintain a strict scientific protocol with his research. He was embarrassed at how he had negated his own credibility. Now it was impossible to know. He had allowed his emotions to overcome the disciplines of science. With more than three hundred trips under his belt, he was confident with the procedure, but his records were far too sketchy.

*   *   *   *   *

It was late. Jonathan had e-mailed all the results he had from his trips to his office computer and had driven to the office to collect and save the files in their proper locations. The program he had written was designed to analyze data and arrive at predetermined evaluations to document his research. If he was ever afforded the opportunity to present his findings, significant documentation would be required.

Jonathan stretched and yawned. He leaned back from his work station and squinted to look at his wrist watch. It was eleven thirty. Cataloging the supporting data was tedious. In addition to his respiration, pulse rate, and brain activity, he decided he should measure all the neurochemical changes as he had with his rodent subjects. But the panel of tests would need to be far more specific and would require more time. He didn't mind the long hours; it was science.

Other people worry about the long hours. I don't. Maggie probably no longer cares anyway. He knew he was in the wrong, that he had ignored her and hurt her. He only hoped that someday she would come around and forgive him. But that hope was distant and fading in light of his discoveries and the advancements he was making in his techniques. This work was groundbreaking in spite of the missing records.

But enough was enough. Eighteen hours was enough. He was still puzzled how traveling to the future never tired him, regardless of the length of his stay. During his trip to the future he was always full of energy. However, returning to his own time left him drained. Tonight, he was tired.

He closed down his testing equipment and turned out the lights. He dragged himself down the hall toward the parking lot and his car. The sidewalk stretched ahead of him in what seemed an endless stream of concrete.

He rounded the corner into the parking lot and saw the silhouette of a woman walking his direction. He looked at her. She stopped.

"Maggie?"

"Hi, Jonny." Her voice was soft and familiar. It was Maggie.

Jonathan let out a breath and smiled. She timidly stepped from the shadows into the beam of the street lamp overhead. He was delighted to see her.

"Hi, Maggie, I've been thinking about you," he said.

"Oh really," she replied cautiously.

"Yeah. I . . . uh, well, I'd like to talk, but I'm just so tired tonight I don't know if I would make much sense."

She took several steps toward him. He could see the concern in her eyes. She stopped seven or eight feet away.

"Even in the dark I can see how tired you are. Why are you doing this to yourself, Jonny? This can't be good for you. You should go home and rest. I'm sorry, but you look dreadful."

He chuckled. "You should see me from the inside." His joke brought no laughter from her. She was right. He needed some rest.

"Go home, Jonny," Maggie said. She turned away and crossed the street, leaving him alone. Her retreating footsteps quickened and it seemed she was running away. He listened to fading footsteps, but she never slowed her pace while he could still hear her.

Jonathan lowered himself into the driver's seat of his car and started the engine. On the way to his apartment, he stopped at McDonald's and bought a two-cheeseburger meal. The first burger was gone in four bites. He devoured the fries and felt a fog of slumber moving over him.

He always slept better after eating, especially if he ate a lot of starchy food and ate it very quickly. He knew it wasn't the best diet, but his research was almost complete. Pushing himself a little at this point wouldn't matter. He could always change his diet later, after all the work was done.

"After everything is done, I will reclaim my life and fix it all," he said out loud, climbing the stairs to his apartment. "I'm not finished with me yet."

He fell into his bed, still fully dressed, and was immediately sound asleep.

19

Dr. Mark Vaughn had not seen or called Jonathan since the ballgame at Maggie's apartment. He had no interest in seeing his longtime friend ruin himself or continue to break Maggie's heart. It was one thing to work diligently on a project, but it was something else altogether to ignore people who cared.

He saw Maggie sitting at the table waiting for him and Rachel.

"So this is the wonderful bistro Rachel has been raving about," he said walking to the table next to the planter in the sidewalk café.

"Hi, Mark."

"I can't believe you've never invited me here before," he said as he pulled a chair back from the table.

"That might explain why we called it *our spot.* You know what I mean . . . before."

"Nice, but it'll be too chilly to eat here in a month. November isn't known for outdoor dining, you know."

"When it gets cold, they put up a canvas tent, you cynic," she said. He bent over the table and kissed her on her cheek. "Rachel called a minute ago and she's probably on her way here from the library by now."

"Good." Mark sat back and looked across the café. "I don't know if I can handle two beautiful women. Sure don't want folks thinking I'm a pimp or something."

"Mark! That's terrible. Don't talk that way. Ladies will tire of hanging around with you."

"Maybe. It's just that I am so darn good looking, I really don't think it will stop. The ladies love me, don't they?"

"Well, I can only speak for two ladies on that subject, and we both are hopelessly stuck with you." She reached for his hand, grabbed it, and squeezed it firmly.

Mark appreciated her warmth and friendship. And in all honesty, he didn't want to let go of her hand.

"Hey, what's goin' on here?" Rachel said as she entered the café patio. "Lady, are you runnin' off with my man?" She broke into a smile and sat at the table.

"I keep telling you, sweetheart, I have to chase them away all the time. It's a burden I must bear. I mean, look at me. Gorgeous, am I not?" he said spreading his arms, presenting himself for inspection and admiration. "Where among humankind might one find a more marvelous example of masculinity and charm, or—"

"Hang it up, Sherlock," Rachel said grabbing him by the collar. "I have you in my web, and I'm keeping you under wraps, buster."

"I do love to be loved," Mark sand and smiled broadly at the women, then leaned forward and kissed Rachel deeply and passionately. She groaned, either in protest or approval, it really didn't matter, and kissed him back.

"All right, you two grab a little air and order some coffee. I mean—for cryin' out loud. Get a room," she said hiding her face in her hands.

"Coffee sounds perfect right now," Mark proclaimed with an arrogant flair. "After that kiss I think I'll have mine black, no sweetener or milk is necessary."

"Why do I put up with him?" Rachel asked Maggie. "Insufferable. Handsome, gentle, and tasty," she smacked her lips. "But insufferable."

"Okay," Maggie began. "I think I need a latte . . . or a scotch," she said scanning the menu.

"Philip, oh, Philip," Rachel called over her shoulder. The waiter appeared instantly wearing a broad grin.

"Wait a minute. Why do you know the waiter? Something going on I don't know about?" Mark said sitting up straight acting shocked.

"Sweetheart," Rachel said drawing her face to his. "Even if there was something going on, you'd *never* know about it."

"Everyone ready?" Philip asked. He took their orders, each accompanied with the same level of teasing and double entendre. Philip walked to the kitchen and returned carrying three steaming mugs.

Mark watched Maggie stare into the hot, frothy mixture as she stirred it in silence. He noticed how quickly her smile faded. Something was wrong.

"Maggie?"

"I ran into Jonny last night." Her eyes remained on the cup in front of her. "Just off campus by the parking lot."

"Where we saw him this summer?" Rachel asked touching her arm. Maggie nodded.

"I wish I knew a way to help you move on," Mark added.

"I can't. I just can't get past this point. And when I think I have, something like that happens, and there he is again, right in my face."

"Do you want me to go beat him up? I could, you know," Mark said half in jest.

Maggie laughed and at the same time sobbed a little. "No, Mark, you may not go beat him up. Are you clear on that?"

"Aw, Rachel, make her let me beat him up." Mark put on a pouty face trying to lighten the mood. Rachel rolled her eyes.

"No. You're such a girlie-man you probably couldn't anyway." Rachel turned to Maggie and put her arm around her shoulders. "Did you talk? Did he just walk by? What happened?"

"Oh, he said he was thinking about me, but he looked sick. Worse than the night he almost knocked us over. He was thin and pale. He even said he was tired. Sometimes, I fear this project of his is going to kill him. It just makes me *sick*."

Watching Maggie suffer made Mark's stomach tie in knots. He had vowed to stay on the sidelines where it concerned Maggie. He had resolved to let the situation work itself out and not become involved. But he had not counted on this.

"Okay, that settles it," he said pushing away from the table. "I'm gonna go beat him up."

"Mark! Don't you dare," Maggie protested.

"No, I'm kidding."

"I'll go," Rachel offered.

"Rachel!"

"No," Mark said as he looked toward Jonathan's apartment, "this is bad business, and I need to do something for my two friends. Maggie, I won't hit him, but I am going up to his apartment and give him a piece of my mind. You two can wait here. I'm on a mission."

Rachel shook her head and grinned. "Mark you are such a protagonist, even if it's only in your mind. But you're right. Someone needed to slam the brakes on this mess. Go ahead Sir George, do your worst. Go save the world."

He stood. "I'm off! I'll be kind, Maggie, I promise. I just cannot sit here and do nothing."

"Okay. Thank you Mark," she said touching his hand.

*   *   *   *   *

Rachel and Maggie watched as Mark walked determinedly toward Jonathan's apartment.

"I'm glad he still cares for Jonny," Maggie said.

"You know he's in love with you, don't you?" Rachel said watching Mark as he half jogged toward the apartment.

"Oh, Rachel, stop that," Maggie swatting her shoulder playfully.

"No, I'm serious. I suspected it from the start, but the longer Jonathan is away, the more Mark asks about you and suggests we get together."

"Rachel, that's friendship. We have been friends for years. He and Jonny go way back. Mark is like a brother to me. I mean, sure he loves me. I love him, but like a sister loves her older brother."

"I understand, Maggie. But you don't see what I see, and I'm telling you, my boyfriend has a serious crush on you. I don't know if I can win that game."

"Then look at it as if it were a game. I assure you, I will not, nor do I have any intention of trying to steal your man," Maggie said gripping Rachel's hand tightly.

Rachel smiled and looked at Maggie. She knew it wasn't in Maggie's heart to take Mark from her. She feared he would simply slip away on his own.

*   *   *   *   *

Mark took the stairs to Jonathan's apartment two at a time. First, he rapped his knuckle on the door. He didn't hear any noise in response. He knocked harder. No response. The third time he firmly pounded and called out for him.

"Jonathan! This is Mark. Are you in there?" He paused to listen. Soft shuffling then a bump echoed in return. "Jonathan?"

"Yeah, yeah, yeah, I'm coming." The door swung back to reveal a much thinner, almost ghostly image of the man Mark knew as Jonathan Walsh. He tried to cover his shock and hoped he was successful.

"Hey, Mark. Good to see you. Come on in," Jonathan said as he turned back into the living room and dropped himself into an overstuffed chair. He rubbed his forehead and eyes trying to shake the sleep from them. His hair was a mess, he was unshaven, and the apartment smelled stale.

"Did I wake you up?" Mark asked ignoring the obvious. He was shocked by the man he was looking at. Jonathan's appearance was more of a man approaching fifty than of one in his late twenties.

"Yeah, I think you probably did," Jonathan said with a half smile. "What time is it anyway?"

"Eleven forty-five."

"In the morning?"

"Yes."

"Wow. I think I've been sleeping for more than twelve hours."

"Buddy, it looks like it should have been more. Are you okay? I mean are you eating enough?"

"Probably not. But isn't that what mothers are for?"

"Honestly, I wouldn't know. But I think you could use one about now, Jonathan. Can I get you something?"

"No. I ate last night and can get some cereal here in a minute. What can I do for you? I mean, why'd you come by?"

"I was concerned about you. We haven't seen you for weeks."

"We?"

"Okay, I was just having lunch with Maggie and Rachel. We're all concerned about you, Jonathan." Mark regretted the irritation in his voice, but it reflected his feelings.

"Oh, I get it, so the three of you get together and talk about me."

"No, not at all. In our conversation Maggie said she ran into you last night, and it really upset her."

"I don't know why. She didn't stick around long enough to let me tell her how I was feeling, or what I was doing. She walked off. I called after her, but she ignored me."

"Jonathan, you lock yourself away for days, weeks at a time. We don't hear anything from you. Even when you promise to call, you don't. What is she supposed to take from that kind of behavior?"

"I love her!" Jonathan snapped.

"So do I," Mark answered with more of a challenge in his voice than he wanted. His face flushed, and he turned his eyes away. He had finally said it.

Jonathan turned slowly toward him. His face was contorted with anger and insult.

"I get it," he snarled. "You come up here just to see how I'm doing, like my old buddy, but what you really want is to know if you can go after my girl. That's it, right?"

"No, Jonathan, that isn't it."

"But you just said you loved her, right? You want to know if I'm still interested or able to take care of her, right? You don't know what you're talking about. I can see right through this fakery. And you call yourself a friend."

"No, Jonathan, that's not it. We are all—"

"Oh, so now you and Maggie are *WE*, huh? You two sneaking around behind my back?"

"No, not at all. The three of us are—"

"Now that just makes me sick. The three of you together. You've dragged Maggie into some of your sick perversions. Get out of here! I don't ever want to see you again." He pushed Mark toward the door.

"Jonathan, you're taking this all wrong. Nothing *perverted* is happening! You're acting crazy!"

"Yeah, I'm crazy! Get out of here!" Jonathan shoved Mark backwards hard enough to nearly make him fall. Rage flooded Jonathan's face, and he moved menacingly toward him. Mark held up both of his hands to fend him off. Jonathan stopped.

"Okay, I'm going. But Jonathan, you've got this all wrong."

"Get out!" Jonathan forced Mark out the door and slammed it behind him.

Mark stumbled down the stairs. He hadn't felt so betrayed since he had returned from boarding school to find his parents off on another party trip. He and Jonathan had never fought. *This is bad*, he said to himself. *Something here is very, very wrong.*

*   *   *   *   *

I did not find the last one. It is still around. I hear it cry. It would be better if I killed it. Less noise. It is weak. It has no food. I will not feed it. I will not help it.

I am going through again. I must understand what is there, and why It goes there.

I do not need to go fast. I can walk through the gray and into the closet. I like it there. I like it very much.

This time I will wear different clothes, softer ones. I will pick what I like. I will look like the others. I will not be frightened. I will be like them.

I enter the gray. The gray and darkness is very thick. The farther I walk the harder it is to push through. Here it is. Push hard. Harder!

I am in the closet. I like warm clothes.

The room is clean, straightened up, neat. I put on the clothes I like. The ones that make me warm. Clothes feel good on me.

What is that? Yes, I know what that is. A reflection? A mirror.

What is this? No. That isn't right. No. It cannot be that, I am not that. What am I seeing? It moves like me, but . . . NO!

Touch it. TOUCH IT!

It cannot be. I cannot be. It is me.

I am It.

*   *   *   *   *

When Mark sat down at the café table by the planter, Maggie and Rachel were just finishing their lunch. Philip brought Mark's meal to him with a bit of irritation on his face.

"This isn't as hot as when you left," he said flatly.

"I know, I'm sorry. There was something I had to do. This is just fine," Mark said with a half smile.

"Was he home?" Maggie asked.

"Yeah, he was there all right," Mark said, and then he took a huge bite of his sandwich. Rachel sneered.

"Isn't that just like a man. Ask him a question, and he stuffs his mouth with food." Maggie laughed. The bite turned out to be more than Mark had bargained for. He held up his hands as a gesture for peace as he chewed vigorously. Both Maggie and Rachel laughed and looked away. However he planned to swallow that amount of food, it wasn't going to be pretty.

"There," he said after he nearly gagged. "Ladies, I am a man, not very genteel, definitely vulgar, with a very significant touch of cuteness. You may once again look upon me."

Both women turned to him shaking their heads. Maggie became serious.

"And Jonny?"

"It wasn't pretty. I think I woke him up. I also think you're correct when you say he's not well. He seemed groggy, and he was very short tempered," he said.

"What happened?" Rachel asked.

"He wanted to know why I was in the neighborhood. I said I was having lunch with the two of you, and before I knew it, somehow in his mind we were all having an affair. Some sort of twisted tryst and he went off the deep end."

"Oh no," Maggie said covering her mouth with her hand. "Why would he think such a thing? That's not even reasonable. He would never even joke about something like that."

"I'm not surprised," Rachel added. "I always suspected a pervert behind that nice-boy façade."

"Rachel!" Maggie exclaimed.

"I'm sorry. I shouldn't have said it, but I've been thinking it for months."

"Well, you shouldn't at all, Rachel." Maggie said sternly. "We have to at least hope that Jonny will come through this. I cannot bear the thought of never being with him. I must believe this foolishness will have an ending somewhere. Can we try to have hope for him?"

Mark and Rachel were quiet. After what he had witnessed, Mark had little hope for Jonathan. Rachel had made it clear she never had much hope for him.

"Maggie, for your sake, we can hope," Mark said. He looked at Rachel. She nodded and grasped Maggie's hand.

"Even I can hope a little bit."

"Thanks, Rachel. Now, Mark, you'd better get busy with your lunch before Philip comes back and decides to beat *you* up."

Rachel laughed and grabbed his plate, pulling it away from him. "That sounds like something I'd like to see."

The smiles and lighter mood returned, but one person was missing and everyone knew it. The hope they shared was muted by yet another emotion. Fear.

20

Jonathan was livid after his confrontation with Mark. He could not believe that Maggie would consort with his former best friend. And to add Rachel, another woman, was just sick.

"Maggie, how could you do such a thing? What has happened to you?" Tears of rage burned in his eyes. "If you were here right now, I'd *beat* you.

"It's bad enough that you have given up on me," he cried out loud. "But this, with *both* of them. Oh, Maggie, you betrayed me. I am *done* with you, woman. You are out of my life forever!"

He burned with jealousy inside. For the first time he was certain he had lost her. She was the one who wouldn't give him the time he needed for his work. It was *her*. She had made the choice to leave him.

Anguish, fury, and treachery fueled his madness. He scorned Maggie for her duplicity. They had promised each other that they would be together. Her unfaithfulness was a terrible, wretched shredding of that promise. He vowed it would not happen again. She was on her own. And he had work to do.

He tried to clear his head, to focus on doing his job, and keep proper records. He decided he would leave, go to the future. He began attaching the monitoring cables to his chest, but suddenly stopped. *To hell with that.* He threw the monitoring cables across the room in anger.

Jonathan dropped onto his bed, jabbed the syringe into his stomach, and pushed the plunger on the syringe.

*   *   *   *   *

With a hop, Jonathan landed stark naked in the future. He dressed and headed to the café for a quick lunch. On the way he purchased a newspaper to read while he ate. *Odd they still have newspapers*, he thought.

It also seemed unusual to him that he felt no anger from his confrontation with Mark. He remembered every detail, yet the rage he had experienced was gone. He actually felt refreshed and vibrant.

As he approached the café, Jonathan glanced toward the park across the street. The older man was sitting on the park bench. *What is familiar about him?* He stopped and looked at the man. The man on the bench returned his gaze. His eyes reflected more apprehension than friendship.

Jonathan smiled and took a step toward him. Immediately, the man stood and walked the other way. It wasn't a stroll. It was a fast pace. He glanced back over his shoulder at Jonathan but did not slow down or stop. It was clear he didn't want to talk or meet with him.

Jonathan continued to the café and took a seat at the table beside the planter. A couple of minutes later, the older version of Philip approached him to take his order.

"I assume you want the same thing you always want. Grilled cheese and soup, right?" Philip's demeanor was cool, almost angry.

"Exactly. You have an amazing memory," Jonathan responded with a warm grin.

"Been at this a while," Philip replied. He turned and headed into the kitchen. Jonathan wondered what had occurred in Philip's life to leave him so sullen. He considered asking but decided against it. Too many questions from him would certainly raise questions. He didn't want to go there.

He was also curious about the man on the park bench. Why did he leave so abruptly? And what was it that was so familiar about him?

Jonathan scanned the newspaper while he devoured his meal. It contained little news. Even back in 2007, cable networks and satellite systems were evolving into electronic media. Information was becoming instantly available on personal computers, even the early handheld devices of his time.

In this time, the future, download time was a thing of the past. Streaming entire news programs, not just the articles, or even movies was commonplace. Information was a commodity available to everyone. There was no reason to wait for the morning paper to learn what was going on around the world. The newspapers contained information of legal notices, club meetings, garage and moving sales, but nothing that was news. The world had changed. Everything had changed.

While he ate, he thought about his outburst at Mark. Their fight had inspired this day's trip. Bitterness gnawed at him. *Maggie is no longer my partner. She doesn't support my work. It's clear she doesn't care. Rachel never liked me. And Mark is a traitor. He wants to steal Maggie.*

After lunch Jonathan headed to the library on campus. Now that everyone he had cared about was against him, he cared for no one. But he was going to find out why they turned and what really happened.

He pushed through the heavy wooden doors of the library. A young woman with red hair was busy at the information desk where he had first met Marcia. She looked up and smiled as he approached.

"May I be of assistance?" She was a pleasant natured girl and that seemed to calm him.

"Yes, I was wondering if Marcia was working today."

A grin curled across her lips as she leaned back in her chair. This woman had talked with Marcia. Jonathan could tell she knew something about him. He couldn't think of a way to ask her, however.

"No, she's off today. I think she went out of town. Is there something you need specifically?"

"Would it be alright for me to use the computer?" he asked.

"Of course, select any cubical you like." She waved her hand toward the cluster of cubicles in the center of the main room. He went directly to the unit he had used before and slipped the earpiece over his left ear. The screen lighted instantly.

"This is so weird," he said softly. The advance in technology caused him to marvel every time he encountered it.

"Hi, Jonny," the computer voice cooed into his ear. A shiver ran down his spine. *Why is that voice so familiar?* It had seemed familiar the first time he visited, like someone he knew, but he couldn't place it.

"Hi, Connie. How far back do your databases go?" he asked.

"All the way, Jonny. How far back in time would you like to travel?"

Odd wording, he thought.

"Not terribly odd," she answered. "I do it every day." He had forgotten about the computer's ability to sense his thoughts. "I can take you as far back as the first written texts and provide realistic synthesized reenactments of any historical event. Would you like to visit the Garden of Eden and learn about sin and betrayal? If you prefer we could travel to 18th Century France and experience the Revolution from either side as a rebel in the streets of Paris or an aristocrat visiting the guillotine. And I can take you there in 3D."

"Uh, that's a bit much. Let's start about thirty years ago, okay?"

"Whatever you say, Jonny."

"Wait, why are you calling me that?"

"It's your name, isn't it?"

"Well, yes, but only my very close friends call me Jonny, special friends. I would prefer you address me as Jonathan."

"As you wish, Jonathan. What information do you require from the year 2007?"

"I would like for you to look *me* up. Jonathan M. Walsh. Then list all the information you have on me in the following years." His earpiece was silent. "Did you hear me?"

"Of course I heard you, Jonathan. Are you sure this is the information you want?"

"Yes. You said you could pull up anything. I want to see what you have on me."

"Very well, Jonathan. Beginning with the year two thousand seven, you graduated from Stephens University at the end of the winter trimester. Congratulations, you finished early. Then, you died on November 19, 2007."

"What?"

"Would you like for me to repeat the information? You graduated from Stephens University—"

"No, no thank you. I got it." Jonathan sat in silence. He couldn't believe what he heard. *How did I die?*

"You were found alone in your apartment lying on your bed. No one knew the exact time of death. You had no close personal friends and made little contact with your family. According to forensic records you had been dead several days when your body was discovered. Rigor mortis had set—"

"Okay, stop!" His thoughts spun. *Did someone come in and kill me while I was in the future?*

"There were no signs of forced entry or injuries to your body. The police—"

"Enough!" He saw the redhead at the information desk raise her head at his voice. He pulled the earpiece from his ear. He was terrified, but he wanted one more bit of information. He replaced the earpiece. Connie's response was instant.

"No, Maggie never married. She lived alone all her life after you died. She was heartbroken. She had no friends; she was an old maid, almost a hermit because of you, Jonathan."

"No. You're wrong. She had friends. She was very popular; she was a lot of fun, very sweet and full of life. Nothing you say makes any sense."

"It makes perfect sense. It is what happened long ago."

"No! These are all lies. This is not how it ended. Connie, you are not telling me the truth."

"All I have told you is the truth, except one thing. Would you like to know what that one thing is?"

Jonathan's entire body was shivering. He felt he was falling into an abyss.

"You have lied about everything. What else have you not told me?"

"My name is not Connie."

"What . . ."

"My name is not Connie. I am Rachel."

Jonathan gasped. He pulled the earpiece off and stumbled backward from the computer screen. *Her voice is familiar. How else would she know about Maggie?*

Jonathan tried to stand. He stumbled and his chair toppled and clattered on the floor. He shook his head. *No, that's not what she said! She did not say her name was Rachel.*

Suddenly, the public address system became her voice. "Jonathan, I am Rachel. I am Rachel."

He bolted and ran to the door. The young woman at the front desk stood looking around the room to see where the voice was coming from.

"I am Rachel. I am Rachel."

Jonathan burst through the door and onto the sidewalk. He stumbled and fell, then scrambled to his feet and ran as hard as he could toward his apartment. He took the stairs three at a time and crashed into his bedroom.

Immediately, he was whisked through the flashes, the grayness, and the colors again. Jonathan jerked awake in his own bed. He felt horrible. He rolled to his side and vomited.

*   *   *   *   *

"That wasn't much of a breakfast. Do you want anything else?" Alice asked.

"I don't think so. The older I get it seems the less I need to keep me going," he answered. Martin felt stuffed.

"Well, you don't seem to be wasting away, if you catch my drift." Alice smiled as she moved her skillet to the sink for washing. She always kidded him about his success in storing her magical meals right out front for everyone to see.

"I do. Losing weight simply does not appear on my agenda. Even when I've tried, it ends in futility. You know that."

She did. Martin's tummy was an ever present reminder of her culinary skills. It was his one imperfection he could comment on with little pain.

"How's your search going?" she asked over a clatter of dishes and utensils.

"It would be much easier if you simply told me what it was," he said.

"Now you know there wouldn't be much fun in that. What would you learn? Where would the thrill of discovery come from? How would that help you grow as a man, or a human being for that matter?" She was challenging him and he knew it.

"I know . . . I have to find it for myself. It's just doing the church thing over and over, or continually going through the motions isn't really getting me anywhere. I feel about as much progress as when I wash my hands. It needs to be done but what does it accomplish?" His voice was colored with irritation.

"You are such a sweet knuckle head," she said with a smile as she walked toward him. Alice pulled back a chair and sat, then propped her elbows on the table. Her eyes bore holes in his forehead. "Martin, what is it that we have shared all these years that has made our time together worthwhile?"

It was the simplest of questions. He knew the answer in an instant.

"Well, it is not one thing, if that's what you're getting at. It's friendship, love, respect, and sometimes honest disagreement." He smiled and looked at her and said, "And sometimes it's a knock-down, drag-out fight before we come to terms. Or at least until I come to your terms."

She smiled. "Honesty. That's a good start. In your search for what I found, apply all you said coupled with honesty. You're doing real well, sweetie. That is, for a knuckle head."

She grinned, stood and walked to the sink full of dishes. "You know, these won't get done until I start washing them. You won't finish your project until you actually start, either."

Suddenly she was right in his face, almost nose to nose. He longed to take her face in his hands and kiss her. She was so close he could feel her warmth.

"Honey, it is lovely here," she said. "I don't want you to miss this."

Martin's eyes popped open. It was 3:00 a.m. He sat upright and picked up the notepad and pen he kept on his bedside table. He wrote the words friendship, respect, love, and honesty.

It was time to start.

*   *   *   *   *

I have come to understand there is much I do not know. I do not know why I look like It. I cannot imagine why It streaks through the gray with such horrible noise. I do find pleasure in eating food and wearing clothes. I go through the gray often.

"What is it you don't understand, One?" the Man asks.

"You surprised me. I did not hear you coming," I say to him. I am embarrassed he was able to approach without my knowing.

"You know you have nothing to fear from me, don't you?" he asks.

"Yes, I do not fear you. You are not like the large creatures I see and hear in the gray smoke and mist."

"No. Those are the Watchers. They go from here into time to help the people I know and care about. They are my workers."

I do not know what he means, but I am no longer afraid.

"You will need to learn a great many things now," the Man began. "A time is coming soon when you will no longer stay here. I have some things you will need to take care of for me. Is that all right with you?"

"It is fine, but I cannot imagine how I can help you," I say feeling very puzzled.

"You will understand when the time comes," the Man says. He places his hand on my shoulder. I like his hand touching me. It is warm and makes me smile.

We talk for a very long while about what is happening around me. I have kept many questions for him. He answers every one, but the plans he tells me about are too great for me. I complain, but he tells me I will be ready.

As he walks away, my heart pounds in my chest, excited about what is coming. It will to be a great adventure. When it begins, I will leave this horrid place and never return.

21

When Jonathan woke the next morning, he was sure it had all been a nightmare. A very real nightmare. He was certain it could not have been true.

But it was like the other trips.

He ate, he touched things. Those things were real.

Is anything real anymore?

Slowly, he sat up on the edge of his bed. His foot landed in a pool of cold vomit on the floor. He recoiled. Chunks of his last meal dripped from his bare foot. That part was too real.

He wiped his foot clean with a tee shirt. He slid to the end of his bed before swinging his feet to the floor. His balance was off. He staggered then gingerly pulled himself erect. He winced from the pain that shot down his back and through his right hip.

Jonathan felt woozy and weak. His vision was slightly blurred, and his head throbbed.

"What a mess," he said to the empty room. He cleaned the floor by his bed, pulled the sheets into a bundle, and tossed it all into the laundry basket.

The video equipment stood in its customary place. Jonathan shuffled to his desk and sat carefully so as not to hurt anything. He felt unstable and he was afraid he was going to knock something over or break his equipment.

The computer fired up, whirred for a few seconds, and opened on the scene of his room with his vital statistics along the left side of the screen. The recorded information indicated all his systems were functioning normally. Physically he was perfect.

"Why do I feel this way?"

The entire video of his "trip" was just under four minutes. He rewound to the beginning and watched it to the very end.

"The orb." The words came into his mind and out of his mouth in the same astonished moment. Something was wrong with the orb, his life force.

He cued the video to the moment of departure and watched frame by frame. Slowly the orb rose from his chest and formed into a ball. It was faint. Very little light flickered through the smoky apparition.

Jonathan's mouth opened. His face contorted in a silent scream of despair.

"I am dying," he whispered. His hands shook as he split the screen to view his very first high-definition recording of the orb. He stopped the frame-by-frame advance at the fully formed orb an instant before it left the screen.

The difference was shocking. The first video showed an orb filled with bright colors of every shade and hue of the spectrum. It was spectacular. The most recent recording revealed an orb that was practically bare.

"What have I done? What have I become?"

The last thing he wanted to do was lie down on his bed and die. He had to do something. He had to try. He had to go back and find Marcia, then force her to tell him the entire story. He had to know what he did. He had to know what had happened.

This time he didn't care about the measurements of his vital signs. If his estimation of the situation was correct, this could be his last visit. Something had gone dreadfully wrong and maybe, just maybe he could still fix it. He had to find Marcia.

He filled the syringe to the precise amount of formula and took his position on the bare mattress. The laundry could wait. Without a moment's hesitation he jabbed the needle into his stomach and pushed the plunger, emptying the contents into his weakened body.

*   *   *   *   *

I am It. I am the same. I do not know how that can be, but I look exactly like It. I wear Its clothes, and they fit me perfectly, but I am *not* It. I am different. I need to eat something so I feel better. That will help. I will go through the smoke and eat.

It is easier to go through the smoke than before. Am I stronger than I was then? Do I understand more? Is that what makes it easier?

I know I can go to the place It goes. I will go to the place where I have watched It eat and do what It does. I will go to the café and act like It.

I must be calm and walk as I have seen It walk. Head erect. Don't slouch. Don't hide. Walk like It. People smile at me just like they smile at It. I nod. I smile.

Now, sit where It sits.

"Good morning. Back so soon? I'll get your paper and the regular."

"That will be fine, just the regular." I sound like It. That man knows It. I don't think I will need to kill that one. He's different from It. His name is Philip. How do I know that?

I like this place and the beautiful green grass and trees. I understand why this is a favorite place, and why It comes here. I enjoy sitting, watching all the people, hearing the birds sing, and seeing the children play.

"Here you are, sir. Can I get you anything else?" he asks.

"No thank you, Philip. This will be fine." I am amazed how my voice sounds like It. Calm, smooth, real.

The paper. I know this. It is for reading and contains information. This must be why It comes here. I will read it.

Numbers. The date. Yes, that is the date. November 6, 2037. That must be today. It is November 6, 2037. I will learn and know what It knows. Then, I will understand and be as wise as the Man told me I should be.

The food is hot. I eat slowly. I am calm and relaxed. It won't come soon. It won't come now. I hope It won't come here now.

Who is that? That man, the one sitting on the park bench looking at me. He is watching me, and I must be calm. Don't panic. But I am afraid. I must not look at him. Why does he just sit there staring at me?

I will finish my meal and slowly walk to where It lives. I know that I need to return there soon, but I must not hurry. I will walk calmly and enjoy the day around me.

The old man is still watching me. Why is he doing that? Why is he staring at me? He is coming toward me. No, I must go.

He grabs my arm. "Jonathan? No, you're not him are you." I turn to look at him, but I do not know him.

"Wait! Please," he says.

"I do not know who you are," I say trying to move away from him.

"I know, but I am a friend. Please, listen for just a moment," the older man says holding my arm firmly. "Please."

I stop and turn to face him. I look at him, trying to understand why he is familiar, why he wants to talk to me. He stops and steps to me. He is smiling. I am not afraid.

"I will listen to you," I say. The Man told me I would learn things from other people. Even though I was afraid at first, I am no longer frightened. I decide I need to hear what he has to say.

"I know you're not Jonathan, but somehow you look exactly like him." The older man's voice is shaky and urgent.

"I do not know this Jonathan. Who is he?"

"The one you followed all the times you came from the apartment. His name is Jonathan," the old man says.

"I know him as It, but you must know this Jonathan."

"I do. I know him and love him as a brother," he says earnestly. "Now, please listen. You must stop coming here. This is not the place for you. You must go to the other side. You must follow Jonathan when he goes back. He has damaged and hurt many people. You must go the other way and correct his mistakes."

Suddenly the words of the Man began to make sense. I know I must go back to the other side and help. I would be helping the Man. I know the old man is sending me to do a great work and help heal people in their pain.

"Do I know who you are? What is your name?" I ask still a little confused.

"I am Mark Vaughn, Jonathan's best friend. Please, go back and help the others."

"I will. I will go back," I say. I turn and run hard and fast, around the corner, and down the street. I run into the house and up the stairs, two at a time. I run into the room and take off Its clothes. Then I run into the closet, into the gray. I am home.

*   *   *   *   *

Mark sat on the loveseat in Maggie's apartment resting his elbows on his knees and staring at the floor between his feet. He felt terrible. He had told Maggie almost everything that had transpired in Jonathan's apartment the day before. He couldn't tell her everything; he wouldn't tell her everything.

Maggie sat across from him in her winged back chair. "What should we do?" she asked softly. "I mean, the thing I have feared most, the thing that grips my heart, is happening before my eyes. It's like I have watched someone drown in slow motion and did nothing to help. How can we help him?"

"I don't know," Mark sighed. "I really don't know. Maggie you've done more than enough. You begged him. You dragged him out of that place. You waited for him."

"Did I? Did I wait enough?"

Mark reached for her and gripped her hand in his. He looked into her red, swollen eyes. Passion swelled within him. Prudence weighed against it.

"Maggie, Jonathan has made some poor choices. We cannot undo those choices, nor can we force him to change them. I'm the one who argued with him. I made him angry. I'm the one he misunderstood." Guilt crushed Mark's heart. He knew the words he had uttered had been like a knife to his best friend. His words cut an irreparable rift between him and Jonathan, and at the same time severed all hope in Maggie's heart. His offense had wounded everyone.

"I don't know, maybe if we give him a little time, things will calm down, and we can talk some sense into him," he offered. It was a failing effort to plant a seed or two of hope, and it faded quickly.

"Yeah, maybe. I feel it's gone too far. I feel like I've lost him, and I don't know how to live without him." Maggie melted into tears and buried her face in the crook of her arm.

Mark opened his mouth to offer some consolation, but nothing came out.

He heard a gentle knock on the apartment door, and it opened slowly. Rachel peeked into the room. Mark stood and walked to her. They embraced. It was as if they had all returned from a funeral. The room was buried in grief.

"I'm finished here," he said softly to Rachel. "Some girl time is probably the best thing at this point."

Rachel nodded and moved to Maggie's side. Mark left the apartment and pulled the door closed behind him.

He felt lost.

*   *   *   *   *

The changes he had witnessed in his orb, his globe of life, sobered him. It was no longer a game. The experiment was somehow expending his life. A side effect he hadn't considered was very real. This had become serious. This trip was bound to be intense, but he promised himself he would get some answers.

He popped into his room in the future and wasted no time. He dressed immediately and left the apartment. The sky was overcast and threatened rain. *Fitting*, he thought. *Just as I get down to some truth, my whole parade is washed out in the rain.*

Jonathan was reticent about returning to the university library. *How could the voice in the computer possibly be Rachel?* he thought. It didn't make sense. Even thinking about the possibilities horrified him. But curiosity won and he decided he must confront both the new terror and the familiar voice.

When he entered the library Marcia was working the front desk. She did not smile when she saw him. Her glare was cold.

"I'm surprised you decided to come back here. Don't you know when you aren't welcome?" she said.

"Sometimes a person needs to find out why they aren't welcome and do whatever they can to fix it." He smiled wearily. "I need to talk to Connie . . . I mean, Rachel."

An odd look crossed Marcia's face. "What do you mean, Rachel? Who is Rachel?"

"So you don't know, do you?" Jonathan walked past her and the front desk and straight to the computer station he had used before. He sat and put on the earpiece. The response was instant.

"Good to see you again, Jonathan."

This time he was certain, the voice was Rachel's. The attitude was hers as well.

"Thank you, Rachel," he said. His voice was flat and unanimated. "You gave me quite a start last time."

"It would be a stretch for you, but can you imagine my shock when you first came here? I can do a lot of things, but electrocuting my clients is not one of them. Why are you here?" Her voice was as caustic and vengeful as he had ever heard.

"I didn't want to believe what you told me last time, the thing about my death. But you were right, I am dying. I don't know how, but this experiment is killing me."

"Did you want applause or violin music with that little confession? We could watch the Pope make nice words over your superimposed corpse. Wouldn't that be fun?"

"You'd like that, wouldn't you?" he replied.

"Gleefully." The earpiece went silent.

"I'm sorry. I was wrong."

"Yes, you were, and now you're almost dead. Soon we'll all be dead. Does that justify everything for you?" she asked.

"No. It justifies nothing."

"Good. Then I'm through with you. Good bye, Jonny."

The screen flicked, and a box appeared with the copyright information. Jonathan nearly jumped out of his skin.

It read: Copyright 2018 by Dr. Mark Vaughn, Foundation of Synthesized Intellect. All rights reserved.

"Mark?" he said aloud.

Marcia was at his side almost immediately. She looked at Jonathan. Her eyes pressed into his.

"Do you know my dad?"

"What? Your dad?" Jonathan knew he must have looked a bit mad, just slightly unhinged.

"That's right, my dad. Mark Vaughn is my dad. I'm Marcia Vaughn," she said drawing frighteningly close to him. "And you're *him*, aren't you?" Her voice was low and almost menacing. "You're that guy that messed it up, aren't you? You're Jonathan, right? *That* Jonathan."

Jonathan was backing away from her, almost falling over the desk behind him. *Mark was her dad? Messed it up? What was messed up?*

"I'm sorry, I'm not sure what you mean by all that. Listen, I need to leave," he said backing away. "Thank you for your help. Thank you so much."

Jonathan walked quickly out of the library. He felt panic rising from deep within him. It was similar to the fear he felt the night he fled from his laboratory a few months before, but not the same. This fear was different. It didn't pursue him. It was inside him.

By the time he reached the street, he was running as hard as he could. The only thing he could think was that he needed to get away, get home, and make it all stop. He rounded the corner by his apartment building and flew up the stairs.

Jonathan burst into his apartment and ran to the bedroom. The instant he entered the room he felt as if something grabbed him and literally threw him into his closet. He saw the flashes of color, the grays and blacks, then more flashes; simple fractions of seconds in time.

Suddenly, as if a switch were thrown to the ON position, he sat bolt upright in his own bed gasping for breath. Perspiration rolled from his body. He trembled from head to toe. He was back. Home. But he didn't feel safe. The fear was still in him.

He slept.

22

This trip was quick and easier than the last one. It was a new day. Jonathan dressed quickly and left his apartment at a light jog toward the library. He didn't know if she would be working. He simply must find her. She knew the answers to the questions in his mind. She could help him fix what he had broken.

The other thing he didn't know was how many of these trips he could complete. What had caused the weakness he observed in his orb? Why did he feel strong and vibrant in the future but weak in his true time? He had to find the answer, any answer.

The jog to the library left him a little winded. He tugged on the heavy wood door and entered the large, quiet, and oddly dark room. Perhaps it was his eyes making adjustment as he moved from bright sunlight to indoors. To Jonathan it seemed darker.

He walked to the check out counter and asked if Marcia was working. It was the girl with red hair he had seen before. The look on her face told him she recognized him. Her look also told him she wasn't thrilled to see him again.

"She's in the stacks," she said backing away from him. The fear in her eyes reminded him of the unusual events in his nightmare. *But she was in the dream. Was it real?*

He turned and walked toward the tall shelves of volumes and books. How many men and women had dedicated their lives to defining or preserving a single truth, or tale of heartbreak or adventure? His conscience stabbed him in his heart. *You have spent your life destroying yourself and three, perhaps four of the people you love the most.*

He shook it off. Sentimentality had no place in today's business. He passed row after row, checking both ways for Marcia or her cart. She could be anywhere in the labyrinth of shelves and books.

Suddenly he heard a voice, a woman's voice. He slowed his pace. He crept toward the sound. He was sure it was Marcia. She sounded as if she was having an argument, and he was hearing only one side of it. She turned to look at him the moment he saw her. An earpiece hung from her left ear. She had been talking to her mother, Rachel.

Marcia's eyes pierced him. The hurt and offense was deeper than Jonathan had imagined. He didn't know if it could be done, but he ached to fix everything.

"Marcia," he implored, "please excuse me, but I need to talk with you."

"So I've heard. I can't imagine why or what you think you can do to make a difference."

"Please, I need your help. Please sit down."

"You are the last person on the earth I ever wanted to see, much less help." The contempt in her tone of voice left no question to the suffering she had endured. She sat.

"I understand. Well, as much as I can. I need to know what happened. What did I do that caused so much damage?"

"What you're doing right now, you jerk."

"What do you mean? Talking to a young woman?"

"No, sponge brain, traveling in time," she snarled at him.

"You knew?"

"Of course, dimwit. I've known about you since I was a small girl. You think I wasn't smart enough to understand something was wrong when I watched grown-ups cry? You think I didn't hear your name when my parents argued about you?"

"No, please, all this mess has nothing to do with you."

"Nothing to do with me, huh? Well, I'll tell you, you piece of human debris, it has everything to do with me. I watched my father crumble in the misery of your aftermath. I watched my Aunt Maggie wither away with a broken heart. And I watched my own mother die, crushed in a love-starved marriage, without any hope of happiness. You have no idea how much this has to do with me."

Jonathan hung his head. It seemed hopeless, but he pressed on.

"What *I* have done has nothing to do with you. You have suffered the effects of things I did years ago that I know absolutely nothing about. When it happened, I was already—"

"Dead? Would you please go back and stay dead?"

"There's a good chance that is exactly what will happen, but I have to try to fix things. Please tell me what happened."

"Only because Rachel told me I had to tell you," she said in a softened bitter tone.

"Rachel. You *do* know," he said.

"I do *now*. She told me everything." Marcia's countenance told him it was a story she did not want to tell. Relaying details so vividly etched in her heart and mind would do nothing to ease her pain. It would dig them deeper and make them fresh.

"You started your experiments in the spring of 2007. My mom and dad had just met. Those were the happiest days of their lives. Dad loved you, and you were his best friend. The secret that you didn't know was that he loved Maggie before you even met her, before you loved her."

"Before we met? I didn't know that."

"Of course not you arrogant wad, it was all about you and your experiment, wasn't it? Well, Maggie fell for you, and Dad decided to take a back seat, keep you as his best friend, and that way he could still be close to Maggie as well. It broke his heart. He knew it would be frustrating and unfulfilling to watch you two fall in love, but it was a noble sacrifice on his part. He couldn't justify life without either of you.

"Then Maggie brought Mom, Rachel, into the picture, and Dad was taken by her. She was beautiful, intelligent, and witty, perfect for Dad. It took the pressure off a bit. He could still be near the woman he really loved, keep you as a friend, and have a fun and full life with Rachel. At least, that's what he thought."

"We did have a great time. You must understand, to me that was only a few months ago."

"Oh, I understand," she said, her eyes brimming with tears. "Trust me, it gets worse, much worse."

He knew the part he didn't want to hear was yet to come. Still, he needed to hear it. He nodded and waited for her to continue.

"So, you started your insane experiments. You began to change. You worked all the time. You didn't call Maggie, you rarely saw your father, and you only saw my mom and dad because Maggie forced you out of your stupid laboratory. Finally, you and my dad had that terrible fight where you threw him out of your apartment. A week or so later they found you dead on your bed.

"No one knew how you died. The autopsy discovered trace elements of unusual chemicals, but none in a quantity large enough to kill you. It would have been better if you'd put a gun to your head, then everyone would know why and how you died."

She paused. He could tell it was painful for Marcia to bring everything back into the light. He dreaded hearing the rest.

"How did you come to know all this?" he asked gently.

"Rachel. She hasn't forgotten anything." Tears streamed down her cheeks. "Dad told me a lot, but the details hurt him even more than they upset me. You want to hear the rest?"

"No, but I need to." His heart sank as he watched Marcia in agony.

"You died, and my dad was torn in two. He was faithful to my mom, even before they were married. He never made any advances or secret rendezvous with Maggie, but Mom could tell. She saw it in him before you died but said nothing to him. Jealousy locked her in a cage, and her heart became bitter over time.

"Dad showed tender affection toward Maggie, and although he felt love for Rachel, it was muted by comparison. She could tell. She loved Maggie too. It was a bad situation without a solution.

"Maggie suffered terribly in loneliness and a self-inflicted solitude. Eventually, neither Mom nor Dad could get her to go out to a movie, have dinner with them or anything. And for some reason they never watched baseball again. My dad loved baseball."

Jonathan sighed. The "proof" he had brought back for his best friends stained their lives forever.

"And poor Mom. She tried everything to win my dad's love and attention. Finally, she got pregnant with me. She hoped it would turn him back from Maggie and bring him into a full life with her. They got married, but he carried the same emptiness into their marriage that he held before.

"Years went by, but their sadness lingered. Mom could never completely win Dad's attention. He knew he was acting strange, but he couldn't separate his feelings for the two different women and his best friend. In some perverted sense, it was noble. He carried on.

"The other weird thing he did was rent your old apartment. He never lived in it, but he went by and cleaned it, kept clothes there, even some money and food. I heard them arguing about it toward the end. When Mom learned he had kept that place for years, she exploded. She accused Dad of having an affair with Maggie in that perverted little love nest."

"No . . . he kept it for *me*," Jonathan interrupted as it dawned on him. "Your father knew I was traveling to the future. I'm not sure if he knew how *far* into the future I went, but he knew I had done it. I'll bet he kept the apartment in the hope of meeting me, you know, like when I came to the future. Maybe he thought he could convince me to stop and prevent the hurt I caused."

She looked at him oddly.

"I know this is difficult for you to understand," he said. "And I know it's hard for you to tell me the whole story. The time I came here to the library and met you was my second trip to the future, to now, this time. I came here to get proof that I had traveled in time. That's why I used the computer—to learn about a very unusual event that occurred two days after I left my present time to come here. If I could tell them about something before it happened, then watch it happen with them, they would know I was telling the truth. I used that triple play in the ballgame as proof to show them my experiment actually worked."

He finally saw the lights come on in her eyes.

"It was that first time I came to the library," he elaborated. "I told them the details before they happened." He was smiling. She was putting things together.

"So, he believed you when you gave them proof. He believed you traveled to the future."

"He must have," Jonathan said. "That's why the room is always neat and clean, and there is always money and food around. He must have felt he would be able to catch me and make me stop all this."

"It seems he hasn't yet," Marcia replied coldly.

"No, but there was this old man sitting in the park . . ."

"The park near your old apartment? He loves that place, and the café," she said coming to life.

"I went after him one day, but he ran from me. Why would he do that? Why would he run away?" Jonathan asked.

"I don't know. I'll have to ask him." Marcia traced her fingernail through scratches on the tabletop, then raised her gaze to meet his. "But there is more you need to know, a lot more. Rachel was hopeful when I was born that things would change, but that hope faded quickly. It was more than five years after I came along that Mom got sick. They fought all the time. It was nonstop, well, until Dad learned of her illness."

"What was it?"

"Cancer."

Jonathan hung his head. Did her bitterness and anger toward him aggravate or even create the cancer in Rachel? Guilt mounted him and pressed on him.

"Where was Maggie all this time?" Jonathan asked.

"Around, but not much. I think she stayed to herself mostly. After your father died, she had no one to care for or visit."

"My dad died?"

"Of course, you idiot. He was old, remember?"

He realized his father had been right all along. The experiments were dangerous and even foolhardy. Jonathan's death probably wounded his dad with grief far greater than he could have ever imagined.

"Yeah, you're right. He was old."

"Maggie's life seemed empty, purposeless, and whatever fire was in her as a young woman was gone, it had dwindled to nothing long before I knew her. She was sweet and gentle with me, and I was always glad to see her. Mom wasn't. Dad was cautious and cool. But I loved Aunt Maggie. She told me wonderful stories about a princess and her prince. I knew she was talking about someone, but I never dreamed it would be you."

"I don't think I'm much of a prince, Marcia." He looked at the floor. "Tell me about your mom."

"At first, it was just a change in her attitude. She was caustic and short tempered. No one knew she was sick until they discovered triple-negative breast cancer. It was very aggressive, and in those days they didn't know how to treat it like they do now. It was a death sentence for her. There was nothing the doctors could do.

"That's when my dad got his big idea. You had proven that a life force, the human spirit and intelligence, could be separated from the body. His research in Artificial Intelligence found a link. He speculated he could do the same procedure you did and capture the life force, linking it to an unlimited supply of digital knowledge.

"He found all your notes in the apartment and studied them thoroughly. With your directions and equipment he was able to reconstruct the formula based on Mom's body mass and weight.

"Since the doctors had given up on healing her, Dad had her moved home to die. She was happier at home than in a sterile hospital room. She was as happy as one could be on their death bed.

"I was only a little girl, but I remember watching a lot of it. They thought I was in bed asleep. Instead, I sat in the shadows in the hallway outside their bedroom and heard it all. Mom just wanted to die and be done with it. Dad begged her to reconsider. At least they would be able to talk if she allowed him to do the procedure.

"He had devised a method of combining your process and the artificial intelligence procedure he had worked on for almost ten years. The fit was perfect. He knew he could couple digitized knowledge and information with a human subject."

"Rachel," he said nodding to the earpiece.

"Exactly. Finally, she relented. He convinced her she would be able to watch me grow up and even talk with me. You know, she could share my life with me. I watched from the shadows that night. He set up all the equipment by her bed. He talked to her telling her he loved her and would miss her. She cried as he sobbed on her shoulder. They kissed, and he gave her the injection.

"I saw the flash that came from her and was captured by the equipment Dad had built. Even though it was an instant, I saw the flash with my own eyes. I guess her body was even weaker without her 'life-force' in it. Anyway, the cancer took the rest of her within hours.

"What Dad failed to realize was that the *person* would be contained in the transfer from her body to the *program*. He had developed a new interactive intelligence, and then made millions from it. But my mother, my *mother*, is trapped in a living, digital hell without hope for any real life. She is doomed to an existence of no touch, no taste, no warmth or love, only data and facts. Imagine a human being encased in a non-human existence for eternity."

Jonathan was speechless. He had succeeded travelling in time, but in the process hurt, or killed everyone he loved. He understood Mark's regret and shame for the way he treated Rachel, and ultimately for what he had done to her. He knew the failure he felt when it came to Maggie. All his mistakes were dumped into the tragic life of this young woman, Marcia, who deserved none of them.

He slumped back in his chair. "Do you see your dad very often?"

"Once or twice a month. Why?"

"When you do, please tell him I'm going to make every effort to fix this."

"Good. Then maybe none of this will ever happen, right? Who do you think you are, God? Of course you do. Anyone who would act as you have acted would think they are a god, or at least as smart as God. And now you think you're going to fix everything? Well, good luck with that, mister."

"I mean it. I know I'm not a god or anything close. I am a *fool*." Jonathan's heart weighed heavily in his chest. His sorrow overwhelmed him. He lowered his head and he wept.

The story Marcia told him replayed in his mind over and over. He remembered the choices he made, how he felt, and he began to see how wrong he had been. His arrogance hadn't hurt those he loved, it had destroyed them.

Jonathan didn't know how long he had been sitting at the table. He had no idea why she was still sitting across from him. She looked exhausted.

"Marcia, I'm going to go back and stop all this. I really believe I can. I am sorry. I am sorry for the pain I have caused you. Please forgive me."

Her hatred burned with new vengeance.

"Yeah, I'll forgive you when I see you in church." Incensed anger flashed in her eyes. "Oh, by the way, I don't go to church. I have work to do." Marcia turned and pushed her cart to the next row.

There was no time to waste. Too much time had been wasted already. Too much had been destroyed.

He ran as fast as he could toward the apartment. Inwardly, he thanked Mark for keeping it all these years. He would repay that kindness. He would make it right and set everything back in place.

Jonathan rushed into his bedroom and was immediately whisked into his closet.

23

Jonathan stumbles, falling against the hard gray wall. Smoke swirls around him. He is encased in darkness. He struggles to catch his breath. Nothing makes sense. He cannot understand why he wasn't on his bed in the apartment.

I jump from the darkness and grab Its throat to choke It. These things are a menace, and I am bound to rid myself of them. They are worthless, and they smell bad.

"I'm going to wring the life out of you like all the rest," I scream ferociously. My face is twisted with hateful anger. Killing these monsters is a horrible thing, but their cries, whining, and smell drive me insane.

"No, please, don't kill me," Jonathan says. "I have to get back. I have to fix the things I've broken. Please, please just let me go."

The Man touches my shoulder and kneels beside Jonathan. The look on his face is compassionate and kind. I feel calm instantly. The rage I felt when I had caught It faded immediately.

"I'm sorry, Jonathan, but you won't be going back this time," the Man said with the gentlest voice.

Jonathan. Now I know for certain that Jonathan, and the creature I call *It* are the same. I feel pity for him.

"No, I must! I've really messed things up, and I need to set it straight. I have to get back." Jonathan collapsed, sobbing.

It, Jonathan, is weak and broken. He will soon die on his own. What do I care if he takes longer to die?

"The others will kill him and eat him," I say to the Man. "I know how they hunt. I do not fear them because I have grown strong. I have learned many things they cannot begin to understand. They are beasts."

"Yes, they are. One, I will take care of Jonathan," the Man says smiling at me. "The others will not harm him."

"Others? What others are you talking about?" Jonathan asks in a whisper.

He opens his eyes and look around. He looks at me and is startled. "Who are you? You look like me."

"I am not you. I am One," I snarl back at him.

The Man touches my arm to quiet me.

"Jonathan," the Man begins quietly. Every time he speaks, it is as if nothing else matters. His words are clear and amazingly comforting. "You have accomplished a great deal, but in the process you have caused tremendous damage. Through your science you managed to arc through time, but you have broken eternal laws prohibiting such things. You traveled from one time to another, and now you are stuck between times, out of time."

"What?" he asks groping for understanding.

"Jonathan, there are times and seasons for all things, an established time for a man to live and for him to die. You violated that law by breaking free of your time. Time itself is much like a coil. Even more specifically, it is similar to the double helix in your DNA models. When you broke free from your natural time, you transferred directly across into a time adjacent to, almost parallel to your natural time, a future time that advances at the same pace as your natural time."

I am surprised that I understand the Man's words. I sense I am at a point of change, a beginning, a view of something too grand for my thinking. I wonder what it is he had done to cause this terrible destruction. The Man continues.

"In order to leave your time, you needed to separate the life that was created to be you, from the body which you were given to live your life. Before you were born, your intelligence, physical attributes, and human spirit were formed together in your mother's womb," the Man explains. "Separating those pieces of life was extremely difficult and dangerous, and to accomplish that severing of life, intelligence, and the physical body was a brilliant act of physical science. However, doing so broke laws of Creation. When your life—you call it an 'orb'—traveled out of your time, your body remained *in* your time just like the rodents in your lab. They seemed to freeze or sleep. That is exactly what has happened to your natural body.

"But when your orb, your life, traveled ahead to a future time, Creation was required to manufacture another body for you, a fresh, new, strong human body. You were able to move, live, and eat in the future time just as in your original time. It seemed the same to you, but that body was a copy, a replica of you.

"When you returned to your time, not all of the life in your orb went back with you. Small fragments of the life given to you at conception remained in the replicated body Creation provided for you."

"So where is my life now? Scattered about in dozens of clones?" Jonathan asks.

"No, not dozens. Hundreds," the Man says. "But most of what you had in your life has found its way to him, One."

"To me?" I ask. I am shocked. The life in me is coming from this man who hurt others and broke eternal laws of Creation?

"Yes," the Man answered. "Human life, the intelligence and persona, is elemental, much like the elements of the rest of Creation but with the capacity to be much more. Within the confines of time, similar particles of matter tend to find their way to each other, much like how oil and water separate and seek out their common elements. Metals, chemicals, even dust and sand, filter together in near elemental companionship. It is part of Creation's law. Even the simple saying 'Birds of a feather, flock together' illustrates the fact. The fragments of your life that have been broken apart into many, many replications of your natural life, have come together in this man, One, the first replica."

"That's why there were fewer lights in the orb in the last video. That explains it," Jonathan says in a faint whisper.

It looks exhausted to me. I have watched some of the others die, but this one is different.

"Here, out of time, human life does not exist. No natural life of any kind. It is void, formless," the Man continues. "It is not made for humans. This is all there was before time was created for the benefit of mankind. So human life trapped outside its natural time finds life that is similar to it and joins it."

"I am the container of that life," I say, realizing why I had grown in strength and understanding.

"Yes," the Man answers.

"What has happened to all these copies of me? Where are they?" Jonathan asks, struggling to catch his breath.

"Many are around us. They are weak and dying," the Man answers.

"I killed many of them," I say before thinking what I must say next. The Man looks at me. His eyes penetrate all my defenses, and I know I must confess what I had done. "I ate them."

This is the first time I have ever known shame. I had to kill or be killed. That is how I survived. My deeds weigh heavily on my conscience, and I am deeply ashamed. The Man touches my shoulder to comfort me. I can only look away and hide my eyes from him.

We are quiet for a while. Jonathan struggles to speak. His voice is fading, and he stammers through dry, cracked lips.

"Who are you? What is your name? I mean, are you the one in charge here?" Jonathan asks the Man.

"I am," the Man replies.

"I have done things that hurt the people I love. I need to make it right," Jonathan says faintly. The color has drained from his skin. His eyes sink deep in their sockets and look glazed and dry.

"You do not have the strength to go back. Someone else can do that for you." The Man glances at me.

My jaw drops. I have no idea how I can help to correct his mistakes. This isn't fair. Why should I have to undo the pain It had caused?

"I cannot do that. I know nothing of his life, or who he has hurt. How can you ask that of me?" I protest.

"Do you remember the first time you followed Jonathan to the future?" the Man asks me. "When you entered his bedroom, you remembered you had been there before. It took a minute, but you remembered. It will be the same with people. You will remember them. You will remember what happened, and you will know what to do. You will know them as well."

I do remember. Names and faces flood my mind. "It is as the old man said, then," I say.

"Yes, Mark has waited for thirty years for you to come, so he could tell you to go back and repair Jonathan's mistakes." The Man's words made my decision for me. It was all true. I must go back.

"You met Mark?" Jonathan asks in a whisper.

"Yes, not long ago. He told me he was your friend," I say. Jonathan smiled and nodded his head. He is very frail. I look at the Man who holds him gently.

"Please forgive me. I was wrong," Jonathan says to the Man. Then he turns to me. "Please, go help them."

His words penetrate my heart and mind differently than any of the knowledge I had gained. This is the event the Man had described to me. I will go, and I know the Man will be with me to help.

"All right, I believe you. What should I do?" I ask. I am both frightened and intrigued. The fact that I can help bring happiness to other people is a wonderful thought. The picture of the older woman at the café flashes through my mind. I know I can help heal the heartache she has endured. I can work to prevent the horrible things Jonathan had done.

"You must go back to Jonathan's natural time and find the people he wronged," the Man says. "You will need to make amends with Jonathan's father, then with Maggie. That one will be interesting, but she will come around. Don't forget Mark and Rachel. They will both need to forgive you. To them, they will be forgiving Jonathan, and that's the way it should be."

"Won't they know the difference between me and him?" I wonder.

"They will all notice something different about you, but they will be eager to have Jonathan back with them. Human love is a very powerful thing. You will experience it and find it rewarding."

"Will I be able to come back here?" I ask.

"Would you really want to come here again?" the Man replies. I know in an instant there is nothing here I want, there never has been.

"One, because you were created here you are able to return to this place outside time. You are a created being, like the Watchers. You can even travel to future times, but that would not be wise. It would be best for you to return to Jonathan's time and work to repair the lives and relationships he has ruined."

"But what about you? How will I find you?" I ask bewildered.

"I will always be with you."

I am uncomfortable with the direction of our conversation. I do not understand and cannot find a great deal of comfort in his instructions.

"If I need to come here, will I know how to find this place?" I ask.

"You will not need to return here. I am preparing a place for you. When the time comes, it will be ready. How will you find it? I am the way. You will see." The Man's smile is comforting, and without thinking about it, I smile back at him. I know I do not understand. I also know it is just fine that I do not.

"What about him?" I ask. I really don't care very much for this sad creature.

"I can take care of things here. You need to head back." The Man's eyes are bright, and he smiles warmly at me. I know things will go well. I don't know how, but I believe him, and I believe that I can help.

"And the body in his bedroom?"

"I've got it, One. I'll take care of it." I know he is right, and I choose to obey his directions and go back.

"Will I get to see you and talk with you again?" I suddenly fear I will never see the Man again, and that I might make mistakes as well.

"I told you I will be with you. Yes, you will make mistakes, but those around you will help you. I will walk through your missteps with you."

I glance at him, this one called Jonathan. He is limp in the Man's arms. His face is ashen. He appears to be asleep.

I take one more look at the Man, and gaze into his gentle eyes. He nods at me and smiles. Then, I turn and step through the gray.

*   *   *   *   *

"I have been looking everywhere and I cannot find my glasses." Alice said as she dug through the stack of newspapers and magazines for the third time. "Martin, have you seen my glasses with the blue frames?"

"No, dear, I have not. That's why my glasses are always on the night stand by the bed or on my face," he replied with a bit of a smirk.

"No, they're on your face because you are as blind as a bat without them. Help me find them, would you please?" He assumed she was just a little cranky about his lack of progress and hoped he would improve the search.

"Where was the last place you had them, sweetheart?" he asked moving the cushions from the sofa.

She turned to him and propped her hand on her hip. That was her stance when she was about ready to blast away with both barrels.

"The last place I remember having them was on *my face*, Dr. Walsh."

"Like I always say, begin with the obvious and proceed to the obscure." He really didn't always say that, but it fit and he thought it was rhythmic and somewhat funny. He chuckled.

"If I wanted obscure I would have put you to work an hour ago looking for them," Alice said. The edge in her voice bothered him.

"Are you upset with something? Did I do something wrong?" he asked.

"Did you find what you are supposed to be looking for?" she replied.

"Your glasses?"

"No! What we've been talking about for weeks. Did you find it yet?"

"Yes, my dear, I did."

Alice stopped her search and stood still. She knew. She could tell by looking at him that he had completed his investigation.

"You did, didn't you? I can see it in your eyes, your face. You did find it." Alice grinned and crossed the room. She stood in front of him, reached up and stroked his cheek. "I'm glad."

"It is a joy I have never known and contentment that reaches beyond anything I have ever imagined. What kept me from looking for Him before?"

"Arrogance. Pride. Bull-headed stupidity. I don't know. It doesn't matter anymore. I will see you soon. Now, just don't mess it up."

Martin's eyes popped open. *I will see you soon—that was what she said*, he thought. Soon.

24

The first time I saw Maggie I was stunned by her beauty. I had never seen a lovelier creature. I must admit my exposure to people was limited and my experience non-existent. I kept my distance. I tried very hard to not stare at her, afraid she might sense someone was watching.

She was sitting in the café with another woman who had jet black hair. *She must be Rachel*, I told myself. From the park bench I could see them clearly. I pretended to read a newspaper, but I found it difficult to keep my eyes off Maggie. It was clear to me that she was the older woman I had frightened on the cold side.

That was when I began to understand how Jonathan must have felt about her. I couldn't grasp the emotion and sensations that seemed to swirl around inside me, but it seemed very human and something I must get used to. In all honesty, I rather liked it.

The two women talked and laughed over their meal for a long time. Several times I saw Maggie look toward the apartment where Jonathan had lived. Now, it was my home. She appeared to be expecting someone to come out of the apartment door. Maybe she was looking for him.

Suddenly, she was looking at me. I could *feel* her eyes on me. I hid behind the newspaper hoping her stare would not reveal who I was. Terror struck me when I considered the possibility of her approaching me. I wasn't ready.

After several minutes the feeling left me. I peeked from behind the paper. The table was empty. The women were gone.

I spent the next two days collecting information and learning about the events that brought me to this point. I viewed all the videos of Jonathan leaving for the future and returning three and a half minutes later. It was repetitious and mind numbingly dull. Perhaps my mind, although it seemed to work quite well, did not hold the same scientific interests as his. I understood his notes, calculations, and conclusions. It all made sense.

What fascinated me the most was the analysis of the life orbs he recorded. I paid a great deal of attention to each one. I concluded the study of the energy and matter that comprised the orb could be a lifetime's work. My second conclusion was that such a study was perhaps beyond the intended capacities of mankind.

The comparison of the orbs in Jonathan's recordings told the story. If he had paid attention to the details and changes in the orbs, he might have ceased his experiments early on. Every trip to the future degraded the activity in each successive video. His experiment was killing him a fragment at a time.

If he had discontinued his experiments, I would have most certainly been lost in the nether world outside the scope of time, present or future. My fate would have been like the dozens I heard in the distance of the gray, crying and waiting for death to claim them. It was too horrible to consider, yet too real a possibility to ignore. It was a possibility I must not forget.

I was surprised at all that I could recall of Jonathan's memories of his life. They were my memories as well. I imagined they were somehow assimilated, along with the knowledge that enabled me to understand his experiments. It was strange to have a memory of something I knew was a certainty, yet in which I had not participated.

The financial picture was interesting and somewhat cluttered. He had made some speculations that offered potential, but I would need to watch. In spite of a significant income, Jonathan had spent very little, and more than half the grant money was unused.

I also managed to become close friends with Philip, the waiter at the local sidewalk café. I enjoyed his company at two meals each day. It seemed enough. I was hungry when I sat down and satisfied when I left. I wasn't sure how many meals were customary. If memory served me correctly, Jonathan's eating habits were rather bizarre and inconsistent. I decided to eat when I felt hunger.

The time came for me to make contact with those in Jonathan's life. It was now my life, and the task couldn't be more difficult. I understood human interaction, but had little actual experience dealing with people—only Philip the waiter, in both the present and future, and the friend named Mark. That was the complete extent of my contact with other people. I decided to begin with his father.

The drive to Jonathan's childhood home was simple, but a bit awkward at first. I knew how to drive but had never gone through the mechanics of it all. I arrived at the house only slightly humbled by my lurching starts and sputtering stops when I forgot to put in the clutch. I walked to the front door with a nervous feeling in my stomach.

"Dad, are you home?" I called through the screen door.

"Of course. Come in, Jonathan, come in."

I opened the door and entered the familiar living room permeated with fragrances from the past and fleeting fragments of memory. The old gentleman stood and turned to face me. For a very brief moment he paused, but only for a moment.

"Good to see you," he said as he approached me. He embraced me and held me tight against him. I also wrapped my arms around him. It was an unexpected expression of intimacy with which I was unfamiliar. I was surprised at the feeling of acceptance, and I liked it.

"What have you been up to for the last month? Classes are about finished for the semester, and I will have more free time after exams. What's your schedule looking like?" He held me at arm's length. His face beamed with a broad smile.

"Not sure just yet," I said grinning back at him. "I think my research is concluded, and I'm considering teaching in the spring. I think I would like that."

"Jonathan, that's wonderful. I am so glad to hear you show an interest in teaching. I think you'd be great in the classroom." He was obviously delighted, and I could tell he was avoiding the discussion that had to come about the research Jonathan had done. I waited.

"Coffee? I just made a pot not fifteen minutes ago. Ground the beans myself," Dad said as he turned toward the kitchen. I followed him through the house. Every room, piece of furniture, picture on the wall, or trinket on a shelf stirred a memory. It was an odd feeling.

I thanked him for the steaming mug. It was tasty and warmed me on the cool autumn day. We sat at the counter on the tall wooden stools I remembered climbing as a child. I knew it was time to talk.

"Dad, I want to tell you about the research that I've been doing for the last six or seven months."

"Oh no, that's not necessary. I want to hear about you, and maybe what's happening with you and Maggie. Bring me up to date, I haven't seen you in far too long."

He was smiling and clearly pleased I was with him. I knew the joy in his eyes was soon to pass. I was not happy about telling him everything.

"No, Dad, I need to explain some things and tell you what has happened. I'm sorry, but I must do this." My tone sobered his countenance. He knew this was a serious discussion that could not be avoided.

"I don't remember if I told you about the initial experimentation with rats, when I injected them with the cocktail serum. Did I describe that to you?"

"No. You were pretty tight lipped on your work, son."

"That's true. Dad, I was wrong. I know we haven't seen eye-to-eye on much, but I was wrong in behaving as I did. Please forgive me."

Tears welled up in the older man's eyes, and it was more than a minute before he could speak.

"I understand, Jonny. For most of my life, I've been just as wrong. I lost years and years of memories with you and your mother by devoting myself to useless endeavors. Of course, I forgive you, but you must forgive me as well. I set the example for you, and it was a poor one indeed. Please, forgive me."

I was surprised, almost shocked. I had not experienced the emotions that framed Jonathan's resentment toward his father. I remembered events, but the hurt had not scarred me as it had him. Forgiving this tender, gentle, old man was without question the correct thing to do.

"Dad, I do forgive you, of course." My words brought instant relief to him. But there was more to tell.

We talked late into the afternoon. As the sun began to slip into the west, shadows stretched across the kitchen. The colors in the room changed to ambers and oranges from the reflected colors of the clouds in the western sky. The older man listened intently as I described the procedures of preparation, what happened physically, and finally the process of separating the life force from the life host, Jonathan's body.

I told him everything I could remember in great detail. Keeping the events in the proper sequence was the greatest challenge. I was not present for most of it, I only shared the memory. I knew Jonathan's plans to make investments and even raid the future of its accomplishments and attempt to advance the science from his present time. It was terribly dangerous and horribly selfish. I was ashamed to speak the story, even fully knowing it had not been me doing the actions or making the decisions.

"The final observation, and what was unknown until toward the end of the research, was the deterioration in the orb over time. What escaped my detection was the degrading of the energy and life force in the orb itself," I explained. I saved the worst part for last.

"You see," I said slowly, "each trip to the future was made by the intelligence and life, or human spirit, not the physical body. And on each trip a new body, a created clone, if you will, was made to accomplish the journey."

"Wait. So while your mind and, I guess, spirit went thirty years to the future, your body stayed here in this time?" His brow was deeply furrowed in concentration.

"Yes, in a sense," I replied. "And every time I traveled, a piece of that life remained in each of the cloned creations."

"That would mean you would have less and less life in you upon your return. How did you survive, Jonathan?"

Only one answer could satisfy the truth. I looked deeply into the eyes of a man with a keenly scientific mind and knew this was the moment I had dreaded.

"Sir, Jonathan didn't survive." My words settled on him slowly. Tears streamed down his cheeks, and he bowed his head. His shoulders lurched and shook as he sobbed, weeping over the loss of his only son.

After several minutes he regained his composure. He dried his eyes and blew his nose. I refilled our mugs with hot tea. As I handed it to him he looked at me and spoke.

"So, you are . . . ?"

"I am the first replica of Jonathan. I am the one who survived the longest, learned the most about him and the mistakes he made. I have been sent here to try and set things back in their intended order, to fix what was broken."

"And who picked you? Who sent you here to make the repairs?" he asked softly.

"The Man sent me," I replied.

"The man? What man?"

I explained my meetings with the Man and how he taught me many things. How he encouraged me to pick up the fragments of Jonathan's life and to set it back on the right course. I told him how the Man held Jonathan is his arms as he fell asleep.

"Jonathan asked him who he was, what his name was, and if he was in charge of the place, and he said he was. I could only assume that he spoke the truth."

"What was his exact response to Jonathan's question?" the old man asked.

I felt naïve. I could tell Jonathan's father expected an answer, a specific answer. I was unsure what the answer could be. I did not understand.

"He said, *I am*. That was all." I watched Jonathan's father closely. His aged face reflected an internal realization I could not put into words.

"Then it's true after all," was all he said. After a quiet moment, he looked at me. "So, what do you plan on doing for the rest of your life, or Jonathan's life?"

"Besides teaching, I'm interested in cancer research, I think. Triple-negative cancers, the more challenging varieties. I believe I could be helpful." I wasn't certain what all might be involved in that discipline of research, but I had a compelling reason to discover what I could.

We sat together quietly as evening dissolved into night. It was a new beginning for both of us. From that moment, life held a fresh understanding between two men. The bond of father and son was forged in grief, tempered in truth, and embraced with courage. At last, he had a son, and I had a father.

25

I spent most of the following week with my father. The transition was less difficult than either of us imagined. Dad had spent most of the last six months resetting his life and reworking his priorities.

Of course, Jonathan was different. I was different. I believe the parts of his nature that were the least useful managed to stay in that nether world between times, and most likely perished appropriately within the beasts that possessed them. I would not miss those character traits.

"So, when are you going to talk to her?" Dad asked over hot chocolate one evening.

"Not exactly sure," I said. "But soon." It was odd because I knew something was close, but I couldn't tell exactly how close. I felt I was about to receive the final lesson to accomplish a great feat. I was waiting for that one more thing that would complete me for the job.

"What about Thanksgiving? It's next week. Should I invite her over?" It was a good suggestion. "She used to stop by for a chat frequently. Perhaps Maggie won't have plans."

"I like that," I said. "If she will come here it would be like . . . neutral territory. Do you think she'll come? I mean, I wouldn't blame her—"

"Oh, she will come." He was beaming. "Don't forget, she'll be watching us. She'll see the difference, I guarantee it." Dad raised his cup. The steam from the hot cocoa fogged his glasses for a moment as he sipped.

"Do you mind calling her?" I asked.

"Not one bit and I can set the stage for a wonderful day, too." Something was cooking in this old fellow's fertile mind that was more than a turkey dinner. I decided to surrender to his greater experience and agreed.

*   *   *   *   *

Thanksgiving Day arrived with all the accompanying festivity and color. I remembered the holiday, but experiencing it firsthand was new and exciting. It was something I had never actually done. I was doing practically everything for the first time. The transition from memory to experience was exhilarating.

Maggie arrived just before ten that morning. She came through the front door carrying a large bag of vegetables and spices.

"Hello the house!" she exclaimed. I knew she was honored to be asked by my dad to come for the day. He had explained on the phone that I was going to be here for the day. As she entered her discomfort with my presence was clear. Still, she came. That had to be positive.

"Come in, Maggie," Dad called in his booming voice as he walked to greet her. He set the groceries on the table in the hall and enveloped her in his arms. He embraced her like a long-lost relative nearly lifting her off the floor.

"Let me take your coat, dear," he said placing her gently back on her feet. She was smiling brightly and quickly shed her winter wrap. Dad hung it in the hall closet. She swept the load of groceries from the table, came into the kitchen and saw me. Our eyes met. Immediately, she looked down. Her face flushed.

"Hi, Jonny," she said. She placed the bag on the countertop and walked directly to me. She put her arms around my neck and hugged me.

I almost fainted. I had never been hugged by a woman. I had never experienced tenderness of this kind. I closed my arms around her in a tender embrace.

"Hi," was all I could manage, and that was a struggle. My voice caught in my throat and with it my breath. *This is new*, I thought in amazement. She was warm against me. She smelled wonderfully fresh and sweet. And though it was but a momentary embrace, time stood still.

"I'm glad you could come, Maggie," I said, returning to the present. That one moment could be a happy eternity for me. I hoped for more.

"Me too, Jonny," she said looking directly into my eyes. "You're looking much better. Has Dad been feeding you well these few days?"

"Yes, he's turned out to be quite the chef," I said smiling at my father who was entering the kitchen.

"No, I'm not. Your mother was the kitchen magician who made copious notes. A blind bat could make your Mother's miracles happen in the kitchen. I just follow the directions."

"Then there's hope, even for me," Maggie said breaking into a timid smile.

We all laughed.

Dad took the helm and directed the activities in preparing the midday meal. The feast would begin promptly at 2 p.m., and the list of chores had a specific timetable. It was the same one Alice Walsh established nearly thirty years earlier, and one that would be maintained for at least the next thirty.

Maggie pitched in and watched closely. I noticed her intense monitoring of every move and mix my dad completed. I knew I must be cautious with my feelings, but her joining in with such interest gave me hope.

At last, the preparation of the feast was complete. It was ten times the amount of food we needed. The turkey was placed at the head of the table in front of Dad's seat, Maggie and I sat across from each other. Bowls of mashed potatoes, green beans, creamed corn, broccoli salad, cooked carrots, hot rolls, and butter and jams spread before us. It was a feast for kings.

We sat, and Dad held out a hand to each of us. I took his hand and instinctively reached across the table toward Maggie. She paused for an instant, and then she took Dad's hand and mine. They bowed their heads. Not sure what was going on, I did the same.

"Our gracious heavenly Father," Dad began. "We thank you for your many blessings. For the food before us and the hearts united around this table of Thanksgiving, we rejoice in the goodness and mercy you have shown us. Bless this food to our strength. Bless this fellowship with your grace and love. In your precious name, amen."

Maggie whispered an *amen* across the table. Inside me, not from my lips, but deep inside, another voice said, *So be it, and amen.* I knew the voice. It was the Man speaking in me. He said he would, and now I knew how he would.

*   *   *   *   *

I could never have imagined the wonder of good food. I was lost in new tastes and aromas. Dad and Maggie laughed. Dad had been telling stories of young Jonny and his many misadventures with his best friend Mark. I could only feign my protests in his exaggerated tales. Every bite was a new experience. I loved the food.

"And then there was the night he sneaked over to Mark's house on some Tom Sawyer escapade they'd cooked up. Jonny threw pebbles against Mark's bedroom window but couldn't wake him up," Dad laughed harder than I had ever seen him laugh. "When he finally came home our cocker spaniel, Pokey, growled and barked and wouldn't let him in the house!"

Maggie was totally taken by the tale and laughed until she cried. She wiped the tears from her eyes. I couldn't help but smile, even if it was at my expense, in a way. Dad went right on with his story.

"Finally, I heard all the noise and commotion and went to the back door. 'Who's out there!' I demanded." Dad nearly choked on his own punch line. "Then I heard this tiny voice, caught red-handed in the middle of the night say, 'Dad, it's me.'" He roared. Maggie collapsed, and I had to laugh.

The memory of the humiliation surfaced. My plan had been foiled, Dad was firm, but he hadn't punished me. The next day we had talked of the dangers of a young boy being out in the middle of the night. I remember learning I had made a poor choice.

Clean-up time arrived with certain somberness. The festival was coming to a close encased in a cherished memory. The dishes must be washed and put away, and the leftovers placed in containers for keeping and dispatched to the freezer or refrigerator. That was when Dad initiated his plan.

"Oh, I nearly forgot," he said drying his hands on a towel. "My seniors group at church is getting together for the football game. You two don't mind if I skip out on you, do you?"

The pause was discernable but not long enough to make a difference.

"No," Maggie said. "We'll be fine here." She looked at me with a pensive smile that asked if we would be fine for sure.

"Absolutely. We're good," I said with a confident, broad smile. "We have some catching up to do. You go along to your old fogies' party and guzzle your mugs of Ensure. We'll be fine." I looked at Maggie. Without any question it was hope that glowed in her eyes.

Dad took no time at all getting out the door. I learned later that the game was on, but no one watched it. The old fogies' club gathered in a circle of chairs and implored heaven for a favorable outcome back at the Walsh homestead. It was part of Dad's plan.

"Jonny, you're different," Maggie said as she sat on the couch with me. "What has been going on with you and your dad? It's a miraculous change. I have never seen the two of you two get along so well."

"Maggie, a lot has changed, and I need to explain it all to you." This would be much more difficult than I imagined. I remembered my dad's words and clung to the hope that grace and love would prevail.

"First, I have to say that I was wrong, terribly wrong. I know it will take time, and I don't expect you to forgive me right away, but I am asking that you forgive me." I opened my mouth to begin my account of events, but she interrupted me.

"Yes, Jonny, I forgive you. I would never withhold that from you." I looked at her and could see in her eyes she meant exactly what she said and nothing less.

"Thank you, but you must hear the entire story. Are you okay with that?" She nodded, and I began my story.

Maggie had a lot of questions. We talked about specific instances, meetings she had with Jonny, things that were assumed and other things that were missed. Then it came to the final trip, and what became of Jonny. I told her carefully.

"So, you're—not really—him?" she asked.

"No."

"But you look like him, you even smell like him. When I hugged you, it was the same as hugging him. I love that. When you talk and laugh, you are just like him. I don't understand. How are you different? How are you *not* Jonny?"

I told her about the Man, and how he instructed me to come here, make amends, and see where life would take me. How he said he would take care of Jonny, and I shouldn't worry for him.

"The Man's concern was that the things that Jonathan had broken, the people he hurt, found an opportunity to be repaired. I have learned that that means forgiveness for Jonathan and his mistakes." I looked at Maggie. She'd sat up straight on the couch the entire time. I could see her mind working, churning the facts and details of my story, and mixing them into her memory of the last seven months.

"But, you're *mostly* Jonny," she said finally.

"Yeah, I guess *mostly* is a good description." My heart sank. I knew deep inside that I didn't measure up. She saw me only as the imitation, the replica, not the real article. I had told the truth as I knew I should, but I realized I was losing her.

"No!" she insisted. "That's not what I meant. It's like you're the alcoholic without the alcohol, the drug addict without the crack. Don't you see? I can tell there is a difference in you, a huge difference. Your dad is different. He's changed in the last several months, and he's full of life and hope. You've changed. You're not the Jonny that was addicted to his research, slavishly pouring his life into an empty, bottomless cauldron that would destroy him. Don't you see that?"

I was shocked. The addict without the addiction. Was there really hope? Could I dare to hope?

"Hum. I hadn't thought of it that way. Am I that different to you?" I asked a little confused.

"Oh Jonny, you *are* that different."

She called me Jonny. I didn't know what to say. The practical side of me came to the surface.

"Listen, I don't want to push you in either direction," I said. "Either away from me or to me. I very much want to spend time with you, be with you. I have never held a woman in my arms. I have never kissed a woman. Can we do this slowly?"

"Yes," she answered almost before I finished speaking.

"May I date you and see where this leads us?" I asked trying to hold my composure together.

"Yes." Again her response was immediate and assertive.

"Well, there ya go. I think I'm going to like this pla—"

Maggie lurched across the couch and kissed me. It wasn't a peck on the cheek, it was a kiss. My insides exploded. I never dreamed of such a feeling. My mind swirled with emotions and passions that were foreign to me. I was off balance and had difficulty sitting on the couch. I was certain if she let go of me I would crumble to the floor. When she did stop kissing me, I was greatly relieved that I did not fall to the floor.

"Was that okay?" Maggie asked shyly.

I could not speak. I looked into her eyes unable to find coherent words. I think I mumbled something and nodded. Then I put my hand on her cheek, leaned toward her and kissed her again.

Somewhere in the background I heard a familiar voice laughing with joy.

*   *   *   *   *

Eventually, I did catch my breath. And since that first kiss I have lost it again dozens if not hundreds of times. From that day forward we were constantly together. It seemed like old times even though they were times I had not lived out. The memories were enough.

Our lives became a constant blur of dinners with Mark and Rachel, afternoons in the sun, and quiet evenings on my dad's front porch. In our long talks I told Maggie the things I remembered of Jonathan's life, the things he felt and thought. I shared with her what he had misunderstood. She told me the wrong choices she had made that separated them further from each other.

It was a time of cleansing, forgiveness, and coming to know each other better. The slate was wiped clean and a new life plan drawn.

We were married the following spring. My dad beamed as he escorted my lovely bride down the aisle. Maggie's eyes brimmed with tears of joy. My heart nearly burst.

It was years later when we told the entire story to Mark and Rachel. I relived the horror of the times in the future. I was able to recount my visits to the library, my encounters with Connie, and even Marcia. The most difficult was telling the story of Rachel's illness and death, and what Mark decided to do with Jonathan's technology that imprisoned Rachel in a human-less hell.

During that time, Mark and I discussed the tidbits of science we had gleaned from Jonathan's notes. We discarded almost all of the research as much too dangerous. We were able to use some of his discoveries in our chosen fields, however.

The women thought we were boring nerds. They shared their own long discussions about marriage and motherhood as each carried their first child.

When Maggie and I shared our story, we measured our friends' reactions. Astonishment gave way to revelation. Fear of what might have happened surrendered to thanksgiving for the lives we shared. Three weeks later, Rachel gave birth to their daughter, Marcia. Our son, Martin, was born the next month.

The secrets we shared bonded us together as family—friends for life.

26

The alarm interrupted my deep and greatly appreciated sleep. I had grown to revel in the simplest of pleasures. Rest and a comfortable bed were among them, and at my right side was my greatest joy, Maggie.

She stretched and rolled to her side. Her hair fell into her face and she smiled through half-opened eyes. The years had not diminished her beauty, but simply made her more lovely, her touch softer, and her lips warmer when we kissed.

"So is this the big day?" she asked with her raspy morning voice. This day had been on the calendar for nearly three decades. This was the day the original Jonathan made his first trip to the future. Everything hinged on today and the many, many days that lay ahead.

"This is it. April 27, 2037," I answered. "Today we will watch Jonathan enter his future." I knew it presented a conflict within Maggie. It signaled the beginning of a new hope and the end of a long and lingering wound.

"If you don't mind, I think I'll stay home and catch up on some email. I really don't want to watch all this happen, and for the life of me, I can't imagine why you and Mark insist on doing this."

I smiled at her. Of course she had no real understanding of the horror that could have been. The history I witnessed and learned from Marcia in the library so long ago had not occurred in our lifetimes.

Deep inside I dreaded that somehow, if something were missed, it could all be undone. I didn't know how, but still it haunted me.

"Well, just consider it something a couple old codgers want to make sure actually happens. I don't want anything to go wrong." I knew my fears were baseless and my long held trust in the Man was more important. Yet, I wanted to watch it all and make sure.

Maggie put her arm around me and pulled herself close to me. It was a sensation I could never take for granted. Having her next to me was always a new and wonderful experience.

"I'll be here waiting for you when you're done. Do you want the left-over chicken for dinner?" she asked.

"We'll see. Maybe some potato soup and a grilled cheese at the café?"

"That's not a bad idea. It has been a while, hasn't it?"

"Yes, it has." I kissed her and held her close. I was as happy as a man could be, and I would never let this go. I would never give up Maggie.

*   *   *   *   *

Mark and I stood beside one of the huge maple trees in the park across from my old apartment. The old park was a silent observer of our past, as a sentinel that remained while our lives had unfolded around it. It was an important day, one we had awaited for a very long time.

The late April sun was warm on our faces, but the air was crisp and cool. Maybe it's that we were older, but the cold seemed to find more ways to creep in, silently invade, and chill us than it did in years past. We kept our coats pulled tight around us.

Quietly, we watched the young man leave the apartment. He was bold and confident, even brash. He jogged across the street and paused in front of Gina's Laundromat that is now a bike shop. We watched as he made his way to the café and to sit in his usual place beside the planter, one we both knew well.

The waiter approached the young man and spoke to him. We are too far away to hear what was said.

"So, this is where it begins," Mark said softly.

"Yes and where it ends. We'll keep watch and see where he goes on his next visits," I added. We watched in silence. "You know, Mark, we're watching the first replica of Jonathan Walsh carry him into the future. That young man is One."

Mark gasped with the realization and turned to me grabbing my arm. He didn't speak. For a moment he was frozen as his physical body caught up with his mind.

"You mean—"

"Yeah, that's me." I smiled remembering the feelings of that first day. It was very strange but I felt and thought everything Jonathan felt and thought. Then I remembered the empty feeling when I found myself in the gray and smoke. The confidence, understanding, and clear presence of my mind were gone. I felt alone and confused. A beast. Everything in that timeless realm was mystifying.

Abruptly, the young man leaped to his feet and sprinted back to the apartment building.

"There he . . . there *you* go," Mark said. "It's a good thing you bought the apartment building. I don't know how we could have managed it otherwise."

"I just looked at it as an investment in the future." We both laughed.

*   *   *   *   *

Through the rest of spring and that following summer, Mark and I watched the young man leave the apartment many times and set out on one of his investigations. Sometimes Mark sat on the park bench for a closer look. Once, the young man pursued him, calling after him to get his attention. Mark knew better. This young man was not the one with whom he would speak.

It was a different future. Jonathan was traveling to a time where those he loved had not suffered from his arrogant mistakes. We were careful to not make contact with him until the right time. Mark was even required to run from him a time or two.

But for Jonathan the result was the same. He was expending his life, believing he was advancing science. I didn't dare interrupt that series of events.

One day while I watched one of the other replicated versions of Jonathan, I wondered if it was one of the ones I had captured and killed. The thought made me shudder. I have learned the precious value of life. It is to be treasured even in its simplest forms. The "Its" that I killed in the gray were what most would call less than human, but they were human. Over time I have been able to reconcile how I had behaved in my ignorance and for my own survival.

Still, I kept my distance. I watched from the hill in the park. I knew the young man's life was on a path of destruction, and I would not interfere. It was sad in a way, but my happiness depended on his failure. If he had stopped his pursuit, I would be lost in a timeless eternity.

In the end it all worked out. I remembered the calamity his choices brought to everyone he loved and those who had loved him. It was part of that collected memory between the two of us. He learned about it, I remembered it.

*   *   *   *   *

I am here on this final November day to assure the necessary events are completed. Summer has come and gone. Autumn is in full color and winter is on its way. I stand alone beside one of the large maples and watch. Mark is sitting on the park bench below.

Another young man is sitting at the sidewalk café beside the planter. He looks nervous and unsure of himself, but he does not hurry his meal. When he is finished, he stands to leave, and Mark makes his move. They meet. Mark holds onto him firmly while they briefly talk.

Then it is done. The nervous young man runs toward the apartment. Mark turns to me and spread his hands to say, *Is that it?* I give him a thumbs-up. He lumbers up the hill to the maple tree where I stand, and takes a moment to catch his breath.

"Wait a minute." Pointing over his shoulder he said, "That was you."

"Yes, it was. And that was the last time I came here from the gray."

I smile. Who knows what might have happened if I had stopped my earlier self to warn me about what needed to happen. I am glad Mark was willing to play along.

It is time for us to go. Maggie and Rachel had insisted we get home early. Our kids, our son, Martin Walsh II, and their lovely daughter, Marcia, have something they want to discuss with the four of us.

Now who can imagine what they might be thinking?

*   *   *   *   *

That day by the maple tree in the park was the point at which my life changed. Although it wasn't the beginning of a change, my life was entirely new. Waiting for the fullness of life was past; life is full.

Every day I remember more of the life I had not lived, but had been given to repair and complete. Things happen very quickly, but never too fast to enjoy, never too fast to embrace. I have never once longed to enter the smoke and the gray on a quest of discovery.

I have looked at life all around me. It is often the same, yet still unique. It is busy, almost too much. It can be hectic, but life can also be tamed. The beauty that surrounds me and the colors and the sounds are always different. Sounds of home, safety, and peace.

There are many sounds and situations that come at me, and sometimes I don't know what they mean. But I am no longer afraid. It is no longer confusing. I love all that is around me whether it is in order or utter chaos. I love this life and the one who gave it to me.

Life is full, packed with action, responsibility, duty, and joy. The size and weight of my responsibilities are meaningless. I have learned that I can do all things through the one who gives me strength, and I am surrounded by many who are willing to help me when I don't know what to do. I love it. I love it all.

I am me. I am Jonathan.

*"You should not be surprised at my saying,
'You must be born again.'"*
John 3:7

www.ingramcontent.com/pod-product-compliance
Lightning Source LLC
Chambersburg PA
CBHW072235170626
46813CB00003B/1242